THE ZENIA WOOD

Carrie Looper Stephens

THE ZENIA WOOD BY CARRIE LOOPER STEPHENS

Published by Illuminate YA Fiction
an imprint of Lighthouse Publishing of the Carolinas
2333 Barton Oaks Dr., Raleigh, NC 27614

ISBN: 978-1-64526-234-3

Copyright © 2019 by Carrie Looper Stephens

Cover design by Megan McCullough
Interior design by AtriTex Technologies P Ltd

Available in print from your local bookstore, online, or from the publisher at ShopLPC.com.

For more information on this book and the author, visit www.carriealooper.com

Brought to you by the creative team at Lighthouse Publishing Of the Carolinas (LPCBooks.com): Eddie Jones, Tessa Hall, Linda Yezak, Kayla Fenstermaker, and Jennifer Leo

Library of Congress Cataloging-in-Publication Data

Stephens, Carrie Looper

The Zenia Wood / Carrie Looper Stephens 1st ed.

Printed in the United States of America

Praise for *THE ZENIA WOOD*

You can't help but fall in love with Gwyn, the strong, complex heroine of this story. Her love for her brother knows no bounds, and she will do whatever it takes to protect him, all the while battling wizards, dragons, and killers. *The Zenia Wood* offers readers a vivid cast, fun splashes of humor, and an action-packed narrative you can't put down.

~Hope Bolinger
Author of *Blaze*

The world of *The Zenia Wood* brims with mystery and political intrigue. Stephens' vivid writing pulls the reader into the pine-scented forests and treacherous stone palaces of Vickland, and we feel breathless along with Gwyn as she struggles to save all she has left in the world. Fans of classic fantasy will find themselves enchanted by this high-stakes adventure.

~Emily Golus
Author of The World of Vindor Series

In her debut novel, *The Zenia Wood*, Carrie Looper Stephens takes us into an intriguing world of wizards, dragons, magic, and the familiar war between good and evil. The story of young Gwyn and her brother Martin will keep you turning pages and leave you wanting more. I look forward to more exciting adventures from this new author.

~Andrea Merrell
Award-winning author of
Marriage: Make It or Break it and *Praying for the Prodigal*

Carrie Looper Stephens

With a complex world full of magic and mystery, *The Zenia Wood* takes readers on a fascinating adventure rife with intrigue and danger. Readers will race to find out what happens to Gwyn, Martin, and Heron. Stephens draws you in and won't let you go. Get ready for book two!

~ **C. F. E. Black**
Author of *Mind of Mine*

CHAPTER 1

THE FADED RED CAPE

As Gwyn floated on her back in the tingling saltwater, seagulls shrieked above and sailors yelled to each other from fishing boats a hundred yards away in the deeper water. Despite occasional pirate attacks, three-hundred-foot sea serpents, and rumors of the Black Wizard, she and her brother lived ordinary lives in an ordinary village by an ordinary sea.

No matter how hard she tried, she could not rinse the smell of fish from her skin. She and her brother should start heading back home. But there were chores at home, and the Borgay Beach's water was so cool and refreshing after a hot day of selling fish in the marketplace for their father.

The sun, though still unbearably bright, started to fade, and the uneasiness Gwyn had been feeling all day returned.

"Oh no!" Martin's head bobbed back under the water.

"What?" Not good. She searched the sea, half expecting the gray-scaled linador to slither by and devour her brother. Her parents would never forgive her. "Martin!"

The water splashed as she jerked from left to right to behind, scouring the surface for the dagger-sized teeth of the man-eating linador. Had one snatched her brother, intent on making him a midafternoon snack?

Martin's blond head popped up beside her and he grinned. "Never mind."

She jumped backward, almost losing her footing. "Stop scaring me like that!"

"Thought I'd lost this. Papa'd kill me if he knew I borrowed it." He held up a coin-sized medallion attached to a coarse string. "He took it off in the morning when he was gutting the fish. I saw it on the kitchen table, so I took it."

He slipped the necklace over his head, and the medallion bounced against his sunburnt chest. The intricate dagger etched into the dark stone caught the sunlight and made her squint. For some reason, the sight of the medallion sent shivers through her.

"Borrowed or stole?"

"I'm starved. Race you home!" Martin grinned and dove under a wave. He popped back up, his hair plastered to his head as he swam to the shore. Gwyn rolled her eyes and twisted her braid behind her head, running as quickly as the water let her. Her skirt stuck to her legs, lying like lead weights as she ran. Once she reached the shore, the packed golden sand burned her bare feet.

They climbed a slippery sand dune. Despite Martin's head start, she beat him to the top. "Papa's going to be mad that—"

"I'll bring it back."

"As soon as we get home."

"I will, I will! Stop acting like Mama." He kicked at the sand. "Just because you're five years older doesn't mean you're my boss." He looked out at the sea and pointed at the ship on the horizon.

Gwyn shielded her eyes and stared at it. By the color of the flag, it looked like Miranda's father's boat. He was captain of the largest ship in the country of Sunday. She frowned. Most of her friends had fathers who could afford larger vessels than her father. Papa's small fishing skiff certainly wasn't big enough to go out into the deeper water. But what grand adventures she could have on a large pirate ship traveling all throughout Alastar.

"Wouldn't you love to have adventures on the sea, like in all Papa's stories?"

"No. I'd miss supper." Martin squinted down at the shore. "You left the satchels on the beach. Ha! Beat you home." He shoved her and ran toward the bustling seaport of Nelice.

She groaned and stumbled down the dune. At the bottom she brushed off the crumbly, itchy sand stuck to her wet skin and hair, then raced to the satchels and scooped them up without stopping. Martin had never beaten her home before. And today was not going to be any different.

He had already disappeared in the loud bustle of Nelice by the time she dashed under the white shell gateway. The bright entrance shone in the sunlight, making her blink and see spots of color.

The copper druthas jingled in the satchel. She tightened the drawstring. If there was enough money left over from today's earnings, maybe Papa would give her a bit to buy cloth for a new dress. Then she could look like the rich girls in Nelice. She deserved it anyway, after all the work she had done today.

The heat shivered on the shell streets as Gwyn darted around the maze of booths and tables. Yelling, red-skinned merchants, marching soldiers, brawny oxen pulling stinking cartloads of fish, red and yellow canopies, and swinging shop signs zipped past her as she dashed down the main street. Nelice was like a mini sun: red, yellow, bright, and hot.

3

As her feet pounded the ground, she darted a glance over her shoulder at the make-believe pirates chasing her, swords drawn, fists raised. Ha! They'd never catch her! She was far too fast and clever.

A bell rang and mournful chants rose from the Aberdeen Temple. She slowed her pace and stared up at the red stone building. Screams echoed from the prison below the temple, and she broke back into a run. She had heard enough stories about the goings-on in the temple to give her reason to stay far away. She stopped as she neared the cloth shop's window. There was the green cloth she'd had her eye on for months. Ten whole druthas.

Miranda sauntered toward the cloth shop with a horde of other girls quick on her heels. Their clean, brightly colored dresses swished as they walked, and their neat, bouncing curls flowed in the wind. Gwyn stifled a gasp. She didn't want them to see her all sandy and sweaty like this.

She swerved onto Cabana Alley and continued down the dark, narrow passage strung with clotheslines that sagged with breeze-rippled shirts and stinky fishnets. Maybe Martin had forgotten about this short cut.

"I'll never be like them anyway," she muttered as she slowed to a walk so she could navigate the maze of laundry. Selena had looked so stylish with her long blue dress, complete with a blue ribbon tied in her hair.

She heaved a sigh at her faded, sandy clothes. Hopefully, the others didn't see her. She loved running, but now her cheeks burned. She must have looked like a silly little kid instead of the mature fourteen-year-old she was supposed to be.

Why couldn't she have been born to an apothecary or soldier or captain instead of a poor fisherman? Then she would have enough money to buy cloth for new dresses and blue sashes and bracelets.

Miranda's words still cut deep. *Fisher brat, dirty girl,* and *childish* were just some of the names Miranda had called her. She kicked at a clucking hen meandering into the alley. Her eyes filled with tears and her throat ached.

The alley was cool and shadowy. Darker than usual. She ducked under a fishnet and was about to climb over an overturned basket, but a thick arm clamped around her waist.

The man started dragging her into a dark house. She screamed and thrashed until finally he let go of her. She fell to the ground and crawled to the back wall. Dust-filtered light spilled through cracks in the wall, making the white lines of sunlight look like prison bars along the floor. In the doorway stood the outline of a man with a hood shadowing his face. The door closed with a wooden thud that shook the house. The lock snapped with a metallic rasp.

"Gwyn, that you?" Martin's squeaky voice came from the corner.

"Yes. You all right?" He nodded and came to her side. His teeth started chattering. The man turned toward them and walked closer, his boots clomping on the wood-planked floor. Gwyn stood in front of Martin and clenched her fists. She bit her bottom lip and tried not to tremble. Who was this man? Was he from the temple? Would he take them away?

"Who are you?"

The man lit a small lantern, but she could see only shadows across a young face with dark features.

"You both are in grave danger." He spoke quickly and glanced at the door. His accent sounded Surdayan but with a hint of something clearer and less rough. "You must flee from your home and never return to Surday."

She frowned and slid the moneybag behind her. "So you can steal our money, right?"

5

He took a step back. "No, I mean no harm."

"Then let us go!" She grabbed Martin's hand and tried to push past the stranger, but he caught her arm. His grip pinched her skin. Her heart raced faster.

"At least let Martin go." Her voice cracked. Martin's teeth chattered behind her. She caught a glimpse of his bright eyes resting on the medallion around Martin's neck.

"I am not going to hurt you." His voice was calm. Gentle. "I know everything about your family. I know who your father is. I know the danger you all are in." He frowned and turned back to Gwyn. "But it doesn't matter what I know. Do not return to your home."

He slipped a key into her hand. "This will be of good use later. Do not lose it."

Seconds passed as he drew several wavering breaths. Then he turned abruptly and walked out the door. Sunlight streamed in, causing her to blink.

"Was he a crazy?" Martin asked.

"I don't know." The key's black metal glinted in the flecks of light filtering into the alleyway. She shoved it in her skirt pocket and stepped out the door. She and her brother meandered through the narrow passageway, ducking under the fishnets and laundry. None of it made sense. Why would they be in danger? Their family was like any other family. Her father was a fisherman, and her mother cooked good food. They were not rich at all. It had to be a trap.

What if the man was telling the truth? She pictured her father's big, welcoming smile and her mother's loving hands attempting to help her fix her hair.

She broke into a run and Martin followed.

"Gwyn, was he a crazy?" His voice rose to an urgent pitch.

"I said I don't know!" She tried to swallow the panic rising in her throat. Her eyes stung, and she had to blink several times as they burst out of the alley and ran toward home.

The bustle of Nelice faded behind them as they tore through a field. The long, sharp grass grabbed her arms and legs and clothes, like thousands of tiny-boned fingers trying to hold her back. The wind rippled through the field like an invisible giant running his hand through the landscape. They ran another mile and crested the hill shadowing their home. The sun set, painting an orange-purple stain above their tiny tabby cottage. Something prickled inside her and she held out her hand to stop Martin.

The cottage's blue shutters were drawn in. Her father was not sitting on the fence untangling fishnets. Her mother was not shaking out rugs or working in the garden.

An unfamiliar black horse pawed the ground, straining against the rope tethering it to the gatepost. The faded blue door lay in splinters on the front porch. A breeze caused the wind chime on the porch to jingle eerily. Suddenly, a figure emerged from the door.

It was not her father.

Gwyn crouched and yanked Martin down beside her. Her heart pounded, and despite the warm day, she shivered. She peered through thick, whispering blades of grass, squinting to see who the intruder was.

The man's pale face wore a frown as he sheathed what looked like a bloody sword. He fell to his knees and grunted in pain. He obviously hadn't seen them—yet. A torn and faded red cape draped across his bent back. After a moment, he crawled to his horse and galloped away in a cloud of dust.

Every muscle in her body tensed for action. She slipped her hand from Martin's, and they ran down the hill to their home. They stopped on the front porch and peered past the broken blue door. Splinters sliced like daggers into her bare feet as she stepped over the threshold. Her stomach lurched at the smell of cooked fish and some other odor she did not recognize. The purple light streaming into the windows faded to gray. She picked up a stubby candle by the door and felt along the doorway for the little nook where her father kept flint.

"Lemme do it," Martin said after she tried twice to light the wick. He took the flint, lit the candle, and a small stream of warm light cast dark, bouncing shadows above their heads. He stuffed the flint in his pocket.

A light flashed beside them. They screamed and swung around to their pale, wide-eyed reflections in a cracked mirror along the wall.

"Just the mirror." Martin clutched the candle in his shaking hand.

"I know." She took his other hand and clenched it. "Come on."

They crept into the kitchen, stepping over debris from broken furniture and pitchers littering their once happy home. But this was not home. She did not feel like Gwyn. She felt like a girl in another story—in another world.

A gasp caught in her throat as she knelt by her mother's still body in front of the fireplace. Mama's face was so pale. Gwyn checked her pulse, like her father had taught her. Nothing.

"She's dead," she whispered. Chill bumps prickled down her arms. Martin sobbed. She touched her mother's soft dark-brown hair. None of this seemed real. It was a dream. It wasn't happening. Tears blurred her vision.

She fingered the locket around her mother's neck. It had been a present from Papa.

"Papa," she whispered. She removed the necklace and stuffed it in her pocket, then searched the room. Her father lay near an overturned table. She leaped over a smashed chair to kneel by his side. Martin knelt beside her. Her father's eyelids flicked open, and he groaned. Gwyn started trembling. "Where's your wound? What do you need? What medicine?"

"No medicine." Her father took her hand, his sticky with blood, and the warmth of his grasp flooded comfort into her, despite the panic rising in her throat. "Go! Run, hide. He'll be back."

"You're not going to die!" She squeezed his hand tighter, longing to somehow bring life into him, to ease his terrible pain. How many times had he healed her scratches and bruises? And now she could do nothing for him.

She looked over her shoulder toward the door. "Who was that man?"

"Doesn't matter now ..." He took a deep, rasping breath and trembled. "Go. He'll be back."

"Mama's gone," Martin whispered.

"I know." He touched Gwyn's face. "She was so brave. You look so much like her, Gwyn. So much." His eyes shone. "There was nothing we could do. They'll be after you now. You must leave. Go to Uncle Edwinn in Seatress."

"Uncle Edwinn?" Martin said. "But we've never met him. What if—"

Papa clenched Martin's arm. "Protect your sister." Then he turned to her, rubbing his thumb along her face and wiping away her tears. "Gwyn, protect Martin. You two look after each other." He stared at them with shining green eyes, the eyes she and Martin had inherited.

Papa rested his head on the floor. "I told myself I would never let my children be orphans like I was." He clasped Gwyn's hand. "Promise to think things through. Don't be so impulsive. Promise me you both will be brave."

His eyes caught the medallion around Martin's neck. He touched it and gave him a weak smile. "So that's where it was. That's why he came ... Never lose this. Never give it to anyone. Keep it secret. If that man finds it ..." He shuddered. "Go! He'll be back."

Warm tears slipped down Gwyn's cheeks, and her father's face blurred. "You must hurry. Be strong," he commanded. "Do not give up hope. Remember—"

He gave a final shudder and stared blankly at the ceiling. His limp hand slipped from Gwyn's grasp. No pulse.

Martin put his head on the floor and wailed.

"No," she whispered.

Time slowed, yet everything spun out of control. Pangs of fear and grief ripped through her like stinging ice. But her tears were warm as they slid down her face. This was not real. She went numb. This must just be a dream or a story she had created in her mind. She bent down and kissed her father's forehead, smelling the familiar sweat and stale scent of freshly caught fish, and tasted the bitter sea salt on her lips.

Martin shivered and moaned. "No, no, no."

The wind blew a shutter open and it knocked against the wall. Gwyn shook herself and looked over her shoulder.

Something in her mind shut down. She couldn't deal with this now. Fear replaced her grief. She didn't want to leave, but she had her brother to think about, and she wasn't going to let anything happen to him.

"We need to go."

"We can't just leave them here." He sat up. His face looked like he had rubbed poison ivy all over it.

"That man will be back."

Gwyn scooted her back against the wall and let her head fall into her arms. Her tears spilled down her cheeks. She couldn't do this. She couldn't go on. But she had to.

"Go pack." She stood and pulled him to his feet. "Come on."

She spoke more roughly than she intended, but the roughness in her voice boosted her confidence. She forced herself not to look back. She had to focus on Martin. They hurried to their room and stuffed a few clothes into satchels. Martin lay down on his cot and stared up at the dried dragonflies and spiders and beetles pinned to the wall on his side of the room. Gwyn stood by her unmade bed. She wanted to crawl under the covers and wake up from all this. She longed for a candle's light to appear, for her parents to come running in and tell her it was all a dream and to go back to sleep.

She picked up her journal lying on top of a small wooden crate serving as her bedside table. She ran her hand over a drawing of a ship she had sketched on the front. The worn parchments, scraps of paper, and pieces of birch bark were sewn together with knotty brown thread. Her mother had helped her sew it. She shook away the memories and slid the journal in her satchel. Her charcoal pencil was somewhere. She found it in a chipped clay pitcher with her shell collection. She fingered the familiar rough wood before sticking it in the satchel. Her worn shawl was right where she left it this morning, crumpled on the floor. The soft material caressed her skin as she wrapped it around her shoulders.

She shouldered her satchel, then Martin's. "We need to go."

"I don't wanna go back in the kitchen. I don't wanna see ..." His lips trembled. She heaved a deep breath.

"We'll go out the window, then." She pushed open the window in their room and held it as he jumped out, then scooted out and closed it behind her. Sharp sand spurs in the grass poked her bare feet. She rested her hand on the side of the house, feeling the familiar cool tabby against her forehead. She clenched her teeth and turned away. They plodded up the grassy slope and stared back at their tiny cottage, now shining with the full moon's light. Shadows stretched across the porch like phantoms, and the wind chime played a mournful song, as if telling them goodbye one last time.

"Someday" — Martin's voice trembled and his frowning brow shadowed his tear-stained eyes — "I'm going to kill the man who did this."

She turned away and placed her hand on his shoulder. "Let's go."

CHAPTER 2

UNCLE EDWINN AND THE MAN NAMED ANDULZA

From the journal of Gwyn of Nelice, in The Season of Warm Suns, year 1227:

Uncle Edwinn is strange. I don't trust him. When Martin and me first came to him last year, he said he didn't want us and sent us to the Aberdeen Orphanage. It's not really an orphanage. More like a workhouse. We had to serve the monks by cleaning the temple for about a year. If the girls in Nelice saw me then, I'd be mortified. Thankfully I've been able to avoid going into town. The only bright side: Martin and me were too skinny to become sacrifices to the gods. But last week, Uncle Edwinn came back and asked the monks if he could adopt us. It's nice to be able to sleep in a real bed again and not have to scrub floors and dishes and basins from dawn to dusk. Uncle Edwinn's food is the most lavish we've ever had. Fish, pork, beef ... all with the fanciest spices. But it's still not home.

Cyrilla Coastworthy has sentenced us to our rooms again because we tracked mud on her freshly cleaned floor. I'm so sick of her. Are all maids as crabby as she is? Her long nose reminds me of a witch's. From the time she was hired—just after we got here last week—she has done all she can to make our lives as miserable as possible. I guess she was hired so Uncle Edwinn wouldn't have to take care of us. He is never around to see how evil she is to us. But I doubt he would do anything to stop her anyway. He seems scared of her too.

I'm suspicious of Uncle Edwinn. He said he buried my parents' bodies at his own personal expense and said it like he was annoyed by having to spend so much money on something so trivial. I don't think he even liked my father. He didn't seem sad when we told him the news. If he didn't like Papa, then why is he helping us now? What changed his mind?

I've been sneaking around his office today. The library is there, and I've found some strange books. Black Magic Demystified, Secrets of the Kothir Elm and She Who Dwells Within, Poison and Cures from the Skull Forest, *and* The Art of Wizardry. *I noted* The Art of Mind Reading *and told Martin I'd read it to him today. But this afternoon, after Uncle Edwinn left for Nelice, I stole an opened letter addressed to him. I found it tucked away between two books on his desk. He thought he was being so clever. He underestimates me.*

I wasn't able to read the whole thing, because I heard Cyrilla's clippity footsteps in the hallway and I burned the letter in the fireplace quick as I could. Here's what I remember of the letter:

"I am now well enough to travel to Surday. I will be there tomorrow evening to inspect the children and medallion. Your cooperation will be rewarded and your debts canceled in full."

It was written in fancy handwriting, fancier than Mama's. I haven't told Martin about it. I don't want to scare him. But it definitely scares me. Why would anyone need to inspect us? Why would anyone care about the medallion? Every time I see it, I feel sick. It reminds me of Papa. I wish Martin would stop wearing it around his neck. But anytime I mention it, he yells at me and locks himself in his room. He gets upset anytime I mention almost anything. But I honestly can't blame him. Even after a year, I still have nightmares.

Little things upset me. Watching Martin look more and more like Papa as he grows. Seeing my uncle's eyes. They're similar to Papa's, but they aren't kind. He always wears a sullen look on his face, like he has never known happiness.

Everything that happened last year has shaken me to my very core. After my parents' deaths and after enduring the eerie Aberdeen Temple, I wasn't frightened, but something seemed to happen inside me. It gave me courage and strength, yet I can't quite put my finger on it. I have learned so much since that day.

In the gathering darkness, Gwyn placed her worn charcoal pencil down on the window seat beside her and closed her journal, running her hand over the ship drawn into the bark.

Martin was playing with a spinning top at the other side of the room. His blond hair shone in the orange candlelight. She slid the journal and pencil into her skirt pocket and looked at her reflection in the window. Her hair had grown longer. She had learned how to tame it somewhat. Instead of silly girlish braids, she had started pulling her hair halfway back with a ribbon or string. She also liked pulling it into a bun. Tendrils of her hair often fell into her face, but she looked at least a little prettier than she did last year. She had grown several inches taller as well. Poor Martin had grown only an inch, if that. But she was still "as skinny as a fishing spear," as Miranda had described her several years ago. Eating nothing but thin oyster soup the past year hadn't helped.

"Can we read that book you told me about?" Martin asked.

"Sure." Any excuse to keep him distracted from their situation.

He stuffed his spinning top into his pocket but then frowned. He pulled out several chocolate dates. "Oh, I forgot I put them in there after dinner."

They left the room and walked down the hall. Voices filtered through one of the doors near the library.

"They must have the medallion with them," Barnaby, the cook, said.

Gwyn held her hand out to stop Martin and cocked her head toward the door.

"It's important." Cyrilla's voice. "We need to show it to … him. You know of whom I speak. He will be here soon."

"Did you hear that?" Gwyn said once they had shut themselves in the library.

"They want my medallion." Martin slid it out of his shirt and frowned.

"It's *Papa's* medallion."

He winced. "Right."

"Why do they want it?"

He shrugged. "Perhaps it's magical?"

"Everything's magical to you."

"Papa told us not to lose it, so it must be important." His lips trembled.

"Let's not think about it." She motioned toward a high-back chair in the corner of the room. She sat in the chair and Martin climbed onto the arm. She opened *The Art of Mind Reading* and placed it in her lap. Martin licked the chocolate off his fingers while she flipped through the crisp, smooth pages, past pages of mathematical equations, diagrams of some sort, and a drawing of a man who looked like he was in pain. His eyes were glassy and bloodshot. According to the description under the picture, this was how someone looked when possessed by a mind reader. Martin shuddered and Gwyn turned the page.

"Here it is," she said. "'To block the mind-reading process, one must build mental barriers. This process is accomplished by visualizing a rock wall. One must think through the process of building a rock wall and build it around the secret thoughts. While visualizing the construction, also think thoughts opposite to those you are trying to hide. This takes years of practice but is priceless once mastered.'"

Gwyn ran her hand over the page. "I wish I could block my own thoughts sometimes."

"What would you block out?" He touched the medallion and his shoulders slumped.

If only she could get rid of the images of her parents' bodies and the strange feeling she'd had right after her father died. Something in her mind had shut down, just like it had last winter during the plague, when one of her friends died. She'd been so overwhelmed with grief that she refused to think about it, even when her parents tried to get her to talk about it. Maybe her mind was trying hard to block out what had happened to protect her emotions.

"I would block out carrots." Martin returned to eating his chocolate.

"Is that the only thing you'd block out?"

"No." He frowned and shook his head. "Let's practice." He pointed to the book and closed his eyes. "What am I thinking? I see a wall. Building it …"

He probably thought about supper. He was always hungry. She laughed and whopped his head with the book.

"How am I supposed to read your thoughts, silly? We're both learning how to block mind readers, not read minds."

"Oh." He rubbed his head. For a shred of a second, the flicker of a smile on his face made the pain subside a little. Just a little.

"We're going to be all right." The words tumbled out of her mouth without any forethought. His smile faded, and he stared blankly at the open book. "I hope so."

Gwyn played with the stitchwork her mother had done on her old skirt to repair a tear. She smoothed the hem over her knee, out of sight. "At least we have each other."

Martin wiped his nose. "I wish Papa and Mama were here."

She sighed. "Me too." She looked up at the map of Vickland hanging on the library wall. "It looks like a nice place."

"Not as nice as Surday." Martin's voice was squeakier than usual.

She rolled her eyes. Why did she even try to change the subject to cheer him up? It almost never helped. But he was right. She had never tasted food as good as what she'd eaten at Uncle Edwinn's house and had never taken fancier baths. But all this nice stuff did nothing but paint over the hurt still twisting inside her. This silly, fancy stuff no longer attracted her.

Footsteps sounded outside the hall. Gwyn grabbed Martin and they slipped behind the armchair. His teeth chattered. She elbowed him and gave him a shut-up-or-else look. The door creaked open.

"What do you mean you can't find them?" The voice was deep and angry. Unfamiliar.

"Patience, Andulza," Uncle Edwinn said. "It's not easy to be around the little brats. After all, they descend from my brother. All you have to do is rid the earth of them and claim the medallion. That is, if they still have it."

Martin craned his neck toward her, squishing his cheek on the back of the chair. His eyes were wide and a muscle bulged in his jaw.

"*The Secrets of Darkness* by Rook J. Nefarious," the man said. "I need it now."

"Ah, actually, there's a slight problem ..." Uncle Edwinn's voice was barely audible.

"What? Have you lost that too?"

"No, the book's been, well, stolen. Last night someone broke in and—"

"Last night? Don't you find that odd?"

"Yes, but—"

"In the wrong hands that book is dangerous."

"Yes, yes, I know. But it's gone, and—"

"Forget the book. It's the medallion I want most."

"You want me to actually touch it?" Uncle Edwinn's voice sounded like a whimper.

"Yes, of course. I cannot touch it because ... Oh, never mind. You don't need to know. The king of Vickland is also involved in this."

"Donavan?" His voice rose to a pitch almost as squeaky as Martin's.

"He doesn't want the medallion. He wants to see Dylan's spawn, specifically the girl."

"Right." Uncle Edwinn cleared his throat. "It's just that you neglected to tell me the bit about the king. We're presently not on the best of terms."

"I've met with him several times. He is trustworthy, as long as you don't get on his bad side."

Uncle Edwinn uttered a noise that sounded like a nervous laugh mixed with a groan.

"He asked for a high price for the girl," Andulza said. "The medallion is nothing to him. But everything to me."

Why did he want it? Why did her father have it in the first place? And why did the king of Vickland want her?

"A whole year I have had to wait as my wounds heal." As the guest paced the room, Gwyn stared at his sand-covered boots. "I will not let any more time escape me before I have the medallion out of their possession. They will pay for what their father did to me. The Black Wizard is never crossed."

Uncle Edwinn cleared his throat again. "Follow me. I have a key to their rooms."

Boot steps clomped to the door. She dared a look around the chair right as her uncle and his guest left the library. She sucked in a breath and ducked back behind the chair. She'd seen her uncle's guest before—on a horse, galloping away from her parents' house, his faded red cape billowing in the wind.

CHAPTER 3

HERON OAKHEART

Heron dug his spurs into his horse's sides and glanced over his shoulder. A border patrol crested the hill and gained speed on him.

"Not a moment alone," he muttered. He gritted his teeth and ducked lower. "Faster, boy." The horse leaped over a creek, and Heron steered him toward the Zenia Wood. His steed slowed, but he kicked him. His horse snorted but obeyed.

Everyone in Alastar was too superstitious to enter the Zenia Wood. It was a sort of no-man's-land between Veritose and Vickland and would be the perfect hiding place. Tall indigo field flowers whipped against Heron's knees and his steed's legs as if trying to hold them back.

"Stop!" yelled one of the men. Captain Fletcher's voice.

Heron clenched his sword's hilt. If only he had his bow with him. About a dozen or so cavalrymen rode less than fifty yards behind him. He looked ahead and urged his mount into a full gallop. Almost there …

His steed leaped through a barrier of brambles and entered the safety of the forest. He turned and made a rude gesture to his father's soldiers, then urged his horse through the thick undergrowth. The cavalry halted on the outskirts of the wood.

Fletcher called to him, "Running won't make your father less angry!"

Going back wouldn't either. He ducked under a branch. It caught him on the side of his neck, and he swore.

He had to get away from the stuffiness of the castle. From Father, the almighty King Donavan the Oakhearted. From all the pressure and expectations and fake smiles. A mental image of Father's angry face sent shudders convulsing down his back.

After going a safe distance into the wood, he let his horse drink at a small creek. He let go of the reins and leaned back in the saddle. "Heron Oakheart, never let go of the reins," his mother would say if she were here. "Your steed might step on them, and you'll lose control of your mount." She had been an excellent rider and had taught him how to ride from an early age. He swallowed the lump in his throat and pushed away the memories.

He looked into the wood. When he first came into the forest, the undergrowth was thick. Now it had cleared out, and he could better see the enormous trees. They were bigger than the columns at Lyris Castle.

Lyris. Just the sound of the word brought so many memories, thoughts, and fears. The stone walls echoed with the voices of servants and guards and his father's anger. He clenched his jaw when he imagined Father's stern, unyielding expression before Heron slammed the door and stomped off to the stables. There was no room for weakness or failure in Lyris. No time alone. No opinion other than Father's. No path other than what Father had already planned for him. Deviation was not tolerated.

But here there were no angry voices. No angry faces. No expectations. Just the faint chattering of some sort of rodent with a bushy tail and the soft sound of leaves crinkling in the wind. He had never heard so much silence in his life. He breathed a sigh and closed his eyes as a breeze cooled his sweaty face.

A twig snapped in a thicket to his right. Chills trickled down his neck—the same feeling he got every time he was with Father. But this was different. He had never been alone this long in his life.

Without a single howl of warning, four gray wolves tore out of the distance toward him. He yanked his sword out of its sheath, but his horse reared and sent him tumbling off. He hit his head hard. The forest grew blurry and darkness shrouded him.

...

Heron woke feeling as if Lyris Castle had fallen on his head. He groaned.

"You had quite a nasty fall, young sir," a deep voice said.

His eyes snapped open. A solitary candle lit a room smelling of wood smoke. From the pot hanging in the fireplace came the bubble of something smelling of dirt and spices. A tall man with a gray beard bent over him, deep wrinkles etched below smiling brown eyes.

"Who are you?" He leaned away from the man, straining against the rope that tied his arms to the bedpost. His glanced down at his belt. His sword was gone. "Where's my sword? Where am I?"

"Lie down or you'll make yourself sick, young sir. You have a rather dreadful head wound, though it could've been much worse. I am Bromlin of Vickland. Well, I used to be Bromlin of Vickland. When your father killed most of his father's councillors, I ran away and have become Bromlin of the Zenia Wood."

Heron frowned. "My father's many things but not a murderer."

"Ah, I suppose he wouldn't have told you about his past, would he?" Bromlin sat on a stool near the bed and stroked his beard. "Hiding the past is a wise move for some kings, especially if they want to stay alive and remain popular."

"Who told you I was the prince?" He strained against the ropes to sit upright, but the knots held tight.

"You did. You look just like him. You have his dark eyes. The same serious expression. The spitting image." A worried look darkened his features. "Your father is alive and well, I hope?"

"Unfortunately." Heron winced and lay back on the pillow.

The wrinkles in his forehead softened. "I must say I am pleased to have company. I have not had another human in this cabin since my wife died last year."

He glared at him. "If I'm your company, why am I bound?"

"So you cannot escape."

He gritted his teeth. "Where am I?"

"That is a question I cannot answer. If you do escape, you might tell your father where I am."

"What do you have against him anyway?"

"I take it you do not like him?"

"Who would?" He pulled against the ropes and swore. "He never lets me do what I want. I can't be alone for a second. His minions are always watching. Always. It's like he's afraid I'll do something stupid."

"I see." Bromlin's brow furrowed and he stroked his beard.

He pulled against the ropes again. "If you don't let me go, the whole of Vickland's cavalry will be at your front door."

Bromlin raised an eyebrow. "And how would your father's cavalry know where to look if they don't know where you are?"

"Because—" He stopped. His memory trickled back to him. "The Zenia Wood," he said with a groan.

"Smart boy. And now that you remember where you are, I cannot let you go."

A prick of worry twisted in Heron's chest. Would Fletcher tell the king he went into the Zenia Wood? Would Father be brave enough to send troops to rescue him? The last time a group of soldiers entered the wood several years ago, a horde of giant spiders attacked and killed them all. All two hundred. He had heard ghosts living in the trees liked to steal the souls of the curious who dared enter the wood. These were surely just superstitious wives' tales told to children to keep them from wandering into the forest and getting lost. But the way Fletcher had quickly reined in his troops once Heron entered the wood was more than a little disconcerting. He had never seen the captain act in fear.

But the real question was whether Father would take the risk of sending troops into the Zenia Wood to save him. It would not be a smart move politically, especially with the Zenia Wood being so close to the neighboring country of Veritose. And it always seemed like Father cared more about politics than his only son. Bromlin stared at him with a piercing, thoughtful gaze. Heron twisted the ropes so he could lie on his side.

"I won't tell my father you are here." He tried to keep his voice calm. "I'm sure he doesn't care about a crazy old man anyway."

Bromlin chuckled. "Perhaps."

"You never answered my question—where's my sword?"

"Oh, you mean the dull little butter knife you had with you? I have it in the hall."

A gray wolf trotted into the room and sat near the fire. Heron jerked back up to a sitting position.

"Marrok will not hurt you."

"He looks a lot like the wolves that attacked my horse and me." Heron glared at it. The wolf stared at him in a serious, humanlike way.

"They were hungry."

"Where's my horse?"

"He came looking for you a few hours ago, and I tied him up in my barn. He is quite all right, though jumpy. I wouldn't blame the poor creature. Wolves are intimidating. They gave your steed quite a scare! You're fortunate that Marrok and I came upon you right after you fell." He walked over to the fire and inspected the bubbling cauldron. "Now, then. How about some mushroom stew for supper, young sir?"

"Would you stop calling me that?" He glared at his captor. If his head didn't ache so much and if he weren't bound … Bromlin's eyebrows rose, creating deeper wrinkles on his forehead. "You never told me your name."

"It's not your concern."

"Then I'll continue to call you 'young sir.'"

He scowled as Bromlin stooped by the fire and stirred a pot. "Heron."

"Heron Oakheart." Bromlin sat the ladle down and turned back toward him. "An interesting name. A modern name, if I'm not mistaken. Your father used to be an excellent hunter and often kept stuffed blue herons in his chambers. I'm sure he transferred his esteem for the bird to you."

Heron studied his face, unsure how to respond.

Bromlin left the room. His voice echoed from what must have been the kitchen. "Do you like mushroom stew? It is made with only the finest mushrooms in the wood. My wife used to call it Bromlin's Stew. It's quite tasty, if I do say so myself."

Mushroom stew? Was he trying to poison him? "I don't want anything. Just let me go. I won't tell my father where you live."

"And how do I know you are telling the truth?"

"Because I'm a prince!" This peasant was maddening. Didn't he get it? If Father were here, he'd be singing a different tune.

He came into the room with two bowls. "That tells me nothing besides the fact that you are rich and spoiled and will someday be king of Vickland." He sat on a stool by the fireplace and spooned soup into the bowls. "You know, Heron, after my many years in this land—and it has been many years, I assure you—I know with a firm conviction that everything happens with a purpose. I believe your coming to the Zenia Wood was no accident, and I believe I found you for a reason."

Heron rolled his eyes. "Of course it wasn't an accident! I came here on purpose. Listen. Just let me go. You're playing with fire here. My father's troops could bring you down before you could take another bite of that mushroom slop."

He chuckled. "You'll have to get used to me and my mushroom stew, because you are staying here until you forget where you are."

Heron groaned and fell back on the bed. This man had eaten one too many mushrooms.

"Besides, it'll do me good to have some company. I've been rather lonely this past year. Mushroom stew?"

CHAPTER 4

THE BLACK WIZARD

"What're we gonna do?" Martin whispered as they squeezed out from behind the chair.

"I don't know." Gwyn's heart pounded. With a shaky hand, she twisted a strand of hair around her finger and glanced at the maps lining the walls. As long as they were far away from Uncle Edwinn and Andulza, it didn't matter where they traveled to. Going back to Nelice or any part of Surday was the most obvious option, so they couldn't go there. Her eyes rested on Veritose and, even farther away, Vickland. "Let's take all the maps so we can decide where to go."

They rolled up the maps and crept out of the room. Surely it was justified to steal if it meant getting them to a safer place.

Behind them, a book slipped off its shelf and crashed to the floor.

"Run!" She pushed Martin toward the door. They dashed down the hall and slipped into a room near their bedrooms. Through a crack, they watched as Uncle Edwinn and Andulza burst out of Martin's room, ran down the hall, and entered the library.

"Pack your bags," Gwyn whispered as they sneaked into his room.

"We don't have time!"

"We need supplies if we want to escape. Pack!" She pointed to his empty satchel, which was left hanging on his bedpost. She ran to her room, packed her bag, and returned to help him shove his things into his satchel. She stashed the maps, her journal, and pencil in his bag. He glared at her.

"My bag's too heavy. You barely have anything in yours."

Martin picked up the satchel. "Now it's too heavy."

"Stop whining."

She peeked out the window. Night would give them some cover.

They shouldered their bags, and Gwyn slipped on her shawl. She peeked out the door. Andulza stormed down the hall. He was dressed in black, except for the faded red cloak. She clenched the doorknob. If only she could kill him right here, right now. She'd do it with her bare hands. He didn't deserve to live. Uncle Edwinn stood to the left of them, yelling down the stairs for Barnaby and Cyrilla.

Martin slipped and banged his elbow against the door. Andulza turned.

"We meet at last." His pale features and hungry smile brought bile to her throat. A white scar traced down his cheek like a stray lightning bolt.

She remembered the smell of blood. Her parents' bodies. She shook herself. She had to think fast. "Take the medallion!" She opened the door wider and threw her satchel at Andulza.

She and Martin dashed down the stairs toward the front door, but Barnaby and Cyrilla blocked them. Barnaby clutched a mattock in his hand. The chiseled edge looked sharp enough to slice a brick in half. Cyrilla brandished what looked like a pair of knitting needles, but it was her glinting gray eyes that disturbed her most.

They ran back up the stairs. Uncle Edwinn and Andulza stooped over the bag.

"Search their bags," Andulza ordered Edwinn. He blocked the way to the other end of the hall.

Trapped.

Andulza glanced from them to the bag, then lunged toward them and grabbed the back of Gwyn's neck. She yelped and drew her shoulders up.

Martin looked past her to the safety of the stairs, backed away from Barnaby and Cyrilla closing in, and then looked at her for direction.

"Run!" she yelled. She winced at Andulza's grip around her neck.

By the time Martin made his decision to run toward the stairs, Barnaby caught him. Martin's face turned as white as fresh sea foam.

"The medallion's not in the bag." Edwinn stepped toward Gwyn and ripped her necklace off. He looked with disgust at her mother's locket and threw the chain to the floor.

"Not it," he said.

Andulza held his dagger to her neck. His eyes bulged. "Where is it? Tell me where it is or I'll carve your pretty little face off. No one hides anything from the Black Wizard."

"Why'd you do it?" she demanded. A surging hatred pulsed through her like a raging sea. "Why'd you kill our parents?"

"Your father would have done the same to me, I assure you."

The dagger's point made it hard to come up with a plan. Barnaby and Cyrilla blocked the staircase leading down to the front door. Her eyes darted to the left, where stairs led up from this floor.

Andulza must have noticed her glance and tightened his grasp on her neck like he was trying to squeeze her head off. She let out a groan. He brought his ugly face near hers.

"Does your brother have it?"

She stiffened. She imagined her brother lying on the ground, as bloody and lifeless as her parents. She struggled against his grip. "Hurt him and you'll drop dead!"

Cyrilla backed away from Martin, her eyes wide. Barnaby released him as if he'd suddenly grown porcupine quills. Gwyn looked at Martin. If only she could get his attention.

"She's just trying to scare you," Andulza said. "They don't know how to use the medallion yet."

Gwyn finally caught Martin's eye and flicked her hand toward the stairs behind them. He darted away while she kicked backward, hitting Andulza in the knee with all the strength she had. Andulza yelped and dropped his hand. She ducked under his arm and followed Martin up the stairs, rubbing her sore neck. Candles along the walls lit the staircase with faded yellow light. Andulza's loud cursing sounded from below.

"Faster, Martin!" she yelled.

Uncle Edwinn and Andulza pounded the staircase. She ripped a huge painting off the wall and sent it crashing down on them.

"Remember, they have magic on their side," she said.

Martin groaned. "We're gonna die."

"Don't panic." Hopefully he didn't hear the tremble in her voice. She took three stairs at a time and grasped his hand. "Keep up!"

"I'm trying!" He clutched his side.

Panic made her short of breath and dizzy. There was no way they were going to escape. The stairs must have been freshly polished, because both she and Martin kept slipping. Martin stumbled and slid down two stairs. She yanked him to his feet and dragged him to the landing.

"Come on!"

"They're right behind me!" His voice rose to a squeal.

"We don't want to end up like Mama and Papa!"

His eyes widened and he picked up speed. Gwyn pulled another painting off the wall. It bounced down the stairs, ripped on a lit candle, and set the canvas ablaze. Perhaps the flaming painting would give them some extra time.

The two siblings charged into the top-floor room and latched the door behind them. Another library. She spotted a door at the back of the room. A tree was outlined in the pale sphere of the moon outside the window. The latched door crashed to the floor and Andulza rushed in.

"Out here." She opened the window. Martin leaped onto the windowsill and crawled onto the roof. Andulza seized her around the waist and wrenched her hands from the window.

"If you escape, your sister dies," he called to Martin as he threw Gwyn against the wall.

His sharp, cold blade pressed against her throat. She sucked in her breath and stood still.

"Edwinn!" Andulza yelled down the stairs.

From his position on the roof, Martin looked back through the window at her.

"Go!" she called. "Don't worry about me."

His lips trembled and he shook his head.

"How touching. I remember your father saying the same to your mother right before I stabbed him. Keep it up and you'll end up just like your father."

"Leave her alone!" Martin yelled. He leaped onto Andulza's back and clawed at his face.

A bright blue light flashed and Andulza fell to the ground, writhing in pain. Uncle Edwinn rushed in and pulled Martin off.

"Sir!" Uncle Edwinn knelt by him. "Are you all right?"

Gwyn jumped to her feet. "Hurry, Martin!"

Andulza pushed him away. "Get the boy, fool! He has the medallion."

They opened the door at the back of the room, dashed in, and slammed the door. There was a window at the far side of the room.

In a burst of adrenaline and without even thinking, Gwyn took out the key the mysterious man had given her and fit it into the lock. It worked.

They leaned against the door, gasping for breath. A second after the door locked, an eerie green light shone from the crack underneath it. The door rattled as if a strong wind were trying to rip it open, but it stayed locked. The mysterious man had warned them of the danger ahead. How had he known she would need this key?

They ran to the window. She unlatched it, and they slid out onto the roof. Bitter wind and icy raindrops chilled her skin.

"Now how are we going to get down?"

"You should've thought about that before we climbed out here." Martin peered down the side of the roof and pulled back, wincing.

"Would you rather go back inside?" She glared at him.

He shook his head vigorously. The grating of a tree branch scraping against the roof made her shudder. "Trees. We can climb down the trees." They balanced along the ridge of the roof and hurried toward the trees.

A light mist of rain, finer than salt and colder than ice, pelted them. The wind picked up and whipped her hair in her face. Thunder rumbled and a streak of lightning lit the rooftop.

"I hate storms." Martin's teeth chattered.

"Only stun them with the poison arrows!" Andulza yelled from inside. "I want them both alive." Arrows swished past them. One bounced off the roof beside Gwyn's bare foot. It was dulled with a rag reeking of something sickeningly sweet. They scurried faster along the roof and finally neared the trees.

"Wait. These branches aren't big enough to hold us." Gwyn held out her hand to stop him. An arrow whizzed past her ear. The sickening smell made her dizzy. Not good. She looked up. "This one looks strong enough. Here, you first. Can you reach?"

Martin jumped into the air, took hold of the branch, and angled toward the trunk. She grabbed the same branch and followed him down the tree. Something cracked, and her heart skipped a beat.

"Martin!"

"I'm okay. It's so dark."

"Don't slip."

Her heart pounded hard when she imagined him falling. The knobby bark cut into her hands and bare feet. Another arrow hit where her head had been a second before. She pinched her nose to keep the putrid smell away. Her eyelids grew heavy. No, she couldn't pass out now. Martin needed her.

She crouched and fell to another branch, then crawled to the opposite side of the tree, the side away from the house. "Stay on this side of the tree."

"Cyrilla, Barnaby!" Uncle Edwinn called out. "They're climbing the trees. Run down to the front door. Andulza and I will keep to the roof."

Gwyn looked up at the roof. Cyrilla and Barnaby climbed back into the window. Andulza was pointing a bow at her. She slid down a few branches and tried to keep the tree in between her and the arrows.

A sharp limb caught her on the cheek. She blinked back tears and wiped the blood away. A few feet from the ground, Martin yelled and a thump sounded below her. She dropped to the ground where he lay.

"My foot hurts!" He massaged his ankle and started crying.

Great. Could this get any worse?

"Get up. They'll kill us if we don't run." Gwyn helped him to his feet and let him drape his arm over her shoulders. "They'll be down here any minute. Come on. The road is up ahead."

A door opened and slammed. Two people stormed out to the grounds. Barnaby's swaying lantern glinted off his mattock, and Cyrilla still clutched her knitting needles.

Gwyn half dragged Martin into some bushes near the house. They rested their backs against the wall, and Martin rubbed his ankle. It looked like he had twisted it. No blood. No arrow protruding from it. He shivered in the night air and tried to control his chattering teeth and pain-filled whimpers. She wrapped her arms around him.

"It's going to be all right," she whispered. If only she could believe her own words.

Cyrilla and Barnaby passed the bushes, but Cyrilla no longer looked like a maid. Her tight bun had come undone, and her curly black hair swirled in the wind. She wore a long, flowing purple cape, and black goo dripped from her knitting needles.

"Poison?" Martin whispered.

Cyrilla and Barnaby shone the lantern into the branches of the tree they had just climbed.

"Follow me," Cyrilla said. "I smell fear in the bushes." Martin pointed at Gwyn's head. She had completely forgotten to try to block mind readers. Why had she been so careless?

She watched as the two stepped closer to the bushes. The slight chink of the knitting needles and the scent of something like putrid acid wafted nearer. Gwyn backed closer to the wall. Something cut into her heel—a rock. She picked it up and tossed it across the lawn. It fell with a thump near another line of shrubbery.

"What was that?" Barnaby asked. Cyrilla turned away from the bushes and ran toward the other shrubbery, Barnaby close on her heels.

Something rattled down the road. Gwyn pushed a branch away and squinted toward a rider bouncing on the seat of a horse-drawn cart. A lantern swung from a handle on the cart.

"Follow me." She stood and dragged Martin to his feet. They slid out of the bushes, and she helped him run to the road in the cover of the line of shrubbery. They ducked behind the gate in front of the road and let the cart pass by. She couldn't get a good look at the driver. Hopefully, it was too dark for him to see them too.

She helped Martin over the gate and jogged after the cart. He hopped on one foot and clenched her hand for support. At the back of the wagon, she lifted a sheet covering the cart, and they jumped in. The cart smelled of rotten fish.

She pulled the sheet over them and lay on her stomach. Martin's teeth chattered almost as loudly as the cart's wheels. He held up a limp mackerel and groaned. As the cart ambled down the road, Gwyn lifted the sheet a few inches to see Andulza step out from her uncle's house. In the moonlight, he looked to the road. If only the cart would sprout wings and fly. It wasn't moving fast enough.

A shrill scream sent shivers down her spine. Humpbacked creatures skittered through the shadows along the road and limped to the front of the house. Many of them came within a few feet of the cart, but they passed by as if they couldn't see it. Andulza drew his sword and addressed them.

"Witches of the Skull Forest." His voice grew fainter as the cart's rattling wheels and the horse's *clomp-clomp* spirited them away. "Whoever brings me the children will be rewarded generously. I only ask they be brought to me *alive.*"

Gwyn shuddered and placed the sheet back over her head. She let out a long, relieved breath. The stuffy cart rattled and bumped down the road, taking them farther away from Uncle Edwinn and Andulza. For now.

CHAPTER 5

THE WHITE RIVER

The next morning, warm sweat trickled down Gwyn's face. She opened her eyes and blinked in the sunlight filtering through the sheet on top of the cart. The cart hit a pothole, and she banged her knee against the side. Her whole body ached.

Martin. She sat up and breathed a sigh of relief. He was still fast asleep on a pile of fish. She gagged and pinched her nose. The cart smelled like dead skunk, rotting fish, and hundreds of peeled bananas. The cart stopped, and she lifted the sheet, watching as the driver stepped down from the cart and knelt to take a drink at a nearby creek. He wore a black hood, and his back was to them. She turned and shook Martin.

"We need to go," she whispered.

He rubbed his eyes and sat up. His face shimmered with slime from the fish. He took his bag and they stepped out of the cart. "Where's your bag?"

"I left it at Uncle Edwinn's, remember?"

"Oh, right. The delusion." He winced and hopped on one leg.

"Diversion," she whispered. She pulled him behind a wide oak tree and peeked out at the creek.

The man with the hood pooled water in his hands and wet his face. He flipped back the hood and looked up at the sky like he was wondering if it would rain. Or listening to her pounding heart. Or trying to read her mind. She bit her lip and swallowed. Martin looked up at her and she forced an *it's okay* smile. She turned back toward the creek, but she could see only the side of the driver's face. He filled a canteen of water and returned to his seat on the cart.

Gwyn ducked back behind the tree and waited until the cart's rattling wheels faded in the distance. "Let's wash in the creek." She and Martin walked toward the bubbling current.

"That man in the red cape was the same one who—"

"I know." She had been thinking over everything last night while riding in the cart. If their parents' murderer was searching for them, then he surely had the same intentions. But he had several chances to kill them, and he didn't. He seemed more interested in the medallion.

"Why did Uncle Edwinn want to give us to that man?"

"I don't know." She firmed her jaw and kicked at a rock near the creek bank. He hadn't seemed clever when she and Martin first met him. She had underestimated him, and it had almost cost them dearly. She wouldn't do that again.

"I knew Cyrilla Coastworthy was evil," Martin said as they slid into the creek and attempted to wash off the putrid fish smell. "She has scary eyes."

She nodded. "Let's look at your ankle."

They climbed onto the bank, and he plopped his wet foot in her lap. His ankle was swollen, red, and warm.

She fingered the bones around his ankle. "Does that hurt?"

"No, you touching it makes it feel better."

She gently massaged it. "Good. It doesn't look as swollen now. Resting in the cart probably helped some."

"Thanks. That feels much better. You're like Papa. Sometimes." His gaze dropped.

"How?"

"You take care of me when I'm hurt."

She smiled. It was nice hearing him say she was like Papa. It was the kindest compliment she had heard in a while. "But I'm not like Mama?"

"No, Mama took care of me when I was hurt on the inside." He pointed to his chest.

She stopped massaging his foot and heaved a deep sigh. Mama had a way of understanding how she felt and soothing away worries, fears, and anger. Gwyn was not like her mother. If only she were. But did she really want to be like Mama? Should she force herself to become someone she wasn't, for Martin's sake?

She placed his foot back in the creek and untied her hair, letting it flow into the current. If she were more like Mama, she would be able to sort out her emotions and Martin's and give him the comfort he needed. They needed Papa's practical, fast-thinking, and loving leadership and healing skills, but even more they needed Mama's calming love. Especially Martin. But as much as she tried to view herself as being more like Mama, she couldn't see it. She was not her mother. She was more like Papa, yet different. She didn't have his wisdom or kindness. Then who was she?

"That key sure came in handy," Martin said before dunking his head into the creek.

"It did." She flipped her hair out of the creek and shook off the water droplets.

How had the man who warned them of their parents' deaths known they would need the key a year later? The man with the black cape looked similar to the driver of the cart. If he was the same, why did he keep helping them? What did he want? Who was he?

"What now?" Martin asked as he splashed his arms.

"Maybe we can go to Vickland," she said, "where Papa's best friend lives." In the cart's swaying lantern light, after Martin fell asleep last night, she studied the maps, which had thankfully endured the journey in his satchel. It looked like it would be a fortnight's journey, but it would get them far away from anyone who wanted to hurt them.

"The one with the funny name?" He turned toward her. "Gwyn! What happened to your face?"

She touched her stinging cheek. "What?"

"You have a cut." He touched her face. "Right here."

"Ow." She slapped his hand away, then peered into a puddle that had formed near the creek. A red gash sliced from her left ear to her jaw, and dried blood caked around the cut. She touched it and her eyes watered.

"It must have happened when I was climbing down the tree." She splashed water on her face. The cool water soothed the sting some. It looked more like a pink scar now. Would she have this mark forever?

"Makes you look like a warrior," Martin said.

"A warrior?"

"Makes you look tough. I always wanted a scar like that."

Gwyn sighed and disturbed the water with her hand. Ripples blurred her reflection. The girls in her village would make fun of her if they saw her now. Their taunts and teasing still made her cringe. But the opinion of the girls in Nelice didn't matter as much anymore. She had more important things to worry about. Like staying alive and taking care of her brother.

They followed the creek for several miles until it turned into a raging river that churned so quickly the water looked white. Martin was still limping a little, but the sight of the rapids distracted him from his ankle.

"Must be the White River." He studied the map as they wandered along the sandy shore. Martin pointed toward the woods along the bank. "The trees are so big here."

She nodded. "It's different from home, isn't it?"

"Hey, look what I got in my pocket." He grinned at a chocolaty mess in his hand. "It's those chocolate dates I snitched from dinner last night."

They sat down by the river and split the oozing, melting chocolate. It tasted even better than it had the previous night, though it was tinged with a fishy flavor after their trip in the cart and a bit watery after his bath in the creek. It would not be too bad, living off chocolate and traveling on their own. But the chocolate soon ran out. Martin licked the inside of his pockets and she licked her fingers.

Gwyn washed the chocolate off her face and her hands in the river and stretched out on the shore. She didn't hear the constant clatter of people. Gone were the loud cries of screeching seagulls. There was no more putrid fish smell nor the constant bite of mosquitoes, sweat bees, and snipe flies. Gone was the humid, stifling air that made it hard to breathe. Instead, a clean breeze ruffled her hair and cooled her skin. The only noise was the soothing flow of the river. Nelice was familiar, but this place was much calmer. Thoughts of Nelice brought back the painful memories she had tried to bury.

Her mother used to smile up at her father with such loving eyes. Mama was the most beautiful woman she had ever seen. Her eyes were "as brown as chocolate," as Martin described them a few years ago.

When Papa came home from fishing, he used to wrap his arms around Mama's waist and dip her. Mama would

43

giggle like a little girl. He would give her a long kiss, making Gwyn and Martin gag and run to the other room. Then he chased them and tackled them, wrestling and tickling them until they could barely breathe.

She shook her head. She couldn't think about those memories now. She had to focus on Martin.

"Maybe we can live here," she said. "It's so peaceful, and the Black Wizard doesn't know where we are."

"What will we eat?" Martin asked.

A fish leaped up and disappeared in the rushing current. If only she had a fishing spear. The longer limbs of the privet trees along the bank could make a good spear. But once they had caught enough fish, should they risk starting a fire?

Martin studied her expression and frowned. Maybe she could distract him from his hunger. "Want to play the storytelling game?"

"No." He turned his pockets inside out and frowned.

"We've been traveling so long. Let's take a break." She turned toward him and sat cross-legged. She had to get his mind off food. "Imagine yourself as a great and powerful warlord. Your name? Martin the Magnificent," she said. His lips twitched. "You ride a powerful black horse—"

He scowled. "I hate horses."

"Fine. A dragon. A dragon with shiny black scales, little beady red eyes, and wings as long as a ship's sail. One day, Martin the Magnificent was riding his dragon near the White River when he spotted something on the bank. He decided to take a closer look. Your turn."

"But the dragon had enough of Martin the Magnificent," he said as he looked toward the sky. He leaned back on his hands and stretched his legs out in front of him. Chocolate still splotched his face. "The dragon thought Martin was not so magnificent after all. So the dragon shaked very hard and throwed Martin the Magnificent off his back.

The dragon was getting hungry anyway. After Martin the Magnificent had splattered on the rocks, the dragon landed and ate him up."

"Never mind," she said with a sigh. "You always make my main character die."

"Main characters die in all the good stories. Papa's stories ..." He frowned and removed the necklace from around his neck, then handed it to her. "I've been thinking. You can wear the medallion necklace. Even though it was Papa's, it's not very manly. And I have a reputation to keep."

She raised her eyebrows. "A reputation to keep?"

"Do you have any idea how hard it is for a kid with a squeaky voice to keep a manly reputation?"

She coughed to hide her laugh. "No, I guess I would have no idea about that. But I will gladly wear this for you to help you keep your manliness."

He scowled. "You making fun of me?"

"Of course not." She swung the medallion on the chain.

He narrowed his eyes and turned his back to her.

"Gwyn, look!" He hit her shoulder and pointed along the shoreline.

Rubbing her shoulder, she swung around. A man watched them from the woods. He had a black cape with a hood covering his features. Panic seized her. They were vulnerable out in the open. Why hadn't they stayed in the cover of the trees? But as soon as the man noticed them looking, he turned and disappeared into the woods. She slipped the necklace over her head and snatched Martin's bag.

"We better go." They ran for the shelter of the woods near the shoreline, far away from the man with the cape. Martin looked over his shoulder every few seconds. She tried to push away the tremble in her voice when she told him it was probably just a man who had gotten lost.

"But he looked a whole lot like the man with the cart and the man who warned us. Why is he following us?"

"Not every person we meet is out to get us."

He glanced over his shoulder and hiked up his satchel. "Everyone we've met since we left home has been."

She shook her head. "We're in the cover of the woods. We'll be safe."

At least the hooded stranger wasn't a witch.

As they escaped in the cart yesterday, she had caught a brief glimpse of the witches' humpbacked forms and long, talon-like fingers. Her father said witches were once humans who had become consumed with spells and dark magic. In their quest for power, they turned so ugly it hurt to look at them. As the years went on, they formed a sort of race and became uglier and crueler. It was said even witch babies were ugly and tainted with the blackness that comes only with dark magic and cruel deeds.

"Gwyn, why did Andulza say the king of Vickland wanted you?" His voice was barely a whisper.

She bit her lip and tried to ignore the squirmy feeling in her gut. "He must have meant another person." If only Martin would forget about what Andulza had said. She tried to forget as well.

"I'm scared," he said in a whisper.

"Don't be. We're safe now."

They continued hiking the rest of the day along the rocky shoreline near the woods. The cloaked figure never reappeared. By the end of the day, she was too tired to remember to keep looking over her shoulder.

"My feet hurt." Martin's feet were leaving bloody footprints along the sand and rocks.

Her own bleeding feet were beyond painful. They had grown numb. She had never walked this long in her life. "Let's find a thicket and call it a night."

"I'm starved." Martin massaged his stomach.

"I remember Papa telling us pine needles are edible." But he had warned that although yews looked like pine trees, they were poisonous. "Let's find some pine trees that aren't yew."

"Another one of your brilliant ideas," Martin said with a groan.

After finding a knobby old pine tree, Gwyn stripped off two handfuls of sticky green needles and gave him some. He wrinkled his nose.

"You eat it first."

She bit her lip. Maybe she had imagined her father saying pine needles were edible. Maybe this was actually yew. But it didn't look like the yew plants Papa had pointed out to her many years ago.

"This was your idea," Martin reminded her.

She forced a few needles between her lips and bit down. An explosion of bitter resin coated her mouth. "Crunchy."

With a raised brow, he pulled out one needle and slid it into his mouth. He chewed and made a face.

"If we want to survive, we have to eat this." She pointed to her handful and Martin's. "All of it."

After supper they found a camping spot along the bank, hidden in a thick patch of wild privet and brambles. She cleared out a spot for them to sleep and settled down on the ground, watching Martin study a small spider crawling along the forest floor. He poked at it with a stick, turning it over and studying its movements. Little glittering fireflies sparkled in random patterns in the growing darkness. The gentle sound of the river made her eyes heavy. She lay on her back and watched the stars flickering above.

"Do you think we'll make it?" he asked.

"What?"

"We're by ourselves, and our uncle and that creepy Andulza are trying to kill us. All we have to eat is pine needles. It's not looking very good right now."

"Of course we'll make it." She rolled over and faced him. "We have a map, and we have each other. All we have to do now is find Vickland and Papa's friend, River. Maybe he will take us in."

"Papa told us to be brave." His voice was barely audible. "But I'm not brave."

"You're brave," she said. "Remember that time when there was a pirate attack and Papa was in Nelice? You and me and Mama ran into town to warn him."

"That was different. Mama was there." Martin turned over on his back and stared up at the sky. Even in the darkness, she could see tears slipping down his face.

"What about the time you hit that sick dog with a stick when it attacked us? It ran away with its tail between its legs. Mama wasn't there then."

"That was different too." He sighed. "It was just a dog, and it was sick. What if the Black Wizard attacks us? Will I be brave enough?"

"You leaped onto his back to save me when we were escaping Uncle Edwinn's house. Remember?" She brushed his hair out of his eyes. His hair and face were sticky with tree sap. "Maybe we're bravest when we see people we love in danger."

He gave a wavering sigh and sniffed a few times.

"I love you."

"Mm."

He never said *I love you* back. Hopefully it was just a stage ten-year-old boys went through. He was almost eleven. When was his birthday? She counted the days. She had lost count, but it was coming up soon.

"You go to sleep. I'll stay up and keep watch."

She bit her lip to hold back a laugh. "Thank you. You're a good brother." As tired as he was and at his young age, he wouldn't be able to stay up all night, but it was a sweet thought all the same.

"You're a good sister. Sometimes." His voice held a smile. She laughed. "Don't worry. Everything will be okay. We'll find River."

But how could everything be okay? They were alone. If only they could make it to Vickland. Maybe Papa's old friend would take them in. Surely he would want to help his best friend's children.

She gave up trying to get comfortable in the prickly thicket and drifted into an uneasy sleep, her stomach churning after the unfamiliar meal of pine needles.

CHAPTER 6

THE TRUTH ABOUT THE KING

Thunder rumbled outside and rain smeared the window. A drop of water splashed in Heron's eyes. Roof must be leaking. He groaned and pulled the quilt up to his chin.

He rubbed his wrists for a few seconds before realizing his hands were not bound. He tried to climb out of bed, but his feet were still tied to the bedpost. In his struggle to free himself, he fell halfway off the bed and found himself hanging upside down. He swore and reached up to untie the knot.

He stared at a mirror on the wall across the room and moaned at how ridiculous he looked with his feet tied to the end of the bed and the rest of his body on the ground. His shirt and pants were smeared with dirt and a little blood from his fall, and a bandage was wrapped around his forehead like a cloth crown. He ripped the bandage off and grunted as he tried again to untie the knot. But it was stuck fast.

Bromlin stepped into the room and smiled. "Good morning, Heron." He lowered a pile of wood to the hearth and began making a fire. Heron glared at him and scrambled back into the bed.

"What would you like for breakfast?" Bromlin asked as he arranged the logs.

Definitely *not* mushroom stew. It tasted like dirt. "Normal food."

He chuckled. "Ah, I see. Like bacon, a couple poached eggs, a bit of toast and jam, and perhaps a glass of red wine to start the day?"

His stomach rumbled. "You have all that?" Bromlin's booming laugh echoed through the room. "Your love for food is just like your father."

"I am not like my father." His tone sharpened. "Why does everyone say I'm like my father? I don't want to be him." He reached to untie the knot. He was getting out of here. He refused to be insulted by this common villager any longer.

Once the fire was started, Bromlin turned to warm his back. "Many sons endure the pressure to be their father. I myself remember well when others wanted me to be like my father."

Heron didn't want *I was like you at your age* talks. People said that to try to get on his good side. What he did want was some decent food. He had never been this hungry in his life. Bromlin pulled on a worn coat. "Luckily for you, my hens started laying again. I can cook up a few eggs if you'd like. I have a delicious omelet recipe with mushrooms."

This man really was trying to poison him. "I'll take eggs *without* mushrooms."

He muttered something about the excellent nutritional properties of mushrooms as he departed through the kitchen and out the front door.

Half an hour later, Heron was eating his eggs—without mushrooms—in bed, and Bromlin ate by the fireplace.

The eggs weren't terrible. A little dry. He had definitely tasted better. And this thing that carried the eggs … was it supposed to be a plate? It looked like he had taken a lump of red mud, smoothed it out, and let it harden in the sun. To decorate it, Bromlin had carved a little flower into the clay. It made it even uglier. His spoon, however, was polished silver. How had he gotten a silver spoon living out here in the woods?

Once he had finished eating, Bromlin took a basket of berries and put them on a pan over the fire. He stirred them with a wooden spoon and hummed to himself.

"Why did you say my father was a murderer?" Heron asked after he had demolished the last of his breakfast.

Bromlin poked at the berries, which had turned a brown hue. "Ah, they are hardening nicely."

"How is my father a murderer? Do you know him?"

"I did know him when he was about your age. I saw him almost every day." He glanced at him. "He looked much like you."

"Why did you say he was a murderer?"

He took a pitcher near the fire and poured water into the pan. A soothing, rich smell filled the air. "Would you like some drink? I call it Bromlin's Brew. I discovered a berry plant on the outskirts of the wood and have invented quite an invigorating beverage."

"No. Answer the question." Heron's anger bubbled up again. This old man was definitely hiding something. Up until now, this decrepit peasant had wanted to talk for hours about mushrooms, wolves, and history.

Bromlin poured his brew into a mug and sat on a stool by the fire. He took a deep draft and rested his mug on his knee. As he stared into the fire, his kind brown eyes—so unlike Heron's father's—glimmered like sparkling embers. Father's were always angry and shifting, like he expected someone to jump out of every corner and confront him.

Bromlin heaved a sigh and ran his hand through his gray hair. "I have always believed in telling the truth, especially about the past."

Heron rested his head on his arm. Bromlin cleared his throat a few times and looked at him.

"There was once a time, many years ago, when children could run safely in the fields and streets. There was no fear of dragons or soldiers. The borders were secure. No threat of war loomed on the horizon. During this brief time of peace, I was your grandfather's main councillor. Not only his councillor, but a trusted friend. King William Oakheart and I were childhood friends in the Eldridge Mountains ... but that is another tale for another time. During your grandfather's reign, Vickland had a powerful military, a thriving agriculture, and a blossoming university that taught the ancient languages, the art of war, and Vickland's heritage. I was Vickland's main historian."

Heron rolled his eyes. This was just going to be another history lecture. "Yes, but what about my father?"

Bromlin frowned, and a stern, teacher-like expression crossed his face. "I'm getting to that part." He cleared his throat again. "Your grandfather had little to no time for his family, and this was his downfall, his worst and most grievous mistake. He often ignored his son, who began to resent him. I watched Donavan become rebellious and bitter toward his father."

Heron tried to imagine his father as a young man, but his imagination had its limits. "One night," Bromlin said, "my late wife and I were asleep in the castle. All was quiet. Too quiet. I woke and listened to the silence, wondering where the soldiers were. Usually I heard the occasional marching of the soldiers' and servants' footsteps down the hall." He looked up at Heron. "I'm sure you are well acquainted with the sounds in Lyris Castle."

He nodded. He could picture the castle's hallways painted in the orange light of torches, bouncing light trying to pull the shadows from the walls. He had never passed through the halls of his home without the sound of soldiers' clinking weapons and the servants scurrying around. Silence in Lyris would be suspicious.

Just the thought of the darkness and trepidation of Lyris made Heron shudder. His best friend, Gressette, with his mischievous grin, was the one bright light there.

"I got up to investigate." Bromlin poked at the fire as he spoke. "Before I could reach the door, the general of the army, Lysander Launder, knocked. He was bloody and faint. I pulled him into my room, and my wife, who was the most knowledgeable healer at the time, tended to him. But alas, his wounds were mortal. His last words were 'Escape while there's time. The king is dead.'"

Heron's heart pounded faster. The fact that Bromlin was telling a story that had happened in his own home made the tale all the more eerie. "How?"

"I'm not finished." Bromlin frowned again. "I took my wife and escaped down the halls. I saw your grandfather and grandmother dead in their chambers. I will not go into detail, but it was a brutal slaying. Their ashen faces … the blood …" He swiped at his eyes. "The silent assassin followed, and we had a heated sword fight. Of course, you probably don't want to know the details of the fight …"

Heron did want to know the details, though he was trying to maintain an air of indifference.

"When things were going badly for the assassin, the coward fled. We escaped but not before we heard all your grandfather's councillors had been slain. My wife and I fled to the Zenia Wood, and I have not set foot in Vickland since."

"Yes, but what of my father? You still haven't told me why you say he's a murderer."

"Oh, but I have." His eyes glittered. "*Your father* was the assassin who killed your grandfather, King William Oakheart of Vickland."

Chapter 7

An Archer in the Woods

Gwyn woke the next morning and blinked in the sunlight. She could not smell her mother's breakfast cooking, so she must have slept too late. She rubbed her sore ribs and pulled a pine cone out from under her. Martin must have put it there as a prank. She lifted her head, expecting to see his bug collection pinned to the opposite wall. Did she fall asleep outside again? Her feet had fallen asleep. She reached down to massage them but found a bit of dried blood on both.

Then reality crashed into her like a hundred-foot wave. She heaved a sigh and lay back down. It didn't seem real. A whimper escaped her, and she quickly turned it into a cough, afraid Martin would wake and hear. She didn't want to get up.

She rolled over. He was curled with his knees against his chest. He had a line of dried blood on his foot as well. His satchel rested under his head, and he groaned in his sleep. The lump returned to her throat. She had to go on. For Martin. She must protect her brother. At all costs.

A dense fog shrouded the thicket, birds sang noisily above, and squirrels rustled through the leaves in search for breakfast. She stood and brushed the leaves from her clothes. Light scattered the fog as she walked out of the brambles. The raging rumble grew louder as she drew near the riverside.

She pulled her hair into a neater bun and smoothed out her dirty skirt and shirt. Thorns had snagged her clothes, and mud and pine sap stuck to the cloth. If her stylish friends, with their brightly colored dresses and perfect hair, were here, she would laugh at them. She could imagine them tiptoeing through the thick underbrush, whining about the thorns poking them and snagging their dresses. She snickered. They wouldn't survive a day out here.

Before she left the woods, a twig snapped. A scowling, skinny boy with a drawn bow pointed the arrow at her.

She drew in a breath and stood rigid. "Who are you?"

"If I tell you, I'd have to kill you."

Judging by his slightly shrill voice, he was probably a few years younger than her. He was almost as skinny as the narrow tree he hid behind. He had a spattering of black freckles covering his red-splotched face.

Her shoulders relaxed, and she shrugged. "Then don't tell me who you are. I couldn't care less."

"Aren't you even a little afraid?" He frowned and lowered the bow a fraction of an inch.

She folded her arms across her chest. "If your parents had just been killed and you were on the run from witches and wizards, then you wouldn't be scared of little things like a skinny boy with a bow."

"I would never shoot a girl anyway. My uncle would kill me." He lowered his bow and placed his arrow back in his quiver. "Witches and wizards, you say? You must be in a load of trouble to have them after you."

She winced. She shouldn't have said that. "What are you doing here?"

"Running away."

"Why?"

"Because my family is the most boringest family in the whole history of Alastar. They live on the Eldridge Mountains, 'bout five miles from here. Did you know my ancestors—and now my cousins and aunts and uncles and me—have been keeping a stupid secret for hundreds of years? And we're supposed to guard that secret and stay on the mountain and not go anywhere, unless you're a warrior, and I'm not old enough to be a warrior yet. And all I do is study about people who have been dead a long time."

"That doesn't sound so bad. At least you have parents."

"They're not my real parents. Just my aunt and uncle."

He held a knapsack smelling of bread and maybe some apples. She licked her lips and cleared her throat. "What's the secret you and your family are hiding?"

"If I told you, I'd have to kill you." The boy grinned, revealing crooked teeth.

"Of course." She rolled her eyes.

"I take classes at school to learn how to fight and shoot." He let his knapsack fall off his shoulder and fingered his bow. "I'm not very good at it, but it's funner than reading dumb books all day."

"Is that so?" She feigned interest as she stared at the knapsack.

"Yep. My uncle teaches all the boys my age. But he makes me sit out and watch a lot. Says I get hurt too much. But I'm still learning. I'm a fast learner."

"Are we near Vickland?"

His expression darkened. "Why would you want to go there?"

She glared at him. "Are we close or not?"

"Not too far. But I would stay away if I were you. The king there is nasty unpleasant." The boy shuddered. "He likes killing people more than otters like rivers."

Martin stumbled out from the thicket. The boy took an arrow, strung it on the bow, and pointed it at him. Gwyn stiffened. "It's just my brother." She stepped closer to the skinny boy. "Lower that silly bow. Go home and leave us alone." Instead of him lowering the bow, his fingers slipped and he let go of the string. The arrow whizzed toward Martin. Her heart skipped a beat.

"Duck!" she yelled.

He dove into a pile of thorns as the arrow thudded into a pine tree three feet away.

"Oops. Good thing I'm a bad shot." The boy gave a nervous laugh.

She hurried over and helped Martin out of the pile of thorns.

"Who's he?" He pulled a thorn out of his hand and brushed blood away from a scrape on his cheek.

"Some miniature highwayman who refuses to leave," she said with a groan.

"Well, fine! A guy as important as Morin Launder does not want to associate with fugitives." Morin yanked his arrow out of the tree. He placed it back in his quiver. "I don't want to get involved with witches and wizards. Nasty creatures, I've heard they are. They eat people. I don't intend to meet any of them. Besides, we're near the Zenia Wood, and an evil ghost haunts those woods." He strutted off into the forest.

"You think he knew how to get to Vickland?" Martin asked.

"I doubt it. Pine needles?"

"Ugh." He massaged his stomach. "Not me."

"How about some apples and a loaf of bread?" Gwyn held up Morin's satchel.

His eyes brightened. "Where'd you get that?"

"That boy dropped it when he was showing off his bow. He's not very observant. I snitched this while his back was turned."

"Is that stealing?"

"If we're starving, it doesn't count." She shoved away a prick of guilt and searched the satchel. "Looks like there's some dried meat too. Pork?"

Martin yanked the bag out of her hands and stuffed a piece of the meat into his mouth. He grinned. "Yep!"

They sat on a fallen oak and devoured their breakfast. Gwyn had not seen him smile like that for days.

"How far are we from Vickland?" He licked breadcrumbs off his arm.

She slid the map from Martin's sack and unrolled it. "Not sure. Maps have always confused me."

"That's 'cause you have it upside down." He whipped it out of her hands, turned it over, and studied the river. "Vickland should be somewhere that way." He pointed behind him. "Because the river is in front of us. So the Zenia Wood must be that way." He pointed behind him and to the left.

"It looks like a good place to hide."

"But that highwayman we just saw ..."

"He wasn't a highwayman. I was being sarcastic," she said. When he frowned, she explained what *sarcastic* meant.

"He said something about ghosts in the Zenia Wood. Do you think he was being sarcastic about them?" Martin looked behind him again. "I don't wanna see a ghost."

Gwyn crunched on the apple core and spit out the seeds. "We'll find out, I guess."

She swallowed the fear twisting inside her and tried her best to feign confidence. He heaved a sigh and followed her as they traveled deeper into the woods away from the river.

The scent of sweet, musty leaves and clean, cool air wafted through the forest. Sure, they didn't have a home. And the Black Wizard and Uncle Edwinn were probably still searching for them. But at least they were alone in a quiet, peaceful wood. They didn't stop until midafternoon, when Gwyn found wild blackberries.

"Are you sure these aren't the poison kind?" Martin asked as he pulled a thorn out of his finger. His hands and face were stained purple-pink.

"I didn't know there was such thing as poison blackberries." She slid a handful of the berries into his bag.

"I heard there was a kind that made your insides explode."

"I guess we'll find out." She popped another berry in her mouth.

After collecting at least a pound of berries, they continued to hike toward the Zenia Wood.

"The Zenia Wood should give us cover." Martin studied the map as they walked. "We can stay near the border so we don't lose sight of Vickland. But not be too close to the ghosts."

"I don't think there are ghosts." But she couldn't get the image of a ghost out of her head.

"Better safe than sorry. Where do you think River lives?"

"I haven't thought that far yet."

"That's why you need me around," he said with the air of a ship's captain. "I'm good at looking at maps and thinking ahead."

"But I'm good at thinking fast." Gwyn held up Morin's knapsack. "Fast thinking gets us food."

"That's important."

She crawled over a log laden with fuzzy moss, then helped Martin over.

They traveled in silence for several moments, then Martin said, "Maybe we can go to Jalapa and ask round to see if anyone knows River."

"The boy said that Vickland has an evil king. We should try to stay hidden as much as possible."

He stopped. "If the king's so evil, why're we gonna live there?"

"Do you have a better idea?"

He shook his head and continued walking.

By nightfall, she found another thicket surrounded by a fence of brambles. Not that it would keep them safe from any wizards or witches or ghosts. But it gave them enough cover to ease her mind. They snacked on pine needles and blackberries.

"My back hurts." Martin lay down on the forest floor.

"Do you want me to find you a bed and a nice fluffy pillow?"

He groaned. She cleared out a few branches from under her and lay on her back.

"Listen, everything is going to be fine. We will find River. We won't have to sleep on the ground and eat pine needles and stolen food forever."

"Mm." Martin turned away from her. "I hope so."

The crickets chirped and her eyes grew heavy.

"Thanks for taking care of me." Martin's voice was quiet.

She turned toward him. "Of course I'm going to take care of you."

"I'm not very fast. What if the Black Wizard catches us because I'm slow?"

"Even if you're not fast enough, I'm not going to leave you behind. We're in this together. I'm not leaving you." She pulled a few sticks from under him and laid her shawl over him, tucking in the corners. "Now get some sleep and stop worrying."

Chapter 8

Traveling Along the White River

It's day six since we escaped Uncle Edwinn's house. If Martin complains about eating pine needles, berries, and acorns one more time, I swear I'm going to scream. I'm so hungry my stomach aches. We can't keep on like this. It's funny—as a kid I remember telling Mama I was starving when her supper was late. I didn't know what starving meant back then. I do now.

I don't want to keep going. I'm exhausted. I want to give up. But I can't. I have to keep going. For Martin.

He is throwing rocks into a creek as I write. His feet keep bleeding, so we're taking a break in the shade of an acorn tree this afternoon. At least, that's what I call it. These trees are all so new to me. By the looks of the map, Vickland appears to be a little more than a week's journey away. At the rate we're going, it'll take longer. I wish we had a horse.

What if River doesn't take us in? Where will we live? How am I supposed to protect Martin? It's only a matter of time before the Black Wizard finds us. He's powerful. I don't know how I would protect Martin from a monster like him.

Carrie Looper Stephens

I've been trying to put all the pieces together to solve this puzzle. The Black Wizard killed my parents. Why? Was it because he wanted the medallion? Because he wanted us? If he killed my parents because of me, I'll never forgive myself. Uncle Edwinn sold us to the wizard. Why? Why would he betray his own niece and nephew?

"There's nothing special about us." Gwyn set her pencil and faded journal down.

Martin stopped midthrow and looked at her.

"There's nothing special about you or me or Mama or Papa." He turned back to his rock throwing. "Then why are Mama and Papa dead, and a wizard and a king want you and our medallion?"

"I don't know."

She picked up her pencil.

The king wants me. The Black Wizard wants me. And Papa's medallion. Why? Why don't they want Martin? Why me?

Before Papa died, he saw the medallion around Martin's neck. Papa said something like "That's why he came." I don't want to mention it to Martin, but could he be the cause of their deaths? I want to know if he wonders the same thing. This could be all his fault, but there's no way I'd tell him what I think. It would crush him. I couldn't do that to him.

I'm trying to remember all the things my parents said about the medallion. Papa always wore it. He never took it off. When we asked him about it, he said it was nothing and not to touch it. The Black Wizard seemed scared. Said he couldn't touch it. And how did Martin hurt him just by touching him?

I feel different. I'm changing. But I don't know what I'm changing into. Who am I? I feel stronger. More in control. I just got my brother and me away from a dangerous wizard. I can do this. I'm not the scared little girl I was when my parents died.

But then the small voice reminds me … Everything's up to me. I have to figure everything out. I have to get us to safety. No one is here to help us.

"What if the man who warned us comes to save us again?" she asked.

"The crazy?" Martin finally succeeded in skipping a rock more than once. "I don't want his help."

"But he has to be on our side. He warned us."

He shrugged.

"We need to keep walking."

Martin groaned. "My feet are falling off."

Gwyn stuffed her journal and charcoal pencil into the bag and strapped it across her chest. "Come on. Let's get some more traveling done before nightfall."

After another hour of walking along the creek, they came to a valley where the creek filtered into a small pond. Martin lagged behind and she put her hands on her hips. She was about to scold him, but she saw the tear tracks on his face. He looked down to avoid her gaze. His feet were bleeding again.

"Happy birthday."

Martin looked up, smiling. "Is it really?"

No, she had lost track of the days. But now was as good as ever. They both needed a break, especially Martin. She nodded. "To celebrate, no more walking today. But first, let's go down to the pond and see if there are any fish."

Martin's eyes brightened. "I hope there are fish!"

She smiled as he ran ahead of her toward the pond. Once he reached the edge, he turned back to her. "Fish! Little ones, but they look delicious!"

She could already see his mouth watering. She laughed. "Go collect some wood and start a fire."

"Really?" He frowned. "But won't the smoke collect the witches and Andulza?"

"You mean *attract*. And don't worry about it. We're far enough away that they won't be able to see us." She hoped her voice sounded confident enough to convince him.

Carrie Looper Stephens

Martin ran out into the woods, collecting twigs and leaves. Gwyn broke off a privet branch and made sure the edge was nice and sharp. It wasn't as sharp as Papa's fishing spear, but it would have to do. She walked to the water's edge. Little blueish fish flitted through the murky water. They were no bigger than a radish. She sighed. This would be hard, but she had already gotten Martin's hopes up.

"I wish we had honey. I miss Mama's honey fish." Martin dropped a pile of twigs behind her. "Can we find a beehive?"

Gwyn waved for him to be quiet as she crouched by the water, privet branch poised above a swarm of fish. Her reflection was motionless as the little fish darted through the shallows. Martin's fire crackled behind her. Several long moments passed as she waited for the perfect moment. The largest fish swam by. Now. Her arm darted forward, flinging the spear into the water.

Martin jumped to her side and clapped. "You got one!"

She pulled the spear out, a wriggling fish the size of a pear speared to the end of it. She breathed a sigh of relief. Even after a year, she hadn't lost her touch. She found a thinner privet branch and took the fish off the spear and stuck it on the branch. She handed it to Martin, who eagerly ran it to the fire. He perched it over the fire, licking his lips and grinning ear to ear.

She caught eight more little fish. After cooking them, they devoured them. They were bony and there was very little meat. It paled in comparison to Mama's cooked fish. But this was exactly what they needed.

"Best birthday present ever." Martin licked the bones of the last fish.

Gwyn smiled. "Those fish were pretty good." She looked up at the fading light. "Let's find a thicket and call it a night."

Martin put out the fire before they traveled a good distance away from the pond. As Gwyn cleared out a space for them to sleep in a deep thicket, Martin chattered on about the fish they would eat for breakfast the next morning and how he'd find some berries and a beehive and make a honey berry sauce to go on them.

He curled into a ball and yawned. "Thanks for supper, Gwyn."

"You're welcome. Get some sleep."

Gwyn stared up at the sky until she couldn't keep her eyes open any longer. As she drifted in and out of sleep, she kept getting a feeling that grew tenser as the night wore on. The fire caused a lot of smoke. Too much. Would anyone be near enough to see them? The look on Martin's face as he drifted off made her smile. But was it worth it if they got caught?

CHAPTER 9

A NOISE IN THE THICKET

Gwyn's eyes snapped open. Her heart pounded and sweat traced down her face. She turned to check on Martin. He was still fast asleep. A typhoon could have raged, and he would have slept through it. She tried to focus on the loud, high-pitched noise that woke her, the same sound she had heard just before she saw the witches the night they escaped Uncle Edwinn's house.

An eerie white mist shrouded the dark forest. Was she in a dream? If so, it was shadowy, terrifying, and lifelike. A scream echoed through the forest as if a ghost had ripped through the ground and wailed an eternal cry of despair.

She lowered her head closer to the ground. She could not stop trembling. The sweat grew cold as it trickled down her face, and goose bumps formed on her arms. Something scurried in front of her. Not good. The dark night made everything ten times more horrifying. If only she had a candle or torch. The darkness was thick, like an invisible monster encircling her, readying to pounce.

Martin was still curled in a ball, sleeping soundly. Emotion clogged her throat. It was up to her to protect him and get them safely to Vickland. If anything ever happened to him, she could never forgive herself. Losing him chilled her more than the ghostly scream. She shook his shoulder.

"Wake up," she whispered.

Hoofbeats thundered outside the thicket and stopped about a hundred yards away. A horse snorted and pawed at the ground. Martin groaned in his sleep and mumbled something about fish. She slipped her hand over his mouth.

Torchlight flickered and illuminated the horse and rider. The rider lifted an instrument to his lips and blew a long, shrill scream.

"Martin, we have to go," she whispered. More hoofbeats. But they weren't galloping as fast as her heart was.

"Five more minutes." He groaned.

"Shh. There's someone following us. We need to go now. Get up!"

He sat up and strapped his satchel across his chest. His ruffled hair was drenched in sweat, but his eyes were far from sleepy.

Several people gathered around the rider.

"They're in the thicket," the first rider said.

Gwyn clenched Martin's arm.

"Burn them out," someone demanded.

Shrill, cackling voices called to each other.

"Oh, yes. We will burn them crispy like toast."

"Then boil them alive and feed them to the dragons."

Crazed laughter filled the night air as humpbacked creatures carrying glowing green torches crawled closer to the thicket.

"I told you witches were real," she whispered.

Martin groaned.

"This way." She pointed in the opposite direction of the approaching witches. The two crawled through the thicket, pushing away thorns and branches in their path.

"Maybe we can outwit them." She kept her voice low. "Papa always said witches were dumb."

"But Andulza's not dumb." He lifted a branch for her to pass under. Smoke filled the air and the thicket crackled and popped.

"What if there isn't a way out?" he whispered.

"Of course there is." Fear trickled up her neck and down her arms. She stumbled on a root.

"Gwyn!"

"I'm fine." She stood and ignored her stubbed toe.

They ran until the thicket opened into a small clearing. She took Martin's satchel from him and strapped it across her chest. The blowing smoke made her eyes water and made them cough. They tripped and stumbled in the darkness.

"Keep running," she said.

Martin clenched her hand. "Don't leave me." His voice sounded like a five-year-old's.

"I won't. I promise." She squeezed his hand tighter.

A flaming arrow zipped past them and thudded into a tree.

"Let's run in zigzags." It would probably stave off the arrows for now, though it would slow them down. Which would be worse, being shot with an arrow or being caught by a witch?

The cackles of the witches grew closer. Their green torches looked like dozens of eyes glowing in the darkness. Martin ducked under another arrow. In the orange glow of the forest fire, he stared at her, his round eyes shining with fear.

"It's going to be all right." If only she could believe her own words.

"Now's time for your fast-thinking skills." His voice squeaked as they ran in wide Z patterns.

Gwyn coughed and waved smoke away. "I'm trying!"

Carrie Looper Stephens

The clearing had ended, and they were running through another part of the forest. They leaped over a fallen log . They could climb trees again.

She looked up at a large oak but tripped over a root and fell. Martin's hand slipped out of hers. She flailed for something to hold on to but continued falling.

And falling.

And falling.

Her knees and hands smacked the ground, and her head hit something hard. She looked up through a circle at the starry sky. She must have fallen into a hole. Great.

"Martin?" she whispered.

The horses and witches and clamor passed the pit.

Martin screamed.

Suddenly, all was quiet.

"Martin!" she yelled.

Her heart pounded as she clawed at the sides of the hole. Dirt and roots and centipedes fell into her face. Her fingers could not find a good hold on the crumbling dirt. It started raining, making the walls of the hole even more slippery. She clambered up a few feet but was still too far away from the top. No! She couldn't let Martin be caught. She had to find him. After nearly an hour of fruitless attempts to climb out, she brushed away the dirt from her eyes and leaned against the wall, burying her face in her hands.

Poor Martin! All alone, in the hands of the witches and Andulza! She had failed her father. She had failed her brother. The only person she had left in the world.

Bits of rocks and dirt slid down. She looked up at a shadow against the hazy morning light.

"Who's there?" she asked.

CHAPTER 10

A ROPE IN THE DARK

"Catch this," a masculine voice ordered. A rope snaked its way toward Gwyn.

A horse snorted nearby.

Most likely this man planned to kill her, but she had to get out to find Martin, and she couldn't get out by herself. She reached up and caught the rope. It grew taut, and before she realized it, he was helping her to her feet. Once at the top, she backed away from him. His hood shadowed his face.

"Who are you?"

"You're welcome." The voice was deep. Familiar.

"Are you the man who gave me the key and warned us about our parents?"

"Maybe. And I might know the driver of the cart who rescued you and your brother from your uncle's house."

"I need to find my brother." She scanned the clearing frantically and hitched up the bag. A steady fire smoldered in little patches throughout the forest, though the rain was quickly squelching the flames.

"You're too late. Andulza and the witches already found him."

She felt like she had swallowed a hot brick. She searched the woods, hoping desperately to see her little brother dash into the clearing and yell, *I'm okay! I'm okay!*

"How do you know?" She turned to face the man.

"I watched it happen."

"And you did nothing?" she yelled.

He stepped back. "I did all I could. You and your brother are dealing with something more powerful than you realize."

"Where will they take him?"

"The castle, if they don't kill him first."

She had to swallow several times before asking, "Where's this castle?"

"On top of the Uziel Mountain that borders Vickland."

She shoved away the fear growing in her heart. She pictured his smile as he ate last night's fish. This was all her fault. She knew she shouldn't have let him start that fire. "I'm going."

"You can't do it alone."

"Then I will go to Vickland and see if River can help me."

"Let me at least take you to the Zenia Wood." He mounted his horse. The steed trotted toward her and the rider offered his hand.

"How do I know I can trust you?"

"I just saved you, didn't I?"

"Maybe you saved me so you could take—" She slid the medallion inside her shirt.

"So I could take the medallion? No, I don't want it. It will do no good for me. But you must keep it safe at all costs."

She stared at his outstretched hand. "First tell me who you are."

"Someone who is risking his life to save you and your brother." His tone grew impatient. "If we stay here much longer, the Black Wizard will kill us both."

She took his hand and he pulled her up behind him.

"Hold on."

Gwyn wrapped her arms around him as he kicked his steed. The animal cantered until they reached a clearing and then broke into a dead run. She had never been on a horse before and had imagined it would be more comfortable than this. Her whole body jolted, and her legs felt like they were about to fall off.

The early-morning light crept over sloping green hills dotted with large pine trees.

"Where are we?"

"Veritose. I will take you to the border of Vickland, at the Zenia Wood. There, you must go alone."

As the sun illuminated the mountainous landscape, Gwyn tried to get a better look at the man, but he had a black cloth covering all except his eyes and forehead. He was dressed in black pants, black shirt, and muddied boots.

As the day wore on, and as Gwyn grew sorer, a chant ran through her head. *Find River. Then find Martin. Find River. Then find Martin.* Perspiration trickled down her back. The horse's sweat glistened in the sunlight. The rider also breathed heavily and wiped sweat from his eyes.

By the time they stopped at a thick forest, the sun cast shadows on them.

"This is the Zenia Wood. You will be safe here, but I dare not go farther." She slipped off and looked back up at him. In the darkness, she had not seen the long white scar tracing across his brow. It made his eyes even sadder. He took a small loaf of bread out of his satchel and handed it to her.

"You must be hungry," he said. "Stay away from the roads. Keep the key I gave you secret. As well as your father's medallion."

"Thanks." She took the bread from him. "What's so special about the medallion? Why does everyone want it? Is it magical?"

His eyes turned serious when he looked back at her. "I cannot give you much information here, but I will say this. It is the last hope of Alastar. And the one who carries the medallion will be much sought after."

"But is it magical?" Gwyn asked again. He looked into the wood and then looked over his shoulder. When he looked back at her, fear clouded his eyes. "Yes. Very."

She fingered the cool metal. "What does it do?"

"Just know that things will not always be as they appear. This is all I can say now." The horse grew restless, and she backed away. The man clenched the reins. "Follow this path faithfully through the Zenia Wood. The path stops at the end of the wood, and you will be in Vickland. Watch out for border guards once you leave the wood. Vickland is swimming with them. Here. I believe these are yours." He handed her the satchel she had left at her uncle's house. Then he gave her Mama's necklace. She gasped and slipped the necklace around her neck over her medallion's chain, then ran her fingers over the smooth heart-shaped necklace. "How did you get them?"

"Be careful." He nodded to her and galloped off.

She devoured the bread as he rode out of sight. He seemed more helpful than informative. Who was he? In her pocket, the key poked her. She pulled it out and slid it onto the chain. It clinked against the heart charm. She poured the contents from her bag into Martin's and stuffed her empty bag into his. Then she faced the forest.

The trees were so thick it almost looked like evening. The branches above overlapped and intertwined, and sunrays filtered into the forest, creating scattered leaf patterns running across the path like little shadowy creatures. It was a quiet, mysterious wood, the type from a dream or a book.

Papa had spoken of the Zenia Wood. He used to speak fondly of reading in a big oak tree near the cabin where he grew up.

Gwyn once had a friend named Zenia. She used to talk all the time about the meaning of her name: *hospitable*. Surely the Zenia Wood must be safe. But why did the man dare not go any farther?

Chapter 11

A Throbbing Head and Restless Heart

Heron leaned against a tree and touched his throbbing head. Bromlin had told him fresh air would do him some good, so he had spent the past hour exploring the small farm.

Bromlin's voice came from a clearing near the cabin. Heron ducked behind some undergrowth and peered through the leaves. Bromlin knelt by a large stone and placed some fresh wildflowers near it.

"For you, dearest love." The old man's voice wavered.

Heron's cheeks burned. Normally, he wouldn't have cared about invading someone else's privacy. But this was different. Bromlin's voice was tender. Affectionate. A tone Heron had never heard a grown man use.

A mouse-looking creature with a fluffy tail chattered in the tree above him. Bromlin looked toward him. "Ah, Heron. You didn't escape?"

He stood and shrugged. "I didn't feel up to running."

"Yes, your horse is still quite tired and shaken up, poor thing. Best to let him rest a bit. Before we go up to the house, help me bring some wood for the fire." He pointed toward a woodpile to the left. They each took a pile of wood and trudged back up the slope to the cabin. Marrok followed.

"That was my wife's grave. She was a remarkable woman. Her eyes sparkled when she smiled. Brave woman. Fiercely loyal. Intelligent. I've never met her equal," he said with a sigh.

Heron averted his eyes and focused on holding his load. After stacking the wood, he sat down on the front porch steps and touched his bandaged head. Even in the cool of the late afternoon, he was sweating.

"Headache again?"

Heron nodded. The crickets chirping in the underbrush sounded like pounding drums. Bromlin stepped inside and returned a few moments later with two steaming cups. "Here's some of Bromlin's Brew to soothe the pain."

He sipped the dark liquid and winced at the warmth. It was like tea, yet stronger and thicker.

"I couldn't escape anyway. I walk for a few minutes, and my head pounds." He cupped his hands around the mug and stared at the black-brown liquid.

"You had a serious wound." Bromlin sat down beside him. "But though you are injured, you are quite capable of escaping my cabin. I think you have remained here these few days because you enjoy being away from your father. Is this not true?"

Heron stared at the brew, then back at his host. "How do I know this isn't poison?"

Bromlin's lips twitched upward underneath his bushy gray beard as he took a sip of his brew. "You don't."

He took another sip to hide his smile. The warm liquid was making it easier to think. He couldn't help enjoying life in this rugged wilderness away from the prim and proper ways of court and courtly manners. It was inconvenient not having his servants available, but it had given him time to think things through.

When away from his father, he had a clear and open mind. If Bromlin's story about Father murdering his grandfather was true, why had he not heard it before?

He looked out at the yard. Clucking, fat hens pecked at the dirt. A small wind chime jingled above. Besides these sounds, there was nothing. No soldiers marching. No servants asking him every five minutes if he needed anything. No court officials arguing. He furrowed his brow. The court officials did argue a lot. Did they know of Father's treachery?

Marrok trotted over and sat at Bromlin's feet. Heron reached out and ran his hands through the wolf's fur. The wolf looked back at him, his bright blue eyes staring right into his. He buried his fingers in the soft fur. This wolf was different from the pets he had owned as a boy. His dogs had been nothing but ornaments. Only the most expensive dogs were allowed as royal pets. Even so, besides his friend Gressette, they were the only companions he had ever had.

"I can tell you are fond of Marrok." Bromlin sat on the stairs next to Heron.

He shrugged. "It would be nice to be a dog with no purpose in life." He stretched his legs out and leaned his head on the post.

"Do *you* have a purpose for your life?"

He shifted on the steps and took another sip of brew. "I guess I'll become king someday." He frowned and ran his hand along the lip of the mug. "I *have* to be king someday."

Bromlin heaved a sigh. "Royal life is full of unwanted pressures and expectations, Heron. I sense you do not want this grave responsibility."

"Who would?"

"If you were not born into the royal family, what would you do?"

Heron glanced at his expectant face and then up at the sky. No one had ever asked what he wanted to do. The question stirred something in him. Freedom. Excitement. Fear.

He took a long draft of the brew. His head wasn't pounding anymore. "What is this?"

Bromlin smiled. "Just roasted berries."

A large shadow darkened the front yard and then disappeared. He barely caught a glimpse of large black wings. Marrok jumped to his paws and growled at the sky.

"Dragon riders," Bromlin said. "I haven't seen them in decades, but the past two nights I've seen several. The Black Wizard is up to no good."

"He's one of my father's main councillors. Father wouldn't allow him on the council if he were up to no good."

Bromlin choked on his brew and slammed the mug down. "What did you just say?"

"The Black Wizard is on my father's council."

He gripped Heron's shoulders. "You're not fooling me, are you? Tell me you are. Tell me this is not true."

Heron shrugged his hands away. "It's true. All of Vickland knows of it. You should get out more. It's common knowledge."

His incredulous expression turned to sadness, the same look Heron had seen his mother give his father. A look of deep hurt. Bromlin rested his hands on his knees and bowed his head. His eyes were clenched shut, and he shook his head as if trying to shake away the truth. "I once knew him as Andulza. But that was many, many years ago. I know his past. He cares only for power, even if it means trampling over those he loves. He cannot be trusted, and no motive he has will be pure."

"How would a crazy old man living in a shack in the woods know of these things?" Heron rolled his eyes.

"This crazy old man has seen more than you know. Ah yes, I have seen more of this world than I would like." He shook his head. "Andulza is a fool to think he can conquer Alastar. He may have conquered Vickland by using your father as a puppet, but he cannot change the hearts of the people. Often a state is changed not by dictators, kings, and usurpers, but by the slow and subtle change of a mindset, a way of life, the erasing of the ancient ways and laws. And most of all, the abolishing of truth. He is too impatient to realize this. He—and your father as well—can beat the Vickland people into submitting to their whims, but they cannot change their fierce and independent spirits."

"You've eaten one too many mushrooms." Heron slung a piece of kindling into the woods, then stood and walked to the front door.

"I'm not as crazy as you think, my boy. If you are not careful, you may find the Black Wizard's poisoned blade in your back someday."

Heron stopped in the doorway, one hand on the door's latch, the other holding his empty mug. "How does my father treat his people?"

Bromlin leaned against the creaky post. "Have you ever been outside Lyris?"

"Not much."

"When you decide to go back home, take a detour through Jalapa or Whitmire, though I recommend going disguised. There you will see what your father's people—*your* people—think of their king."

Heron frowned. He liked the suggestion but didn't want to admit it. Any excuse to stay away from his father longer was a good excuse.

"Things will change for the worst if nothing is done," Bromlin said. "Indeed they will. Mark my words."

"Then what do you want me to do about it?"

He turned toward him, the disappearing light casting shadows over his wrinkled features. "The change must start here"—he pointed at Heron's chest—"before it starts here." He gently tapped Heron's head with his index finger. "You must decide what *you* believe, not what others want you to believe. You must decide your own path, not the path others want you to take. You must seek out the truth, not lies. And you must seek out your people's hearts."

He winced and pushed Bromlin's hand away. He had never cared much about the truth, unless it got him out of trouble. But the truth was usually what got him in trouble, not out of it. And he had never considered his father's people. He didn't even know what they looked like. Probably like the servants in Lyris. Bromlin insinuated that there was something wrong with him and he needed to change. This guy definitely had guts. A peasant insulting the prince? It was definitely a first for him. The anger boiled again.

He clenched his fists. "I'm going back home whether I feel like it or not. I won't tell my father where you live."

Bromlin sighed. "You are free to go. I cannot stop you."

After saddling his horse, he mounted and trotted past the cabin. Bromlin stood on the porch and raised a big, weathered hand in parting. A sad smile darkened his features. Heron glared at him and guided his steed toward the path. But even the adrenaline of riding through a haunted forest couldn't shake away the questions still swirling in his head.

CHAPTER 12

THE ZENIA WOOD

As the morning sky brightened to the color of a peach, Gwyn settled down by a tree and massaged her sore feet. She rummaged in her sack and brought out her journal and pencil.

Today is my second day in the Zenia Wood. It's a peaceful wood. But I can't be at peace until I find Martin. I'm such a horrible sister. I hate myself. I can't stand the thought of him being alone. It's all my fault. If I hadn't been so clumsy, I wouldn't have fallen in the hole. I would rather be captured with Martin and in the Black Wizard's clutches than by myself. I can't stand being alone.

She grabbed a rock and threw it into the woods as hard as she could. It thumped on a tree and fell with a leafy rustle to the ground. She heaved a sigh and rested her head against the tree behind her. Now that she had written her thoughts down, she could put them away. At least for now. She stashed her pencil and journal in the satchel and gazed up at the ancient gray trees of the Zenia Wood.

Thunder rumbled overhead. She looked up, but the thick forest revealed only shreds of the orange sunrise melting into a gray-tinged sky.

After a breakfast of acorns, she situated her satchel and continued down the path.

"Vickland shouldn't be too far away." She frowned at her crackling voice. It had been a while since she talked to anyone, and it reminded her how much she missed having Martin by her side. A thunderclap shot through the sky and made her jump. A few raindrops chilled her skin. She broke into a run, staying as far away as she could from the darker shadows along the path. They were probably just bushes or undergrowth, but she didn't want to stay long enough to find out.

Even after hours of running through the light rain, the adrenaline and fear tightening in her chest kept her from wearying.

She leaped over a fallen tree, ducked under a low branch, and continued down the path of the Zenia Wood. Her necklace bounced lightly against her chest and her knee-length skirt freed her stride as her bare feet hit the leaf-strewn floor.

She had it all planned. Continue down the path until the wood ended and then find the man named River in Vickland, and maybe he would help her find her brother. Surely, if he was a friend of her father's, he could be trusted. And surely, he would want to help his friend's children. Hopefully.

She ducked under a branch, and the soft green leaves caressed her forehead. She was glad it was summer. The leaves provided extra cover.

But what if she met with the Vickland border patrol the strange man told her about? What if she couldn't find River? What if she had just imagined him? What if he never even existed? She often had a hard time deciphering between her imagination and reality. What if the Black Wizard found her? What if she got lost in the woods? And worst of all, what if Martin was already dead? The tightness in her chest constricted.

Why had she fallen into the hole in the first place? If she hadn't, she and Martin would still be together. Maybe she could have gotten them to safety. If only he had fallen into the hole instead.

Guilt gnawed at her. She would tear that wizard limb from limb if he hurt him.

When she leaped over a small stream, she almost collided with a horse and rider. She fell backward and stared up at a startled boy a few years older than her. His mount looked healthy, and she could tell by its glittering tack that the rider was well to do.

The surprised expression in his dark brown eyes changed to one of mistrust as he touched the hilt of a sword buckled to his side. "Who are you?"

"I'm, uh, Sara." Gwyn scrambled to her feet and backed away. She had never seen someone so good-looking. "Who are you?"

He opened his mouth but hesitated. "None of your business. What are you doing here?"

"Just … running."

"*Just* running? No one dares enter this wood." He had a black-and-blue bruise underneath his brown hair, but it just added to his good looks. It made him look tragically beautiful.

"Why? Are the woods magical?" She hated it when her voice cracked.

"Magical?" He considered this for a second and nodded. "Yes. It's magical." The suspicion returned to his face. "Are you a fairy?"

Her face grew warm and she brushed her hair out of her eyes. "What are *you* doing here?"

"I'm, uh . . . riding. I'm taking a ride. Did my father send you?"

"Who's your father?"

He sighed in relief. "Never mind."

"Do you know where Vickland is?"

"Yes." He looked at her as if she had asked where his nose was located. "Why?"

Could she trust him? He could be on the Black Wizard's side. But surely someone so young and handsome didn't have the capability of being evil. "I need to go there. Do you know a man named River?"

"Never heard of him."

"Oh. Well, I need his help."

"With what?" He stared at her ripped clothes and tousled hair. She didn't think it was possible to be any more embarrassed than she already was. She had to pull herself together and find Martin. Why was she so distracted by this beautiful stranger? Her brother's life was at stake.

"None of your business." She folded her arms and forced her most confident expression.

"Fine." He kicked his horse into a trot.

Gwyn's embarrassment turned to panic. "Please. I need to find him. I'm in trouble. My brother is in trouble." The words spilled out of her mouth faster than she could think.

He pulled on the reins. "Why?"

She swallowed a lump in her throat and stepped backward. A few tree frogs croaked near the small stream behind her. She looked down at the leafy floor. What if this guy was on the Black Wizard's side? If so, telling the truth would mean certain death.

"Well, you're obviously hiding something, and I'm not going to tell you where I'm going, so it's an impasse. Why don't you go your way and I go mine and we forget we saw each other?"

She paused, then nodded.

The boy caught her eye and frowned. He pointed in front of him. "Vickland is that way." He turned and urged his horse into a canter and was gone.

She let out the breath she had been holding. Did that really just happen? She looked in the direction he had gone—the same way she was going. She wanted to see him again, but not all dirty like this. Of course she had to meet the handsomest man ever when she looked her worst. The girls in Nelice would faint if they saw him.

She imagined Martin standing in front of her with his hands on his hips and an annoyed look on his face, and the guilt returned. She had much more important things to focus on now.

She continued running until the sun set and the shadows made her stumble. As the undergrowth grew thicker and the forest ended, she slowed to a walk. Her legs ached and her eyes grew heavy. The encroaching darkness didn't make it any easier. But she had to keep going. For Martin. She tried to force herself into a run. A twig snapped in the woods behind her, and she picked up her speed but tripped over a root and banged her elbow against a tree. She slipped into a thicket full of brambles and privet and lay down on the packed dirt. She was so tired her whole body ached.

Leaves rustled. She tensed and flattened herself as close to the ground as she could. A squirrel chattered and clambered up a tree. She breathed a sigh of relief and rested her head on her arm.

Papa and Mama used to check on her and Martin before bed. She could see them now, standing in the doorway, painted in yellow candlelight. Their warm smiles, their soft voices, their loving hands tucking in the quilts around them …

The wind rushed through the woods and blew wisps of her hair into her face. She twisted a few strands around her finger and pushed away the memories. If only her parents never existed.

No! Why would she even think that? If only she could go back in time and stop their deaths from happening.

She must find Martin. He was all she had.

She pulled the map out of his satchel and traced the White River with her finger in the fading light. She was near Vickland. Hopefully. The White River and Surday were far behind like a distant memory. She folded the map and placed it back into the satchel. She tried clearing out some of the underbrush for her bed but gave up. Hopefully these magic woods didn't have poison ivy. She laid her head on the satchel. It smelled like sweat and chocolate. Like Martin.

She was so weary, so tired of the grief and loneliness. A heavy ache settled on her. Before all this, when she had problems, she could run to her parents, and they would solve them for her. Like magic.

When their parents died, she and Martin solved their problems together. They had been a good team. She was good at getting them out of a bad situation fast, but he was a better planner. And he was better at reading maps.

She let a muffled sob escape and turned to her side to rest her face on her arm. Warm tears fell and she tasted the salty moisture on her lips.

"Martin, please be safe," she whispered.

CHAPTER 13

MARTIN HAS AN UNPLEASANT EXPERIENCE

Martin gasped for breath under the stifling cloth tied over his head. The shrieks and screeches of the witches echoed through the forest as they carried him along. He had been jarred so much his arms, legs, and head would drop off any second.

"Wait till Master sees this prize!" a voice croaked. Cackles filled the air.

"He'll be happy with us this time! Perhaps he promotes us to dragon riders."

"I can't wait to see what Master does to the squirmy little creature. I hope he sets him on fire," the chattiest witch said. "The little brute nearly knocked my eye out again."

"Careful now. The border patrol is near. I can smell them." This witch's voice was louder and more commanding than the others. She must be the lead witch.

"I want to watch him burn alive. I want to watch him squirm and wail and scream. And if Master lets me, I will poke him with my stick," Chatty Witch said.

"After they burn him, then we hang him and cut him with our swords." This came from a witch with a hoarse voice.

"And then we boil him alive and make him into soup and feed him to the dragons," Chatty Witch suggested.

Martin clamped his teeth together to keep them from chattering. Where were they taking him? Probably to Andulza. Had Gwyn escaped? Why had she left him? He had called out to her several times after he was taken but didn't hear her call back. They were supposed to stick together. Protect each other. Like Papa said.

The witches croaked on about violent deaths for what seemed like hours. Finally, they dumped him down on a hard dirt floor.

"Is it the boy?"

He recognized the voice. Andulza, the Black Wizard.

"See for yourself, Master," Lead Witch said.

"Yes! See? See? It is the boy," Chatty Witch piped up. "We fought hundreds of warriors to bring him to you. We alone were the strongest who survived."

"He is a wicked little thing. What will you do with him?" Lead Witch asked.

"Patience. First I must speak to him alone."

"But, Master, we want to watch!"

"Leave."

The grumbling witches' voices faded and a door closed, then Andulza ordered, "Search him."

Gloved hands seized Martin by his collar. Someone ripped his shirt, probably searching for the necklace. Another hand roughly searched his pockets.

"It's not here." Uncle Edwinn's voice.

"You may leave now. I am eager to talk to the son of my worst enemy."

Boot steps retreated. Heavy footsteps strode toward him. The steps stopped, and the cloth slid off.

Martin blinked. He was in an empty room with a single torch burning. He looked up into the face of Andulza. His hungry-looking grin sent shivers coursing through him. A deep white scar traced down his cheek. With his disheveled gray hair, pale gray eyes, and pointed teeth, he was exactly what Martin had always pictured a crazy would look like.

"We meet again," Andulza said, stroking his black-gray beard.

Martin sat on his knees, staring at the wizard's black boots.

Andulza clenched Martin's chin and stared into his eyes. "Remarkable. Green as an emerald. Green is a sign of magical presence. You and your sister could learn to do great things."

Martin tried to put on his bravest face, but it was probably more of a wince than a look of bravery. *If Gwyn were here, she would say something brave.*

"Tell me where the medallion is."

"I don't have it," Martin said.

Andulza kicked him in the face, sending him tumbling backward. His nose made a popping sound, and warm blood gushed out.

"Where is it? Where did you put it?" he yelled. His bloodshot eyes bulged in outrage. "I will not allow two puny children to keep the medallion from me!"

"I never had any stupid medallion." He wiped his bloody nose on his sleeve and crawled backward toward the wall. All this over a stupid medallion. It had grown hot the night he jumped on the Black Wizard's back, like it hated the wizard and wanted to kill him as badly as he did.

"Does your sister have it?" Blue-green veins pulsed in the wizard's neck.

"No." He remembered the book about mind reading and tried hard not to think of the medallion or Gwyn. If he thought of either, Andulza would read his mind. He searched for something else to think about. *Chocolate. Gooey chocolate.*

Andulza's face broke into a grin. He clenched Martin's arm to keep him from retreating farther toward the back wall. "You want to know a secret, boy?"

Martin didn't want to know any secret this crazy man had, but he kept quiet. *Chocolate dates. Chocolate apples. Chocolate bread. Chocolate fish. Chocolate medallion.* Andulza brought his face so close Martin could have touched his nose with his tongue.

"I think," he said with a gleam in his eye, "she does have the medallion."

"N-n-no!" Martin clenched his teeth to keep them from chattering.

Andulza stomped to the door and opened it.

"Bring Edwinn here," he ordered the witches piled up at the threshold. They scurried away. Moments later, Uncle Edwinn was thrown into the room, and the door slammed after him. He dusted off his sleeves and glanced at Andulza, who pointed his flaming torch at Martin.

"He claims he doesn't know where the medallion is."

Edwinn stared at the floor. "I know I saw him with a necklace."

"But now it is gone." Andulza's voice was icy, like someone trying too hard to be patient.

"Listen, why don't you let me go?" Uncle Edwinn shifted from one foot to the other. "You won't have to pay me a penny. Look, I tried to help you get your medallion, but I was mistaken. You know I've helped you in the past. I let you store your magic books in my house. It's not easy hiding those books. Do you know how many break-ins I've had? I gave you the information you needed about the medallion." He wrung his hands and locked eyes with Martin, scowling in disappointment.

Like he would actually betray Gwyn to these monsters? No way.

Andulza laughed. "Let you go? No, I have better plans for you." He glared at Martin. "Before your uncle dies, I want you to take a good look at the man who betrayed your father to me. *He* is the cause of your parents' deaths."

Martin's mouth dropped open.

Uncle Edwinn studied him with an expression that seemed almost apologetic. But the expression twisted into a defiant scowl as he backed toward the door. "Your father deserved it, after all the pain he caused me. He was a disgrace to our family."

Andulza took a handful of blue particles out of his pouch and sprinkled them into his torch, which crackled and roared as the flame flashed bright blue. Uncle Edwinn's eyes grew wide, and he leaped toward the door, but he was not fast enough to escape the torch that flew from the wizard's hand, hitting him squarely on the back. He screamed and fell to the ground, writhing in pain. The blue flames engulfed him, growing so hot the heat burned the hair on Martin's arms. He gasped and scooted against the wall. The fire devoured Edwinn as quickly as if he were a piece of parchment. As the flames died, nauseating smoke filled the room. Martin's stomach churned. Andulza's grin shone behind the screen of smoke.

"Witches, enter." He plucked the smoldering torch from the midst of Uncle Edwinn's ashes and relit it.

The trembling witches entered. Martin wrinkled his nose as the creatures came into the light. Their hair was green and frizzy, and their scabbed, slimy faces glistened in the torchlight. The stories Papa used to tell about them never conveyed the evil, hungry looks on their faces or the horrifying dread when in their presence.

"You said you wanted to watch this boy die?" Andulza asked.

Martin gulped. This was it. He would never see Gwyn again.

"Oh, yes yes, Master! Please, Master!" Chatty Witch said. Her long, pointed nose cast a triangular shadow over her face.

Andulza touched Martin's chin with his sword. The pressure of the blade forced him to look up into his face. He looked at the door, hoping beyond hope to see Gwyn rush in and save him.

"Martin, son of the late Dylan of Nelice," Andulza said in a mocking tone, "what do you know of your father?"

Martin frowned and looked down.

"Speak!"

"He was a fisherman," he said quickly, trying to back farther away from the wizard. But his back hit the wall.

"Your father was not just a fisherman." Andulza smirked. "He was much more. But you will never know this, because he is dead, and the dead do not speak. But what you must understand, boy, is that your father was a failure. A failure, do you hear? He tried to kill me"—he touched the scar on his cheek—"but he failed. Say it. Say your father was a failure."

An angry monster woke in Martin's chest. He narrowed his eyes, and his teeth stopped chattering. "My father was not a failure." The sword point pressed sharper, and he gasped in pain but yelled again, "My father was not a failure!"

The monster roared inside him, spurring him on. No one was going to talk that way about his papa.

Andulza's eyes flashed with a demonic anger that suddenly melted into an expression of chilled, calm contempt. "He was a weak fool and a failure. He had great power, and he didn't use it on anything of importance. I have a bounty hunter tracking your sister even as we speak. She will die if you do not obey me. You don't want to be a failure like your father, do you?"

Icy fear the size of a brick clogged Martin's throat. The monster retreated and hid somewhere in his stomach. He pictured Gwyn running through the forest, calling for him. He stared at the ashes that were once Uncle Edwinn. "Don't hurt her." His voice quavered.

"I won't, *if* you say your father was a failure."

His heart sank. He pictured Papa's smiling green eyes. Gwyn's face came into his head. Her eyes were scared, and the cut on her face looked deep. He had no other choice than to do whatever the Black Wizard said.

"My father was a failure," he said in a strained whisper. The sword point's pressure left and the tip stabbed into the wooden floor. All energy seeped out of him, and he fell to his face and wept.

"That's more like it. Now, I think I have had a change of heart. Witches, I have other plans for him. Call for a dragon. Send him to my daughter. Tell her to lock him in the prison with the other children. He will be of much better use to me as bait. His foolish sister will surely come after him."

Andulza took a wet rag from his pocket and clamped it over Martin's mouth and nose. "This will keep you quiet during your passage to the Uziel Mountain."

Martin tried to push his hand away, but the wizard was too strong. There was a sickeningly sweet smell, and his eyes grew heavy. He couldn't breathe. Andulza's gloating voice sounded as if it were at the end of a tunnel.

Panic clenched him, and he desperately struggled against the drowsiness. No, he couldn't die now. He had to find Gwyn. Why hadn't she come? He tried kicking, but his legs felt like bricks. The room started to spin, and everything went dark.

CHAPTER 14

JALAPA

Heron slowed his horse and read a rotting sign. "Jalapa: 1 mile."

His head throbbed, but he wasn't going home until he took Bromlin up on his suggestion to tour part of the kingdom. Any excuse to delay seeing his father again was a good excuse.

The dirt road was pocked with holes and littered with animal waste. Surely the town would be cleaner. The stench made his head ache more. Indigo flowers whispered in the field beside the path, and the sun beat down hard. A peasant driving an oxcart stared at his steed and gear as he ambled past. Heron touched his sword and glared at the peasant, who returned the glare and passed by without a word.

It should be perfectly safe to observe the land. People wouldn't know who he was without his extravagant gear. He didn't want any suspicions or an attack by thieves. His horse stood still as he slid off the saddle and tack and laid them by the path. Some poor villager would stumble upon it and get rich.

He scooped up mud from the road and smeared it on his steed, then cut the mane and tail with his sword until they looked ragged. He studied his reflection in his sword's blade, shaking his head at his disheveled hair and unshaven face. Hopefully, that would be enough disguise. He laughed. He didn't look like himself at all. He looked like a rogue. A thief. He liked the image more than what he was forced to look like at home. He would be excused from the table if he had not shaven or if his hair had not been combed.

His reflection in the sword's blade reminded him of his desire to explore. Go places he had never been. Fight in battles. He stroked his stubble. Maybe he would keep the beginnings of this beard.

But his father had a beard.

It had to go as soon as he found a razor.

Getting up on his horse was more challenging than he expected. He had never ridden bareback. He clumsily mounted and nudged his steed into a slow walk.

Jalapa carried the worst stench he had ever smelled. Everything reeked of waste and sweat. The people looked like they had never seen a bath. Barefooted children ran in between wooden shacks, causing a man on a ladder to totter slightly as he placed hay on top of a roof.

A man carried a torch in one hand and a bale of hay in another. Heron looked from the torch to the roof of a building nearby. Whoever thought of making hay roofs must have been drunk. If he were king, he would make everyone have stone roofs. Or at least wooden ones. The houses were so close together that one house fire could cause the whole town to burn down. Did Father know of this dangerous inefficiency? Perhaps he could bring it up to him to get on his good side.

A young couple walked arm in arm a few feet in front of him. Despite the young man's ragged beard, the woman smiled up at him and kissed his cheek as he leaned down and whispered something in her ear. She giggled and touched his arm. The rings they wore on their fingers looked like hand-carved wood. Underneath the mud and sweat, the woman's eyes sparkled as she stared up in admiration at her husband. Even with a dirty face, she was ten times prettier than the heavily perfumed, painted girls Heron knew.

Sara, the green-eyed girl he'd met in the Zenia Wood, was pretty, even with a smear of mud on her forehead and a scar on her cheek. Why did he find her and this peasant woman more attractive than the rich daughters of lords and ladies? Perhaps they reminded him of Vanessa, a servant of one of the court officials. Because of her excellent riding skills, she was often sent to take messages to the king. There was something beautiful about her demeanor. She didn't expect everyone to praise her beauty or worship the ground she walked on. She just went about her duties with a faithfulness and cheerfulness he had never seen in any other.

Father had voiced his opinion many times on the subject of Heron's future wife. He had already come up with a strategy involving Petunia, daughter of John of Gloushester. Once Heron turned eighteen next year, he and Petunia were to be married, joining the wealthy Gloushester family to the royal family. His father spoke of it so often that he dreaded the banquets the heavily painted girl would attend. She would bat her eyes and talk about her lace, her musical talents, and her ridiculous dog that looked more like a rat. Her rat-dog looked similar to its owner.

A loud shout drew him out of his thoughts. Hoofbeats sounded. The husband grabbed his wife's hand, and they raced into the cover of a nearby store. Mothers gathered their children and hurried inside houses. Men closed the shutters over windows, and someone yelled to Heron from a butcher shop, "Get off the streets!"

Heron groaned when a troop bearing his father's crest galloped down the streets. General Rinalldo was in the lead. He urged his horse into an alley and slid behind a house to get a better view of the general.

The young couple Heron had seen moments ago were standing before Rinalldo. The bearded man stood in front of his wife and glared at the general.

"I gave you a week." Rinalldo sounded exasperated. "Was that not enough?"

"I don't have the money," the man said. "You took my crop. You already took my chickens. I have nothing else."

"So you aren't paying?" the general asked.

"I can't."

"There's one thing that will cancel your debt."

"That's what you said last week, and I gave you my house." The peasant clenched his fists and glared at the general. The woman slipped her hand into his, and his tense posture relaxed some.

"Join the army for ten years, and all your debts will be forgiven."

The man cursed and laughed bitterly. "The king will not keep his promise! He has never fulfilled that promise to any of his soldiers."

Heron never realized how much the general looked like a snake until now. Rinalldo turned toward his troops and nodded.

Two arrows silenced the couple. They lay side by side, still holding hands. Dark red blood fled like liquid serpents away from the bodies and into the filthy streets.

Heron stared at the lifeless bodies for several seconds. Did that just happen? Mother's ashen face flitted through his thoughts.

He wheeled his horse around and charged the general. "Rinalldo!"

Rinalldo's eyes widened. "Well, if it isn't the prince. Your father has been worried sick about you."

He reined in his steed and pointed to the couple lying motionless in front of him. "I will tell my father what happened here! You will hang for this. I will be sure of it!"

Rinalldo's serpentine smile returned. "I highly doubt that. Your father was the one who told me to kill the wretches."

Heron clenched the reins in his hand. Could that be true? Could his father truly be so evil?

"Your father will be glad to see you," he said. He motioned for one of his men to trade horses with Heron. "Let's head back to Lyris."

He was too shocked to resist. "What did they do?"

Rinalldo turned in the saddle. "Sire?"

"What did the couple do?"

"Why do you care what happens to a few lowly peasants?" He waved his hand in dismissal. "A handsome, talented prince like you should be focused on sword training and finding a lady to be your queen."

He hated when his father's officials used flattery to avoid his questions. He glared at him. "That doesn't answer my question."

"They didn't pay the king's taxes," he said with a shrug. "Those who disobey must be killed. We don't want a rebellion on our hands, do we?"

"Just because of money?"

"I wouldn't question the king's methods," Rinalldo said. "You benefit from those taxes too. You wouldn't have food and a bed if it weren't for your people paying their dues. But if you disagree, you can have a little chat with your father when you get back. I'm sure he's eager to speak to you."

The disgust and anger from the murders transformed into apprehension. His shoulders slumped and all energy seeped out of him. In a few short hours, he would have to face his father.

Chapter 15

King Donavan Oakheart

Heron followed General Rinalldo and his cavalry on the path toward Lyris Castle. Always wearing the snakelike smile, Rinalldo checked several times to make sure he was still in the group. He was probably happy he had found the prince so he could continue being on the king's good side.

The couple's lifeless bodies still haunted Heron. Memories of his mother kept attacking him.

No. He couldn't think about that now.

He tried to sort through everything that had happened the past few days. Part of him wished he had never ventured into the Zenia Wood. Everything he had grown up thinking and believing now conflicted with what he had seen. Or was Bromlin just an old man who had been away from things awhile? It was entirely possible that all the mushrooms Heron ate during his stay in the wood could be messing with his brain.

But the events in Jalapa made Bromlin's words seem not so far-fetched after all. Somehow, his revelation of King Donavan's past seemed to clear up several things, like why his father did not want his only son to wander off. He didn't want Heron stumbling across someone who had uncovered the truth.

The riders crested a hill and Lyris Castle came into view. Ancient gray stone contrasted with the pale blue sky and green-and-purple fields. Green flags fluttered in the harsh wind.

The sight of the castle created a whirlwind of emotions twisting in his mind. This was his home. His familiar safe place. No one would hurt him behind the strong, fortified walls. But this was where his father was.

A prick of pain stabbed his head. He winced.

"Are you all right, sire?" a rider said beside him.

He nodded. His heart beat faster as they entered the portcullis. Soldiers and servants scurried out of the way and created a path for the troops.

"The prince has returned!" one of the soldiers called out.

Several servants whispered to each other. Several wore looks of pity when they saw his bruise. Heron pulled his shoulders back and stuck out his chest. He forced a blank look on his face as he dismounted. He couldn't show any emotion. He refused to look weak.

A servant took the steed away, and Heron walked toward the stairs, where the scent of roasted chicken from the banquet hall greeted him. His hunger returned in full force. He could eat five whole chickens right now. And he wanted to sleep for days.

No. Shoulders back. Captain Fletcher and a dozen or so soldiers stood in the stairway. Fletcher caught his eye with a look of sympathy on his face.

"Sire." He bowed. "I was told to escort you to your father immediately."

"I'm hungry." Heron tried to brush past him.

Fletcher put his hand on his shoulder, and the soldiers stood in his path. "I'm sorry, sire. The king has demanded you be brought to him immediately. I sent for Dredo to bring a warm meal and clean clothing to your quarters." He frowned at the gash on his head. "I will also send for the apothecary. However, for now it will go well with you if you follow me."

He looked at the thick muscles on Fletcher's arms and the double swords resting in sheaths on his back.

"Fine." He was in too much pain to resist. Might as well get it over with.

Fletcher let go of his arm and led him up the stairs. The rest of the soldiers followed quietly behind. He heaved a deep breath as they neared the king's quarters. Fletcher opened the door and gave him a quick glance, an *I'm sorry* glance.

Heron stepped into the room, and Fletcher shut the door behind him. Heron firmed his jaw. He wasn't going to look weak in front of his father. King Donavan sat at a long table by himself. Heron compared his father's neat, trimmed, brown-gray beard and clean, unwrinkled, brightly colored clothes to his own disheveled appearance.

The king curled his lip in disgust. He interlaced his fingers and rested his hands on the table. "Do you have any idea how this makes me look as ruler of Vickland?"

Like a terrible king who's so awful that his only son runs away? Yes, that's exactly how you look.

He pushed his chair back, and Heron jumped at the sudden movement. *No. Stay strong. Stay strong.* His father walked in slow, measured steps closer to him.

He swallowed. "Father, I—"

"Do not speak." He glared at him. Anger replaced some of Heron's fear; still, he kept quiet as his father continued. "I want you to tell me exactly where you went. I want the truth."

"I want the truth as well." He returned the glare. "Why were two people killed in Jalapa under your orders?"

"You went to Jalapa? No son of mine should ever step foot in that dung-heap." Donavan twitched his nose and frowned. "The villagers were obstinate and would not pay taxes they owed. I cannot afford to keep up my country if I am not paid. Besides, they were mere villagers. Why should that concern you? Is Jalapa the only place you went?"

"Yes."

"You lie!" He thundered. Veins bulged in his neck and temples. "Fletcher saw you enter the cursed Zenia Wood."

Heron firmed his jaw and clenched his hands.

"You cannot lie to me. I have eyes all over the kingdom. What did you see in the wood?"

"Trees and wolves. That's all."

"You saw no one?"

"No." Heron didn't flinch. He had mastered the art of lying, and it often served him well when speaking to his father.

"Good. The Zenia Wood is not to be touched by either Vickland or Veritose. It marks the border between us. A wood of peace. The prince of Vickland intruding into Zenia would most certainly be seen as an act of war." Donavan turned and paced the room, circling the table. "I don't know how else I can force you to obey." He returned to Heron and stood in front of him. "From now on, you will never be alone. There will always be guards at your door, and you can only leave for meals and training. This rebelliousness will not happen again. Do I make myself clear?"

"Yes." Heron backed up a step and bowed his head.

"I have had to deal with all sorts of probing questions and ridiculous gossip spreading throughout the kingdom. Some say the Veritose army kidnapped you. Others say you ran off with a girl. You have no idea how embarrassing this has been. This will not happen again." He grabbed

Heron's shoulders with a viselike grip. "This will not happen again!"

Heron looked away from the fire in his eyes. Why did he always feel like a five-year-old when he was with his father?

"Are you listening to me, boy?" He shook him. "I have a kingdom to run. I have no time for such foolishness!"

Heron stared at the floor. He choked back Bromlin's accusations. Now was not the time.

"What is it you want? What can I give you to bribe you into obeying me?"

"I just want to be left alone." He returned the angry glare.

"Then you shouldn't have been born in the royal family."

He rolled his eyes. This was the same speech he had heard since he was little, about how royalty never has privacy, blah, blah, blah. "When a prince or king, you must—"

"I don't want to hear it!" He yanked away from his father's grasp and took a step back. "I don't want to be king if it means—"

"Oh, you *will* hear it!"

"No, you listen to me!" Heron shouted.

Donavan slammed him against the wall and held him by the throat. Little red veins bulged in the whites of his eyes. "I am sick of your disrespect and rebellion."

Guards burst into the room, Fletcher and Rinalldo among them. Heron's head throbbed and his legs grew weak. He fell to his knees, staring at his father's polished boots.

"He has a head wound, sire." Fletcher's voice was faint. "I will take him to his quarters. I have already sent for the apothecary."

Arms clamped around him and the loud voices became jumbled. He found himself back in his bed, and as soon as his boots were removed and a quilt wrapped around him, he fell asleep.

CHAPTER 16

A WOODSMAN OF THE ZENIA WOOD

Gwyn woke with a start and squinted in the early-morning sunlight trickling in through the thicket. Was it a dream, or had she really heard a sound in the woods? She lifted her head. Leaves rustled behind her. Not good. Perhaps it was a squirrel again?

A soldier drew nearer as he hacked at the thorns and privet with his sword. Clangs echoed in her ears. The soldier looked way over six feet, though thankfully he hadn't seen her yet. She felt like a small, scared rabbit hiding in a patch of brambles as a fox sniffed its way closer.

She pushed against the ground with her feet and hands, preparing to run. Adrenaline surged through her body as she sprang to her feet and dashed down the path through the thicket, her bare feet slapping the hard red clay. The man yelled and crashed through the brush behind her. She darted through the bushes, wincing as sharp thorns scraped her face and arms.

The soldier whistled, and another whistle replied farther in the thicket.

Reinforcements. Great.

The medallion bounced against her chest as she pumped her legs faster. She scurried over a log and looked over her

113

shoulder. He was much nearer now. His sword gleamed in his right hand. He was less than fifty feet behind her.

"You can't run forever!" a hoarse voice behind her called.

Trembling, paralyzing panic seized her and she picked up speed. This was a nightmare, the type of dream where your legs are like leaden weights. The worst possible nightmare. The branches whipped past her in a blur of green. Was there no end to this forest?

The smell of sweat wafted nearer. She swung up on a low-hanging branch and began climbing desperately, clawing at the rough bark. A hand gripped her ankle. She kicked with her other foot, slapping away the man's hand. Bark dug into her fingernails and branches scraped her arms as she climbed out of the men's reach. She clung to the trunk and trembled. Would they attempt to climb up after her? Were they that desperate? Were these the border guards the black-caped man spoke of? A short, thin man joined the tall man.

"Smoke 'er down," the tall one said. His watery black eyes blinked and a cruel smile spread over his face.

"Ax would be quicker." The shorter one brandished an ax and began chopping at the tree. It shuddered, and the impact made her teeth rattle.

She climbed to the opposite side of the tree and leaped to the ground. Her ankle gave a cracking sound and she yelped. It felt like someone had crushed it with a mallet.

She fell to her knees. Before she could get to her feet, the crushing weight of a soldier's hand pinned her to the ground. Her face smashed into the hard clay. The soldier moved his hand, and she rolled to her back, blocking her face with her arms as the shorter soldier raised his sword.

"Please don't!" she cried.

He sheathed his sword. He mumbled something, but she couldn't hear what he said. She clutched her ankle.

"Why didn't you kill her?" the tall man asked.

"Ye know the edict."

They stood what seemed like hundreds of feet above her.

"Get up."

She pushed herself up to her feet. Her ankle throbbed.

"Walk."

She trudged in front of the soldiers, limping heavily. The point of a sword prodded her on. Why was everyone trying to kill her or capture her or distract her from rescuing Martin? Her ribs and ankle ached, and she could barely walk.

Finally, they entered a clearing. She collapsed beside a large oak tree. "I can't go on."

The tall man raised his sword. "You go where we tell you."

"Where am I going?"

"To King Donavan. All intruders who 'merge from the Zenia Wood must be brought to the king for questionin'," the short man said.

That meant being away from Martin and the Uziel Mountain. She couldn't escape once she was in the king's clutches. And even if she did, she could barely walk, much less climb a mountain.

She forced herself to her feet and tried to rush back into the woods, but the tall man yanked her back.

"It isn't worth dragging a kicking and screaming girl twenty miles." He yanked her hair, forcing her chin to rise, and lifted his sword.

She closed her eyes and shuddered, waiting for the pain to come. Would she die right away or slowly? And what about Martin? What would happen to him? She would be with her parents after this. It would not be so bad. She trembled as she waited for the sharp pain.

There was a whistling sound, then a thump. She opened her eyes and struggled to her feet. The tall man lay motionless on his back, an arrow protruding from his chest. She swung around, looking straight into the face of the short soldier, and took a step back. Her ankle gave way, and she fell. She crawled away backward.

"Who are you?"

The soldier swung an arrow skillfully through his fingertips and then flipped it up in the air and caught it. "I'm a woodsman of the Zenia Wood, who pretends to be a spy for King Donavan—accursed be 'is name forever," he said in a strange, slow accent she had never heard before. He offered his hand to her. "Nori's the name."

"I don't shake hands with strangers." Gwyn placed hers behind her back. "But thank you for—"

"Anytime. Looks like you've 'ad quite a time." He frowned at the cuts on her face and arms and legs. "No offense, but it weren't smart t' get up and run like that when you were hidden in the bushes. He like t' 'ave never seen ye if ye stayed where ye were."

"I panicked." She sat down on a large root and massaged her ankle with tired hands. The pain lessened some.

"Quite un'erstan'able," he said with a dismissive wave. He was short, only a few inches taller than her, and wore the same garb as the tall soldier.

"We watched yer brother get kidnapped by the witches and the Black Wizard—may his name be forever accursed." He spat on the ground. "I saw everything happen. I heard you callin' out for your brother. I an' some others tried to rescue 'em, but the Black Wizard—may his name be forever accursed"—he spat on the ground again—"his ranks were far too great."

"Martin? You saw him?" Her heart skipped a beat. "Was he alive?"

"At the time, he was alive."

She blew a sigh of relief and continued massaging her ankle. The pain continued to lessen until it was a small ache.

She looked over Nori's head. There, to the northwest, loomed a massive black mountain in contrast with the cheery blue sky. That had to be the Uziel Mountain. It was the first time she had seen it, and her heart fell. There was no way she could climb that. It was taller than the Aberdeen Temple in Surday. Taller than at least a hundred Aberdeen Temples stacked on top of each other.

"As I were sayin', we tried to help, but our numbers were too few. The res' o' the woodsmen are in the south portion near the Skull Forest, fightin' off spiders."

"Spiders?" Gwyn imagined a group of soldiers stomping on tiny spiders and frowned.

"Yes, indeed! There are *giant* spiders in the Skull Forest. My men keep them contained there. If it weren't for us, the nasty creatures would overrun all of Vickland. An' what does King Donavan pay us for our trouble? Banishment. Truth is, I think he wants the spiders to attack the villages so he can come to de rescue. That will put him on the villagers' good side. But 'nough pol'tics. Where are ye off to?"

"Vickland." Such a long journey ahead. "To see River. Do you know where he is?"

"Which river? Ye mean the White River?"

"No." She looked up at the sun. Midmorning. Talking to this woodsman was putting her behind schedule. "River is a man's name. He was my father's best friend. He may be able to help me find my brother."

"Ah, ye mean the youngest Glendower brother. River from Glendower Glen. Ye are not far from 'is place. Follow the crest of the hill and then follow the crick 'nother mile. Ye'll come through Jalapa. Then keep following the creek another mile or so. Their place is in de valley. Ye cain't miss it."

"Thank you, Mr. Nori." Gwyn inched away from him.

"Let me 'sist you, least till you're past Jalapa."

She shook her head. "I am fine by myself." She turned away and as she walked, looked up at the Uziel Mountain with a sigh.

"Stay 'way from the roads, now!" he called after her. "Best to stay in the woods. Dis place is swimmin' wid border patrols. That's what this one was," he said, pointing to the dead soldier.

She waved at him and climbed the hill. As she made her way onward, two sentences circled in her head over and over. *Find River. Rescue Martin. Find River. Rescue Martin.*

Chapter 17

The Bounty Hunter

Gwyn didn't want to leave the Zenia Wood. It was safe, but the creek kept running away from it, and she was told to follow the creek. She kept hearing noises behind her, beside her, on either side, as if an invisible phantom were chasing her. She hoped it was her active imagination, because she didn't have any strength to do any more running. Her ankle still ached, though massaging it had helped a good deal. It had healed quickly. Too quickly. It was a bad sprain, yet as she massaged it, the pain began to melt away. Her father had massaged her mother's ankle when she tripped on a fishing net. Mama had been able to go about her day with only a slight limp. Perhaps Gwyn had inherited her father's knack for healing injuries. She had been able to heal Martin's ankle quickly.

After leaving the woods, she started hearing the bustle of a crowd. The noise reminded her with a stab of loneliness of Nelice. So much had changed since then. Gone were the days when all she cared about was trying to fit in with the judgmental girls in Nelice. Now she had more important things to think about. She had escaped an evil wizard, ridden in a stinky fish cart, eaten pine needles, traveled many miles alone, and not brushed her hair in days. She had surpassed all those silly girls.

The creek cooled her sore feet as she waded through it and toward the gateway of a town. A crooked wooden sign read "Jalapa." The muddy road under her bare feet was soft and squishy. The town reeked.

A man pushed past her with a protesting chicken under his arm. A plump woman chased after a little boy, who clutched a little pastry in his fist. A clump of straw slid off a nearby house and fell onto her. She brushed it off and looked up at the roof. A man jumped from one house to the next and began roping down a thatched roof.

Surely she would be safe if there were lots of people around. And maybe she could find some food. The smell of fresh bread in a nearby shop made her stomach grumble, but she didn't have any money. Did she dare sell Papa's medallion for a loaf of bread? It sure hadn't helped her and Martin so far. Perhaps she could sell the key the black-caped man had given her, but it had been more help than the medallion. She touched her mother's locket. She would never sell that. Not for a thousand druthas.

A faded green flag fluttered in the wind above a shop. On the flag was a purple flower crossing a red sword, in the form of an X. Vickland's flag. Her heart pounded. She was in a new country.

A red cape flashed at the corner of her eye. A gasp caught in her throat. A hundred feet away at the entrance of Jalapa, the Black Wizard stood talking to a young man beside him, a man with a black hood. The same one who had warned her and Martin of their parents' deaths and had helped her after Martin was captured. A flicker of hope warmed her. He was here to help her again. But if he was, why was he talking to the Black Wizard?

The wizard gestured with his hands. An irritated look shone on his face, and he spoke in loud, threatening tones in a strange language. Then he turned and left the town. The hooded man strode toward Gwyn and drew his sword. He caught her eye and smiled. But it was not a friendly look. It was the look of a linador before it snatched up its prey. She swung around and forced herself to take a deep breath. She stepped into the streets and blended in with the crowd, attempting to act calm despite her racing heart. She dared a look behind her.

He stared straight at her. What was worse, the crowds panicked at the sight of him, and when they noticed him looking at Gwyn, they stared at her like she had the plague. The streets swarmed with people trying to find shelter. Shop doors closed. Shutters flapped shut.

"Quick, into the house!"

"Bounty hunter!"

"That look on his face."

"Son of Andulza."

"He must want the girl badly to be coming here himself."

"Lock the door!"

She slid between two carts, leaped over an overturned barrel, and ducked under a horse, then glanced behind her. He was running now.

Oh no! Oh no!

Don't panic. Just breathe. Don't panic!

She panted for air and wrapped her trembling hand around the medallion. *Just breathe. Don't panic.*

A bald man with a bulging belly pulled her hair and held a knife to her throat.

"For sale," he yelled. "I ask two hundred druthas for this one, Rylith. Pay up, and you can have her."

The Jalapa villagers continued to scurry into houses and shops, though a few creaked open shutters and doors to watch. Gwyn kicked backward, her good foot smashing into the fat man's knee with a crunch. He bellowed, his rough fingers releasing her hair. She ducked under his arm and scrambled down the alley.

Boot steps sloshed through the muddy streets behind her—Rylith's, she realized with a rush of fear—and they were rapidly catching up with her. Pain like fire shot up her ankle, but she didn't dare slow down. The look in those eyes was enough to keep her racing for hours.

On the street ahead stood a rickety cart piled high with summer hay. She grabbed the wooden handle and hoisted herself up, her feet slipping in the moldy straw. Rylith looked up at her and smirked.

"Trapped," he said. He placed his hands on the cart and hoisted himself up.

The thatched roof was two feet above her head. She pulled herself onto it, but her feet started sliding. She grasped handfuls of the straw and clambered to the top.

Rylith jumped from the cart to the roof, his hand barely missing her as she leaped to the next house. He was fast. That was way too close for comfort. As soon as her bare feet hit the top of the house, she slipped on the loose straw and tumbled downward. She clutched the edge just in time and bashed her forehead against it. Spots of color sprinkled her vision. She looked below at her dangling feet and shuddered. If she jumped, she might hurt her ankle even more.

Rylith ran toward her, his boots clomping on the roof. Her clenched hands could feel the vibration of his boot steps. *Think fast, Gwyn. Think fast.* Below her, she spotted an open window. Perfect. She swung out from the house and angled toward it, then landed on a table where several men drank ale. The air smelled of beer and smoke. They blinked stupidly at her and shouted things she tried to forget. She jumped off the table and

raced across the room toward the door. Before she could
open it, it swung on its hinges, and she bumped into a
plump maid, who doused her with a tray of soup. The
chunky soup scalded her arms and chest, causing her to
yelp in pain.

She pushed past the maid, dashed down the hall,
and found the stairs, taking three at a time. The first
floor looked like a cloth shop. The front door opened.
She slid behind a roll of cloth and held her breath.

Rylith paused in the doorway, breathing heavily.
Hay stuck to his cloak. She bit her lip and tried to calm
her beating heart. She needed to give him a distraction.
If he saw her now, she would be trapped. Men yelled at
the maid upstairs. Rylith looked up and took off up the
stairs. Perfect.

She raced out the door, ran down the street, and slid
under a gate and into a puddle.

A window smashed above, and Rylith dropped in
front of her. He grabbed for her but missed as she swerved
to the right. She dashed down a dark alleyway like the
one in Sunday where she had first met him. So much had
happened since then. Why had Rylith changed?

She dodged a barrel and passed under billowing
clothes hanging on sagging lines. An arrow ripped a sheet
inches away from her head and fell at her feet. The dulled
tip was covered with a dirty rag smelling of an herbal scent
that made her dizzy. Rylith clenched a bow in his hands.

She ducked under another sheet but slammed into a
wall. Dead end. She drew in a breath. *Don't panic.* The
wall was too high. To her right and left stood tall houses.
Rylith guarded the only way past. Not good. She shook
her head to fight off the sleepiness and turned around.

Rylith strung an arrow and pointed it at her. His
eyes looked glazed over, and every few seconds, he
winced as if someone behind him was poking him.

The mind-reading book. He looked like the example in the painting. That was odd.

"Hand over the medallion."

"It belonged to my father." She tried to sound brave, though her voice quivered. This man was ready to kill for the medallion. Was it worth it for her to protect her family heirloom if it meant dying? If she died, no one would save Martin. He lowered the bow a fraction of an inch and frowned.

"Your father..."

"You're the son of the Black Wizard, aren't you?" Her voice grew stronger. "Your father is the reason I'm an orphan. Your father is the reason Martin's gone."

"Martin." He massaged his forehead and winced.

Gwyn inched toward the right, where she could see the shadow of a doorway. Who knew where the door led, but just about anywhere else would be better than this. "Before I die, tell me where Martin is. Is he dead?"

He held his bow limply in his hand. "No. He's not dead. He's—" Suddenly he groaned and held his head. The angry glitter and glassy look returned to his eyes. "Give me the medallion."

"I will, *if* you give me my brother back." She glared at him.

His confused expression returned. He massaged his head and fell to his knees.

She didn't waste her chance. She slipped past him and rushed out of the alley. The streets were still empty as she raced through them. Soon she heard the clomping boots behind her again. Would he ever give up? He was gaining on her, and she was running out of ideas.

A two-story building stood on her right. She pushed open the front door. Empty. She raced down the hall, slipped into a room with a window, and slammed the door. With trembling hands, she locked it with the key given to her by the very man now chasing her. This was all so bizarre. Why would he give it to her if he planned on killing her all along? He pulled on the latch, but it didn't budge. It worked! His retreating steps pounded down the hall. She breathed a ragged sigh of relief. Her whole body trembled, and her heart hammered faster than the wings of a hummingbird. She leaned against the door and slid down to a sitting position.

Why would the same man who warned her and Martin of their parents' danger want to kill her? It made no sense. She had been foolish to believe anyone was willing to help. The anger surged in her and she punched the wooden floor with her clenched fist. From now on, she would trust no one. No exceptions.

The window smashed open. She scrambled to her feet and fumbled with the key. Before she could open the door, Rylith yanked her arm and slammed her against the wall. His eyes blazed a glassy amber-brown.

He looped his finger underneath the chain around her neck and pulled out the medallion.

"That's my father's," she said. Her father's urgent expression came into her mind. It was all she had left of him, and she wasn't about to let it go.

"It's my father's," Rylith said. "Because he needs it."

"Why?"

"Do you know what it is?"

Gwyn shook her head.

"You know why my father can't kill you? Because you have the medallion. And you know why he can't touch the medallion? Because it would kill him."

She gasped. All this time, she had been safe from the Black Wizard. She should have made Martin keep wearing it.

He slipped the chain over her head. She tried to push away his arm, but he was too strong. She was so weak compared to him. There was no escaping this time.

"Are you going to kill me?" she said.

"It would be a favor if I did. You are wanted in all of Alastar. My father wants you. Even the king of Vickland wants you."

The squirmy feeling returned to her. "Why? Why does everyone want me? I'm just a normal person."

He stared at the medallion and reached out to bring it closer. But as he touched it, a flash of blue light threw him backward. Gwyn shielded her eyes from the light and backed up. He lay motionless on the ground.

Where did the light come from? Was he dead? She would have to figure this out later. She took the chain from his still hand. The medallion was warm. She had never noticed it grow warm on its own accord. Something was off. She fingered its dagger etching. There had to be more to this medallion than just a pretty ornament and special heirloom.

The streets were a blur as she raced through Jalapa. She didn't stop running until the town was far behind and she was in the shelter of a meadow. After looking over her shoulder, she leaned against a tree and tried to catch her breath. She had never run so fast in her life, but she still had narrowly escaped. If she could barely keep herself alive, how was she ever going to save Martin?

CHAPTER 18

THE BLOOD WITCH

Pain stabbed into Martin's ribs. He opened his eyes. Twinkling white stars peppered the blackness. The night air made him shiver. A rhythmic *whoosh, whoosh, whoosh* sounded above him.

Everything came back with a jolt. He was separated from Gwyn. The Black Wizard had just been threatening him, telling him he would send him to some mountain, and then had made him fall asleep. He struggled against the tight grip around his torso, but the pain pierced tighter. Warm blood dripped down his sides and he groaned. He kicked his legs, but his feet didn't come in contact with anything. The *whoosh* grew faster, and lights flickered ahead. And he was moving. A deafening roar made his ears ring. This was no bird.

"Y-you're n-not going t-to hurt me, are you?"

The dragon did not respond. That was probably for the best. He didn't want to have a conversation with a dragon anyway.

Without warning, its claws separated, and he fell a short distance and landed with a loud crunch on what felt like a pile of sticks. He struggled to his feet and clutched his sore sides. As he took a step, there was more crunching under his feet. The creamy full moon pushed through the clouds, and an eerie yellow light fell over him and outlined an enormous black castle. Little lights shone over the fortress like thousands of searching eyes. Dragons circled it like buzzards keeping watch over their prey.

He looked down. He was standing on a pile of bones. He whimpered and stood on one leg, trying to keep as much of his body as he could away from the bones. Should he move? Would the dragons attack if he did? Or should he stand still? But standing on bones was just too freaky for comfort. He took one step and winced at the crunching under his feet. Something scratched against his leg. He screamed and ran out of the pile. Crunching and cracking and sliding echoed in the night. He was finally free of bones, but he did not stop running. He stumbled on a rock and fell face first down a ravine, bumping and bouncing down the slope until he banged against something hard.

A shadowy figure strode toward the ravine. Martin tried to sit up, but the gravel underneath him caused him to slip and fall flat on his stomach. He squinted at a tall woman with billowing purple robes standing at the top of the ravine. The moon cast eerie light on a pale face that did not look human, yet was somehow familiar.

"I have long awaited your arrival." The voice was too familiar. No, it couldn't be. How did she get all the way here? The last time he had seen her, she was searching the grounds of his uncle's manor, holding a pair of knitting needles. He flattened himself closer to the gravel. Sharp rocks poked into him.

Cyrilla Coastworthy pointed toward him, and a handful of soldiers trickled into the ravine. Their sharp spearpoints flashed in the moonlight. Running was useless. If Gwyn were here, they would escape together. But with her gone, he didn't have the courage or strength to escape. Or the speed. She was always so fast and so good at getting them out of trouble.

The soldiers pulled him to his feet and clenched his arms as they brought him back up the ravine. They marched him into the front gate of the black castle and forced him to climb steps. They had to have walked at least a thousand miles by now. His legs were about to fall off.

At the top of the stairs, she turned and looked at him. She looked so different from the Cyrilla he had first met when he and Gwyn came to Uncle Edwinn's house. Her simple maid's dress was exchanged for silky purple robes that shone in the torchlight. Her hair, once pinned back in a tight bun, now fell like flowing black water down her shoulders, and a thin silver crown rested on her head. Her bright red lips and glittering gray eyes contrasted with her pale skin. If she didn't look so terrifying—and if Martin were a bit older—he would have thought her beautiful.

"Do you know who I am?" she asked in a voice as smooth as a snake.

"You *were* Cyrilla Coastworthy."

She laughed. "But I am not anymore, am I? I was disguised to ensure your uncle did what my father wanted. I disposed of his old maid, and he hired me, not knowing I was the Black Wizard's daughter. Such a fool."

She drew out the silver knitting needles. A globule of black liquid slipped off the end of the point and fell to the stone by his feet. The drop sizzled and melted away a portion of the stone. Every part of Martin's body shook.

"I save this for special occasions. But this is not a special occasion. Not yet."

He clenched his jaw in an attempt to stop his chattering teeth.

"Do you know, young one, why my father sent you to me? Yes, as bait for your sister." She waved a hand in dismissal. "But my father knows I have a talent. It is said the tongue is more powerful than the sword. The sword merely kills the body, but words poison the heart, soul, and mind. And poison is my specialty."

He looked from her cold eyes to the sharp knitting needles. He preferred the mean and scary words to the killing part. "Swords and spears may break my bones, but words can never hurt me." His mother had said that once.

A bony finger hooked his chin and forced it up.

"One day, you could be a great man. You have many talents. Dangerous talents." Cyrilla frowned and studied him. She was probably trying to read his mind, but he was too terrified to try anything to stop her. How could she think he had many talents? He didn't even know how to whistle. He was alone. He had no home. Gwyn wasn't here. He was a nobody.

"It is my duty and pleasure to ensure you never live to see the fruition of these gifts. And even if you do live long enough to realize your power, my poison will have seeped so deeply into your mind you will be rendered useless against my father."

Martin's trembling grew fiercer and he tried to shrink away from her.

She tsked. "Your father would be ashamed to see his only son shaking like a leaf."

Every instinct told him to flee, but the soldiers behind him held his arms tighter.

"Don't take him yet. You cannot run from me, little one." She stroked his cheek. He shuddered. "No one can run from me. I will *always* be in your head."

Her smile widened. "I have a prophecy to make, young one. By the time you reach your twelfth birthday, you will have seen enough blood to drown an army. You will have great heartbreak. Your whole life will be touched by darkness, and there will be no escape. No light." Her eyes glinted like hot coals as she issued an order to her soldiers. "You may take him to his room now. Ensure he is comfortable."

The soldiers dragged him down the hall, up more stairs, around confusing twists and turns through locked doors, and threw him into a cell. The door clanged and locked behind him. He fell on his face on the stone floor and lay still. If he pretended to be dead, maybe no one would hurt him. A few whispers came from behind him. Someone turned him over on his back.

"He's just a little boy, Will."

Martin stared at a blond-haired boy with blue eyes. He had dried blood on his forehead and a purple bruise under his eye.

"Hullo there," the boy said with a friendly smile.

Martin scrambled to hide in a corner of the cell. He threw his hands over his eyes and peeked through his fingers. The cell was illuminated by a lone torch in the hall near the cell and the moonlight shining through a barred window. There were four people about Gwyn's age in the cell. Two boys and two girls.

"The poor dear, he's frightened," a pretty girl with blond hair said.

"Could be a spy," Will answered.

"Will, that's so stupid," the other girl said. "He's a kid."

The boy with the bruise inched closer. "It's all right. We're all in the same boat. Or same cell, I should say. We've been here about a day. Did dragons drop you off at the front gate as well?"

Martin pulled his hands away from his face and nodded.

"I'm Falcon, and this is my dim-witted cousin, Will." He pointed to a short, stocky boy partially hidden in shadows, then motioned to the blonde. "This is my sister Stream."

She smiled and waved.

"And Clover," Falcon added, indicating a red-haired girl who leaned against the wall and nodded.

"You from Vickland too?" Falcon asked.

Martin inched away from the corner and shook his head. "Surday."

"You're a long way from home," Clover said.

"I just wanna go home." He clenched his jaw to keep from crying.

"What's your name?" Stream asked.

"Martin."

"That's a nice name," she said. "Do you have any family?"

"My sister, Gwyn. She's looking for me. She will find me." But how would she know where he was? Was she even alive?

Something connected in his mind. Clover, Falcon, and Stream. They had strange names. "Do you know River of Vickland?"

"That's my father," Falcon said.

"Mine too," Stream said.

"How do you know my uncle?" Will asked.

"Papa and River were once best friends." He smiled and had a sudden urge to hug them all, despite his hatred of hugs. "Finally some good luck."

"Who's your father?" Falcon asked.

His smile vanished. "He's dead. He and my mother both."

"I'm so sorry." Stream's face shone with compassion. "You poor boy."

"Before they were dead, what were their names?" Will asked.

"Will, seriously?" Clover glared at him. "You have the tact of a pink elephant."

"Are there ..." he started shyly. "Are there really pink elephants in Vickland?"

"Only legend." Falcon laughed. "But if it makes you feel better, you can pretend they're real."

"Here." Stream brought a basket of bread to him. "Looks like you haven't eaten in days. It isn't much, I'm afraid."

He gobbled it up and frowned at the empty basket. He was hungry enough to eat the basket.

Falcon made a bed out of thin, dirty straw for him, and Stream covered him with a tattered shawl.

"There now." Her voice was soft and soothing as she tucked her shawl around him. "Get some rest. You're safe now."

"Safe as one can be in a dungeon," Will muttered.

"Will, can you just keep your mouth shut?" Clover snapped.

"Don't you worry." Falcon knelt beside Martin and brushed a piece of straw off his head. "We're going to take care of you. We're in this together."

Martin closed his eyes and heaved a deep sigh. He curled into a ball and soon fell into a deep sleep.

CHAPTER 19

WILL

Martin woke from a hazy dream. He lifted his head, looked around the dirty cell, and sighed. This wasn't a dream. Sunlight filtered by gray clouds fell into the barred window, leaving long lines of shadows along the floor.

His heart ached for Gwyn. If only she were here. Maybe she was on her way here to rescue him now. And she could rescue the others too. He would see her soon. And then they could all find River together and live in a safe place far away from witches and wizards and eat food that wasn't pine needles.

Stream walked in circles, wringing her hands. Clover glared at Will, who leaned against the wall. Falcon sat near the door, staring at it like he expected it to open any moment.

"We're all going to get killed, and you know it," Will said, returning Clover's glare.

"Shhh." Stream looked toward Martin. Her soft blue eyes were anxious, but when she saw he was awake, she smiled.

Falcon turned too. "Good morning, Martin."

"What's going on?" He rubbed his eyes.

"You being here confirms our fears," Will said. "The Blood Witch is collecting prisoners."

Martin wasn't sure what *confirms* meant, but by the tone Will used, he didn't like him here.

"Will, we all know things are bad." Clover's red hair made her hazel eyes look even fierier. "So just keep your opinions to yourself. You're not smart enough to say anything we don't already know."

He made a sound in his throat like a growl and was about to speak, but Falcon walked over. "That's enough."

Will grumbled and turned his back to them. Martin had not gotten a good look at him last night, but he looked like what his mother used to call "stocky." Neither thin nor fat and somewhat short. Muscles bulged in his forearms. His shaggy, sandy-blond hair fell into his brown eyes.

Falcon jumped. "I hear footsteps." He backed away from the door and stood in front of the others.

Martin did not want to see Cyrilla again. Not now, not ever.

The door opened. When he saw the purple robes and frowning red lips, he stepped back toward the wall. Two guards came in behind her, holding blazing torches, sharp spears, and long whips. Falcon clenched his fists and stayed in front of Martin and the girls.

"New prisoners will be added to your midst in a few hours." Cyrilla's glittering gray eyes rested on each prisoner. She frowned when her gaze met Will's. "The king requested special treatment for you. Your father is one of the leaders of the rebels. Filthy mongrel."

Will's sour expression melted into terror as he leaped backward. He slammed into the wall and let out a mixture of a groan and a whimper.

"The fact that you do not deny this shows it is true. Your father will not last long. He and his followers will be crushed. The odds are against them." She looked at him in disgust. "Look at you. You pathetic, weak dog."

His shoulders straightened, and he frowned. "I am not weak."

"Then why do you tremble?" She drew nearer and grasped his collar. She brought her face close to his. "I can kill you with a single spell. A mere touch of my hand and utterance of a word, and you will fall to the ground and never rise again."

She held her hand out, and a soldier stepped forward with a whip.

"No!" Falcon stepped forward. "Leave him alone. Take me instead."

The second soldier pushed him to the floor. Stream ran to his side. Clover backed up and stood next to Martin, her eyes wide. Cyrilla's whip cracked, and Will let out a cry.

"You are the weak one!" Her voice reverberated through the cell, mingling with Will's screams and the clap of the whip.

Falcon tried to stand, but the soldier's spear poked his chest and forced him back to his knees.

Will writhed along the floor for several moments until Cyrilla finally handed the whip to the first soldier. She picked Will up by his collar and slammed him against the wall. "You are weak and will always be weak."

She left with a swish of her robes, leaving a trail of bloody boot prints in her wake.

Martin did not move for a long time. He trembled in the corner while the others tried to tend to Will's wounds. Will groaned and trembled as his friends cared for him. Flecks of blood splattered the wall. Martin shivered and pulled Stream's shawl over his shoulders. Hopefully Gwyn was in a safer place than he was.

CHAPTER 20

LYRIS CASTLE

Heron swished the red wine around in his silver goblet. He sighed and placed the cup back on the table. Ladies and lords laughed and carried on about politics, crops, and the latest gossip. Lady Darya of Dippleworth chattered to him on his right. He nodded when her tone was questioning but wasn't listening to a word she said.

Silent servants came in and out, offering dessert and wine, topping off goblets, and refilling plates. The yellow glow of candlelight and arrangement of roast duck, salted pork, fresh bread, bright strawberries, hazelnuts, and parsnips on the table did not interest Heron. Nothing in this room interested him.

He found himself staring at the large green flag draped against the back wall. A purple flower crossed a red sword in the form of an X. His father had proudly told him the green flag represented the strong wealth of their agricultural society. The purple flower was the Aidoris, the country's national flower that bloomed yearlong in the Vickland countryside. Like the Aidoris, the Vickland people were resilient, whatever season

139

or crisis came upon them. The red sword symbolized Vickland's military strength and prowess.

Heron often gazed at the flag, though he was embarrassed to admit that what interested him most about it was the Aidoris. There was something sad in the way the stem stood straight, though the petals drooped slightly. It reminded him of his mother. She was strong and always had perfect posture, even when her body was racked with pain.

He glanced up at his father, who flashed his fake smile as he laughed and talked with the lord and lady of Lavender Hill. Lord Lavender was not only the wealthiest merchant, known for his rich purple cloth, but also one of Father's top advisers in the court. Lord Lavender had definitely had too much to drink and was tickled with a fit of laughter over some ridiculous joke his wife had told. Lady Lavender, a skinny woman with pinkish red hair piled at least a foot high, laughed with a high-pitched squeal that grated on Heron's nerves. Ignoring the noise, he stabbed his fork into a juicy piece of pork, but he wasn't hungry. Bromlin's words refused to leave him. He would rather be back in the old, leaky cabin that smelled of mushrooms instead of the banquet halls with their bright lights, lavish food, and polished silverware.

He used to love the castle's banquets but only for the food. He could no longer sit by his best friend, Gressette—a rule Father enforced because of the mischief they caused at last winter's banquet—so he had to sit by old ladies who wanted only to gossip about potential prospects for him.

"Now, Prince Heron, dearie," Lady Dippleworth said in a self-important voice as she placed a chubby hand on his arm. He met the old woman's gaze as she stuffed her mouth with a puffy roll. Her double chin quivered as she talked. Her round bottom was so large that her bright pink dress, though frilly and loose fitting, was bursting at the seams, and fat drooped over either side of the chair. She pointed at the giggling girls across the table. "You must tell me what you think. Which of those young ladies is most dismaying?"

They all had white gloopy stuff caked on their faces, pink powder encircling their cheeks, and ridiculous swishing peacock feathers in their hair. At his glance, the girls' eyes brightened. And there was Petunia of Gloushester, sporting many different colored ribbons and feathers in her hair. She looked less like her hideous dog sitting in her lap and more like an exotic bird with ruffled feathers. Her dress was such a bright purple it hurt his eyes. The lavish lace along the bodice did all it could to point toward the low-cut neckline.

She must have taken his smirk as a flirtatious smile, because she winked at him. He stared at his plate.

"Well?" Lady Dippleworth said.

"They are nice girls." He was used to lying.

"I think Rubella is especially possessing tonight, don't you?" Lady Dippleworth said of her niece.

"Mm." He pretended to be hungry as he finished a rich pastry. It was normally his favorite dish, but tonight it tasted like mud.

"She *is* your age, you know, Prince Heron, dearie."

If she *dearied* him again ... He clenched his teeth.

"She was born only two days after you. Your mother—blessed is the bequeathal of her correspondent name. It seems like she died just yesterday, even though it was nearly eight years ago. Such a shame. I'm sure you miss her more than anyone, perhaps even more than your father." She studied his expression, as if waiting to see if he would show any emotion regarding his mother.

He firmed his jaw and turned away.

"Anyway, we—your mother and I, that is—both thought it was destitute that you two should be materialized someday so as to bring the house of Dippleworth to the throne. Well, she did not quite think this, though I propelled the suggestion to her, and she said in her kindest way, 'That is quite an interesting thought, my dear friend. We can revisit this once Heron is older.' Such a kind and superfluous woman she was."

He continued eating, casting furtive looks at his father. The king was still talking to Lord Lavender. They were speaking with their heads close together now. Father's brow was furrowed and his expression serious. Heron drowned out what Lady Dippleworth was telling him about her niece Rubella losing all her baby fat by the age of twelve but was able to catch only phrases of Father's conversation.

"Annihilation of the..."

"Andulza's meeting place..."

"Consolidation of the..."

"Get rid of..."

King Donavan looked up at Heron. He adverted his eyes and stared at the girls. They caught his eye and blushed. He winked at Petunia and hoped Father didn't catch him listening. He pushed away the noises around him and again tried to focus on what Father was saying, but the corpulent woman beside him would not shut up.

"Did you hear what Lady Mutterfield's daughter has done?" Lady Dippleworth smacked loudly as she stuffed creamy custard in her mouth. Gloopy yellow custard spilled down the sides of her lips and dripped onto her large bosom. "Raynella, I heard, ran off with her family's cook's son! Yes, you heard right! Lady Cordelia of Nephelham confidenced in me just last night at a feast for her grandson." She dabbed at her lips with a large pink handkerchief. "Do you know she has

142

thirty-six grandchildren? Lady Cordelia, that is. That is a bit inappropriate, if you ask me. I suppose if you have eleven children, you are bound to be cursed with thousands of grandchildren. I suppose their family tree is utterly ungrateful and disorganized."

Heron took a deep breath and turned toward her. "Lady Dippleworth, there is Lord Kaptcher standing by the window. I believe he is recently widowed. His wife died in the plague last year, if I remember correctly."

"Oh!" Lady Dippleworth turned a bright shade of pink. "Oh, well, yes, he is unmar—ahem, widowed. The poor dear."

"I saw him staring at you earlier. I think you should talk to him." He forced a polite smile. This was a tactic Father used often. A little flattery goes a long way.

"Do you now?" She no longer seemed embarrassed but brazen. "Well, I do believe I should. Thank you, Prince Heron. You are full of wisdom for one so young." She clomped off to speak to Lord Kaptcher.

He breathed a sigh of relief and tried to refocus on Father's conversation. His expression had grown even more serious. Dredo, Heron's servant, stood by his chair and bowed. Heron glared at him.

"What do you want?"

"A message from Gressette, sire."

He searched the banquet table and found his best friend, just as bored as he was. His reddish brown hair and sparse goatee contrasted with the graying features of his father, General Rinalldo, who sat beside him and conversed with Captain Fletcher.

Heron opened the letter.

Lady Dippleworth uses large words too big for her pea-sized brain.

He grinned at Gressette and stuffed the parchment in his pocket. He passed his plate to Dredo, who was looking thin again. "Here. Eat all of this. I need you to make sure it's not poison."

A smile played on Dredo's lips. "Yes, sire. Thank you."

Heron turned around and refocused on Father's conversation.

"Not to worry. I always plan ahead." Donavan took a draft of wine. "I've put up guards to question all who cross the border or emerge from the Zenia Wood. But it is the children I want." His voice lowered. "Especially the girl. The boy is most likely too young. We must find them before the wrong people do."

"How could a … a … young girl …" Lord Lavender hiccupped again and frowned. "Pardon me. I forgot what I was going to ask your lord—hic. Oh yes, how did she get past the Black Lizard?"

Lady Lavender giggled and Donavan gave his fake smile again.

"It doesn't matter. Andulza knows what he's doing."

The Zenia Wood and the mention of a girl connected in Heron's mind. What about the thin girl he came across in the woods after leaving Bromlin's? Surely she wouldn't be the girl he was talking about. She looked like a mere peasant who hadn't eaten in days. Nothing Father should be interested in. But perhaps her appearance made sense if she was on the run from the king.

"Have the executions been performed?"

"They were all dead by dawn, my king," Lord Lavender said. "No one will dare defy you again."

"Good." The king turned toward Heron again, but Heron looked away.

The past few days he had asked himself so many questions, but he still had no answers. Was Bromlin telling the truth? Did Donavan kill his own father? Was the Black Wizard as evil as Bromlin said? What really happened to his grandfather, William Oakheart?

Chapter 21

The Training Field

The next morning, Heron tightened his belt and rolled up the sleeves of his shirt as he stepped out to the training field. A light drizzle chilled his skin, and puddles of water sloshed up on his boots and black pants. Dozens of soggy soldiers crowded the field, jogging, sword fighting, or practicing archery. Besides the prisonlike ten-foot wall encircling the training arena, the place was liberating. He could cease being a prince and become a mere warrior, practicing equally with the other soldiers.

Dredo appeared in the arena, holding a quiver of arrows and a bow. Heron frowned. The sight of his servant reminded him that he was not—and never would be—a mere warrior.

"Sire, you left—"

"I'm not using it today." He waved his servant away.

Gressette sprinted toward him. His splash of red hair and goatee contrasted with the gray morning. He paused long enough to give Heron a punch in the ribs. Heron grabbed his arm and twisted it. He tackled Heron around the middle and pulled him down on the ground with him.

145

"All right, enough, you two!" Fletcher yelled. "Back to work."

They laughed as they climbed to their feet. It was nice having someone to laugh with. He certainly didn't have that with his father. They jogged side by side around the field. Heron caught a flicker of a smile on Fletcher's face before he turned away to help a younger trainee.

"You look like you have the plague. You're as gray as the sky," Gressette said. "You drink a lot last night?"

"No." Heron brushed the rain out of his eyes.

"Get any sleep?"

"Not much."

"How'd the *Art of War* lesson go this morning?"

"The usual." Heron groaned.

"That bad? Sorry I couldn't be there to help you through the boredom." Gressette did not sound sympathetic.

"Nice excuse, early-morning training. I'll have to use it next time."

"Your father's too smart for that. My father fell for it, but yours knows too much about what goes on round here. He'd see right through it. And even if he didn't, he'd see right through you."

Heron glared at him.

"You been awful grumpy lately," Gressette said as they rounded the bend in the grassy training arena. "Cheer up! The kitchens are cooking fresh pork today."

"My father's been breathing down my neck."

"Nothing new."

"True. But he's doing it more. He's posted guards at my bedroom door at night. He's suspicious." Heron ran his fingers through his soaked hair.

"Well, he has good reason to be. You did just disappear for a few days."

The gate opened, and Donavan entered the field, followed by Rinalldo. Heron's heart skipped a beat. All the

146

trainees halted what they were doing, except Gressette and Heron. Before anyone could bow, the king waved his hand in dismissal. He and Rinalldo stood under an overhang away from the rain, but he was gesturing with his hands, as he usually did when he was angry. As Rinalldo tried to explain something, Father ran his hands through his hair in frustration.

Heron dropped his hand. He had inherited the mannerism from his father.

Gressette cocked his head at him. "Whether you like it or not, you two do look a lot alike. He's just older and not as pretty as you."

What were Donavan and the general arguing about? Did it have to do with the Black Wizard? Did the general know the king's dark past? Heron leaped over a hurdle and continued jogging, but his thoughts stayed behind with Father and Rinalldo.

"Where *did* you go last week?" Gressette asked.

"I'm not entirely sure I can trust you," he said with a grin. "You would betray me for a brass coin."

He laughed. "I could use the money."

They leaped over another hurdle as they rounded the next bend. Gressette performed a somersault while in midflight over the hurdle.

"Show-off."

He shook his head hard, sending droplets of water on Heron. "If your best friend is the prince, you've got to show off or you won't be noticed. For the ladies, you know?" He winked.

Heron smiled but looked back in the direction of Father, and his smile faded. "I think my father is up to something."

"That's also nothing new."

"I know, but this sounds more serious." He lowered his voice as they jogged past Captain Fletcher.

Fletcher stood by a trainee who barely looked twelve. The trainee frowned at the target before him. Several arrows stuck out of the ground in front, yet not one had pierced the target. Fletcher pushed the bow back in the boy's hands and helped him situate the quiver strung across his back. "Keep trying." He eyed Heron and nodded. Heron nodded back. Fletcher never put on the fake expression his father and Rinalldo and other officials wore.

"Well?" Gressette elbowed him. "What's your father up to?"

"I think he might be meeting with Andulza."

"The Black Wizard?" He shrugged. "I've heard he was not as evil as most people thought."

"I've heard that as well. But if he is *not* evil, then why would my father be keeping it secret? Also, I sneaked into my father's quarters last night before the banquet ended. I found an old map wedged underneath his bed. On the map is a room called the Lyris Archive. I've never seen that room or heard of an archive here. It's in a portion of the castle my father always told me to stay away from." He slowed his pace. "I wonder what's in there."

"You're thinking too much." Gressette waved his hand in dismissal. "Why do you even care how your father runs his country or whether he's hiding something? You never cared before."

"You're probably right."

"I know I'm right. Hey, want to sneak off to watch the tournament again tonight? I heard Vanessa's going," he said with a knowing look.

Heron couldn't help but smile.

"There's that ol' Heron back!" He slapped him on the shoulder.

After ten laps, Fletcher called Gressette to help set up targets for a knife-throwing contest.

Heron leaned against the shelter of the wall and drew his sword. Rain dripped on the silver, double-edged blade and trickled down to the hilt. An intricate design of a dragon in midflight swirled around the blade. Father had given the weapon to him last year. He often lavished expensive gifts on Heron but not out of devotion or affection. The gifts were just to make the prince look good. And if the prince looked good, that would reflect well on the king.

Bromlin was right; his sword was a "dull little butter knife." He ran his fingers over the sharp point. Not even a scratch. He kicked at a clump of grass in the field. When he'd complained about this to Father, he received only a glare. "You're too clumsy to own a sharp sword."

He was many things, but clumsy was not one of them. If Bromlin was telling the truth about the king of Vickland, maybe Donavan was afraid Heron would do to him as he had done to his father.

Heron traced his fingers over the dragon on his blade. After speaking to Bromlin, many of his questions were answered. He didn't like the answers, but they cleared up a lot of things. Now the next question: What was he to do with the truth, if it was indeed the truth?

CHAPTER 22

RIVER BY THE CREEK

Gwyn stopped by the creek and looked over her shoulder, expecting Rylith or Andulza to leap out from behind a tree. Satisfied, she knelt by the stream. The water was gritty, but she was so thirsty she didn't mind. It cooled her warm skin as she washed off.

She limped up a hill to her right and looked down into the valley. Vibrant purple flowers dotted the sloping green fields. Her father often told her and Martin of the purple fields of Vickland. Martin would love this. He should have been here, standing next to her.

Why was he the one kidnapped? He was scared of storms and dogs and carrots. She could picture him now, shivering in a dark corner, his teeth chattering, as the Black Wizard loomed over him.

"May I help you?" A man crossed the creek in quick strides. He wore torn, dirty farm clothes but had an amiable smile.

"I'm looking for River." She stepped back, almost tumbling down the hill. The open field did not give her much of an escape route if this man was on the Black Wizard's side.

"I'm River of Glendower. And you are the daughter of Dylan of Nelice. I can tell by your green eyes. How is the man? What brings you to these parts?"

He wiped his muddy hands on his pants before shaking hers. He had what her mother used to call worry lines on his forehead, but his bright blue eyes sparkled with such warmth that she forgot her rule about strangers and shaking hands. Somehow, she felt she had known him all her life. He had a small dagger strapped to his waist. She took her hand away. Could she trust him? She thought she could trust Rylith. But she had definitely been proven wrong.

"How do I know you're River? Describe my father."

River studied her expression. "I see you are not as trusting as your father. Let's see, he has green eyes. A bit on the shorter side, though not too short. Dylan and I were rescued and then adopted by a dear old man named Bromlin in the Zenia Wood. Your father's favorite pastime, besides running and archery, was reading a book in a big oak tree near the cabin where we grew up together."

He was definitely spot-on about her father.

"Yes, I'm Gwyn of Nelice." Sudden sadness gripped her. No, she was no longer Gwyn of Nelice. She was Gwyn of Nowhere and she belonged to no one. After swallowing the lump in her throat, she looked back at him. "My father and mother were killed a year ago. My brother and I escaped, but he was kidnapped by witches later."

"I'm sorry to hear that. Dylan was a close friend." He looked out toward the woods. "Indeed, the dearest friend I ever had."

She studied a purple flower by her feet. The warmth and sadness she had seen in his eyes were mirrors of her own heart.

"Witches kidnapped your brother, you say? Your brother is not the first child to be kidnapped. Come into the house where it is safer to talk. You look like you need rest and a good meal. My wife will have supper ready by this time." They strolled through the valley, where plump cows grazed and a small house peeped into view. He continued to question her as they walked, so she ran through a brief, scattered timeline of all that had happened.

"When Martin and me were in our uncle's library, we overheard my uncle talking with this red-caped man named Andulza," she said. "He—Andulza, that is—called himself the Black Wizard. We recognized his red cape and realized he was the man who killed our parents."

"Andulza, you say?" River frowned. "He is the most powerful man in all Alastar. Why was he so eager to have you and your brother?"

Gwyn shrugged. The medallion, still hiding in her shirt, hit her chest with every footfall.

"You're quite lucky. Few encounter the Black Wizard and survive."

"Papa injured him before he died. We saw the wizard limping away from the house."

"Your father was a powerful man."

She averted her gaze ahead to River's house, a small stone cottage with a faded blue door. A short, slightly plump woman worked in a little garden plot by the house, while two young children sat on the front porch. An infant rolled around on a brightly colored quilt on the grass.

"Rose!" River called out.

The woman spun around but gave an audible sigh of relief. She replaced relief with a scowl and propped her hands on her hips. "Don't you ever sneak up on me again!"

Carrie Looper Stephens

"Papa!" The boys dashed to their father and wrapped their arms around him.

"Gwyn, this is Lake and Eagle," River said.

Lake looked to be about eight and had blond hair and bright blue eyes like his father. Eagle, the younger one, hid behind River's legs.

"And this is my wife, Rose." He kissed her and gave her a playful hug. "This is Dylan's girl, Gwyn."

Rose's exasperation melted into surprise. She looked to her husband for an explanation, and he whispered in her ear. She turned and wrapped her in a rib-crushing hug.

"You poor dear! You must be tired. Come in and get washed up, and I'll have supper warmed in a moment. You can stay in my daughter Stream's room."

The inside of the cabin looked small, probably because of the clutter. Baskets of green beans were stacked up near the kitchen entrance. Clay birds, spinning tops, and homemade wooden swords littered the kitchen floor. It looked like there were four rooms—a kitchen and three bedrooms partitioned off by large quilts. A fire in the hearth crackled, and the inside was hazy with smoke.

Rose took her to Stream's room and left her with a basin of creek water and fresh clothes. After washing, Gwyn slipped on Stream's blue dress. It had a tight waist and was so long she had to pull up the skirts to walk. It would just slow her down once she was back on her mission to find Martin. The Vicklanders had different styles than Sunday. Most of the Sunday women and girls wore knee-length skirts and sleeveless blouses so they could wade in the shallows and help with the fishing. Taking off the dress was harder than putting it on, but eventually she wiggled out of it and put on her old clothes. They were still a little wet from the creek, but she liked the familiarity of the worn cloth. She

154

combed her hair with her fingers and pulled it halfway back with a ribbon Rose had given her.

The commotion in the kitchen was worse than a crowded street in Nelice. The supper table was loud. Daisy, the youngest in the family, cooed and giggled at the faces her brothers made. It wasn't fair that some families could be together while others were so lonely.

Rose dished out bowls of soup. The savory aroma made Gwyn's stomach growl. In her bowl, little chunks of beef and green beans floated like logs in the soup. There were a few moments of silence as the hungry group ate. At first, she was too hungry to care that the soup was watery and the beef was chewy. Mama used to serve fresh bread, baked fish, grain stew, and boiled garden vegetables in pottery she'd made herself. She'd even made pinkish-white shell spoons, which were much prettier than these splintering wooden spoons that poked her tongue.

Remembering her manners, she said, "Thank you for the soup. I've never tasted anything like it."

Rose beamed. "Why, thank you, dear girl. My mother taught the recipe to me, and her mother taught it to her, and so on and so forth. The secret ingredient is to boil a cow's hoof several hours to create the broth. I often forget to wash the hoof, but it adds protein, don't you think?"

Gwyn dropped her spoon in her bowl and clenched her jaw to keep from gagging. If this recipe had been passed down generation after generation, then bad cooking must have been passed down along with it.

River finished his soup and clasped his hands together on the table. "I will not go into details, but Rose and I are part of a group who has gathered together secretly to discuss a rebellion. Somehow the king got wind of it and kidnapped some of our children. We think he wanted to send us the message that he is not to be trifled with." The worry lines in his forehead grew deeper, and his knuckles turned white. "Our son Falcon and daughter Stream are among the children kidnapped two days ago."

Rose sniffed and pushed her chair back. To hide her tears, she fussed over her younger children, cleaning up after them and giving them more soup despite their protests.

"Do you know where they are?" Gwyn asked.

"In the castle on the Uziel Mountain," River said. "That is where all the king's enemies are sent. The Black Wizard's daughter rules the mountain. Some call her the Blood Witch."

Her heart skipped a beat. "That's where Martin is being kept. Why is she called the Blood Witch?"

River averted his eyes. "It's best you don't know."

Rose sniffed a few times as she settled at the table and began wiping off Daisy's face. "Our nephew, Will, and Stream's best friend, Clover, were also taken."

"But there is something strange about the way they were kidnapped." River leaned forward. "We saw no hoofprints on the path they took to Jalapa. There were also no boot prints besides those of our own children. It was a rainy day, so prints would be noticeable. I think—"

"River!" Rose glared at him with pointed glance toward the boys.

"D-r-a-g-o-n-s," River spelled out. "The Black Wizard owns many of them."

Her eyes widened. She had always wanted to see a dragon.

"The Black Wizard is scary," Eagle said.

"He eats people," Lake added. "Slurps them up like yummy soup." He made a slurping sound. "Feeds them to his d-r-a-g-o-n-s too."

River frowned at his son but turned back to Gwyn. "Andulza's name means *darkness*. It is said he was once a powerful member of the Vickland army. His magical gifts

156

inherited from his father were once used for good. Some say he saved the life of King William Oakheart, the father of the present king. But Andulza's lust for more and more power and his interest in dark magic began to twist his mind. He fell out of favor with the king and eventually was banished. His malice and power have only grown since then."

"Why is the Black Wizard chasing you and your brother?" Rose asked.

"I don't know." The past few days had taught her not to trust anyone. whether Rose was her father's friend or not, Gwyn still had to be on her guard and keep the medallion to herself.

"Poor dear. You're welcome to stay here as long as you'd like," Rose said. "The house feels so empty. It's nice to have company to distract us."

"What about my brother?" Gwyn said more gruffly than she had intended.

River heaved a wavering sigh. "I would storm the castle in a heartbeat to rescue my children. The other fathers would do the same. Several of the men and I traveled to the foot of the mountain, but a group of farmers is no match against powerful dragons and the Blood Witch's ruthless magic."

"So we just sit around while Martin is tortured?" Gwyn trembled.

River frowned. "We have a meeting at our village leader's home tomorrow at dawn. You are welcome to come."

"I will." Her cheeks burned, and she looked down at her clenched hands. "I'm sorry. Martin is the only family I have."

Rose put an arm around her. "Dear, we will do all we can."

The warmth from her arm soothed Gwyn's nerves, reminding her of her own mother's warm embrace.

Later that night, Gwyn lay on her bed, staring at the ceiling. One of the boys cried in the other room.

"Mama, I miss Falcon and Stream."

The lump in her throat grew. She came to River's house wanting help finding her brother. Should she help River and Rose find their children?

No. She had to focus on Martin. He was all who mattered.

Since River had no intention of rescuing his older children anytime soon, he was not going to be any help in rescuing Martin. Perhaps her trip here was a waste of time. But she would wait and see what this meeting tomorrow held. She could yet have some hope.

She tried to plan her next course of action depending on the outcome of the meeting, but her eyelids burned and every part of her body ached. She hadn't realized how weak and exhausted she had been until she had collapsed into a comfy bed. A few minutes after closing her eyes, she fell into a bleak, dreamless sleep.

CHAPTER 23

THE FORBIDDEN ROOM

On an unusually quiet evening, Heron sat on the stone railing of the balcony outside his bedroom in Lyris Castle. A cool breeze ruffled his hair, and frogs sang around the small koi pond under his balcony. He studied the faded, yellowed map of the Lyris Archive and fiddled with the old key he had stolen from an elderly, absent-minded servant.

"Sire?" Dredo called.

Heron slid the key in his pocket and folded the map. He turned toward his young servant, whose shaggy black hair and skinny, malnourished appearance normally bothered him. But he had too much on his mind to degrade him for it now. "What?"

"Message from Gressette." Dredo handed him a parchment.

"You're dismissed."

"He asked me to bring back your response."

"Probably wants to know if I'm coming to the melee. Parchment and pen, you dimwitted—" Heron winced when he realized how much he sounded like Father. "Please."

"Er, right. Yes, sire. Forgive me." Dredo scurried back into Heron's room.

Heron unfolded the letter, smiling at Gressette's sloppy handwriting.

You coming or not? Or are you still studying that stupid map? Hurry up. I'm not waiting forever. —Gressette

He took the paper and quill his servant handed him and scribbled his response.

Party without me. —Heron

After folding it, he handed it to Dredo with a nod. His servant bowed slightly and headed toward the door.

"Dredo?"

He stopped in the doorway and looked back.

"Are the guards posted yet?"

"Not yet, sire. I believe they think you are still on the training field."

"Carry on, then. Thank you," Heron said with a toss of his hand. He watched as Dredo disappeared into the bedroom. Why did he always look so thin? "Wait."

After a few seconds, Dredo poked his head back in the doorway.

"Have you sharpened my sword like I asked?"

Dredo nodded.

"My father didn't catch you?"

"No, sire. He does not know."

"Then go down to the kitchen and tell the cook to give you a slab of pork and a loaf of fresh bread. By my orders."

"Are you still hungry, sire?"

"It's not for me. It's for you. And your family if they need it."

Dredo blinked and looked confused, even a little suspicious. "For me?"

"Go before I change my mind."

"Thank you, sire. I won't forget this. My family and I are most appreciative." He bowed, then hurried out of the room and closed the door behind him.

Heron slid off the railing of the balcony and walked across the deck back into his bedroom. He stared at his black cloak lying on his bed, running a hand through his hair as he weighed the options. He could get caught.

Making up his mind, he grabbed the cloak and fastened it around his neck. The torch took a little while to light. Dredo usually took care of these things. When he opened his bedroom door, he peeked out. Still no guards. He jogged around the corner just as the faint sounds of footsteps neared his room.

The torch's light bounced off the stone walls as he slipped down the hall. He thought back to the map he had spent all day memorizing and turned down the confusing and rarely traveled passageways of Lyris. The hallway smelled musty. No torches but the one he held lit the way. He ran into dozens of sticky spiderwebs and had to stop twice to clean them off.

After questioning a few older servants about the Lyris Archive, he learned that no one had been allowed in this hall for over thirty years. The staff were not to have the keys to the archive. The absentminded custodian from whom Heron pilfered the keys kept forgetting who Heron was, but he seemed eager to boast about how he was the only one clever enough to keep a key to the archive hidden.

"Thirty years is a long time, young man!" he had told Heron as he shuffled down the hallway, leaning against a well-worn broom. "Indeed, many years is thirty. Who are you again, now? Ah yes, Aaron. Yes, that's what I said: Aaron. Forgive me. My ears are not as keen as they once were. The new king wanted all the archive keys—excepting his own, of course—to be destroyed thirty years ago. But I kept this one." He held up the rusted brass key. "I just couldn't part with the dear. My great-grandfather made it here. Indeed, he did! And it has passed down through the generations. I was not about to destroy such a precious artifact. Now then, I seem to have forgotten where I was going. Farewell, young man. I must finish my duties. These halls won't sweep themselves!"

It hadn't been hard for Heron to snitch the key off the old man while he bent over to pick up his broom. Now as he fingered it, he mused on what the old man had said. Thirty years ago, Father had become king after Grandfather's untimely death. What was Father trying to hide?

After traveling through several corridors, he came to large closed doors. He slid the key out of his pocket and fit it into the lock. As he turned it, a soft click sounded. Rust from the latch fell into his hand as he opened the door.

Once inside, he locked the doors behind him. He held the torch high and looked at the ancient paintings on the walls of the abandoned hall. The long room featured a small sturdy table standing upright near the front. Another that had been overturned lay behind it in front of rows of narrow bookshelves. Several dusty, flimsy-looking chairs were scattered throughout. This upright table had two newer chairs sitting under it. Strange that the newer furniture did not have any dust on it. Inches of dust covered everything else in the room.

Something crunched under his boot. Kneeling, he studied the broken shards of a piece of pottery. The familiar face of an old man was painted on the plate. The painting looked like Father, but older and kinder.

He walked to one of the dust-covered paintings on a nearby wall and wiped away some of the grime, revealing the image of a baby. "King William Oakheart" was inscribed under it. Heron's grandfather. He cleaned the rest of the painting with his hand, uncovering a king and queen holding the baby.

The scenes depicted in the paintings got worse as Heron looked at each in turn. He saw the deaths of the king and queen, the baby being spirited away by a girl, bloodshed and battles, and the same girl riding a horse while carrying the infant prince. They were standing in front of an old, crumbling stone fortress.

He ventured toward the next painting of three boys with the inscriptions "William" and "Bromlin" underneath them. Under the third boy, the name had been scratched out, though it looked like it started with an *A*.

The next artwork showed the three fighting in battle together back to back, and the next showed William Oakheart being crowned king. Bromlin stood at his right hand, smiling and holding a book. Both looked like they could be cousins or brothers. They had dark hair and handsome faces, though William looked older and taller. A third man stood on William's left side, holding a sword and dressed in a general's garb. He looked similar to the mystery boy whose name had been scratched out.

The last painting was smudged and looked like it had been painted in a hurry. It showed a middle-aged couple in bed, dead. Was it the king and queen? Where were their crowns? The murderer held a bloody dagger over their heads.

The click of the lock interrupted Heron as he cleaned off the dust of the next painting. His heart leaped and he quickly jammed the torch against the stone wall to douse the flame. He stuck it behind a chair and slid behind the overturned table, trying to calm his heavy breathing.

"You should have destroyed this room years ago," a deep voice said. Torches shone on the wall and two men's shadows appeared.

"I own the only key. It is quite safe. Besides, it has its uses to me." Father's voice. Heron clenched his fists. This wasn't something he had planned for.

The two men came into the room and sat at the small table only a few feet away from Heron's hideout.

"You could not bring me the girl, Andulza?" Donavan asked.

The word *Andulza* fell on Heron's ears like a sword point. He sucked in a breath.

The other man was silent a few brief seconds, then said, "The boy is in my daughter's possession, but the girl will be more difficult. Our best hope is for her to take the bait. If she doesn't, she has the medallion with her, which will make it hard for me to catch her. But my witches will assist me."

"You trust the witches?"

"They are not the brightest, but they are loyal and fierce once they have caught their prey."

"The girl escaped my troops as well. I must have her. We cannot wait much longer. Are the other children in your custody?"

Why would Father be interested in capturing children? It didn't make sense. He usually went after people who were more of a threat to his throne, like rebellious nobles or other kings.

"In my daughter's custody, in the Uziel Mountain. She will take good care of them."

"Good," Father said. Heron heard the chinking of coins in a bag and then a loud thump. "Here's something for your trouble. You will receive the rest once I have the girl, which will be soon, I hope."

"It will be soon. Our plan is genius. Killing two birds with one stone, as the saying goes." Andulza's laugh sent shivers down Heron's spine. "In capturing the children and the boy, we have a significant advantage over those rebels as well as the girl who holds the medallion. I do think, Donavan ..." Andulza paused for a few seconds.

Heron's father seemed unusually patient with Andulza. Ordinarily, he coveted immediacy from those he spoke with. Heron peered through a crack to get a glimpse of the Black Wizard. Sitting across the table from his father was a tall man with pale skin accentuated by the flickering shadows. A wicked gleam shone in his eyes and a sadistic smile spread across his face.

Heron gave an involuntary shudder. He definitely didn't want to be on Andulza's bad side. He had heard talk of the powerful wizard but didn't think he would look this sinister.

"No, I do not think. I *know* for certain this girl is not an ordinary child." Andulza spoke slowly. "Her father was powerful. She and her brother will grow up to be gifted young people. I think the sooner we get to them, the better."

"The girl ... do you think she has what I'm looking for?" Father asked.

"She does without a doubt, though she doesn't know it yet. The boy is too young for me to know, but I believe he is promising."

"Do what you must. As long as you obtain her, I do not care what methods you use. However, do not lay a hand on the boy. Just in case the girl does not work out."

Who were these kids, and why did Father want them?

His father frowned at the painting. Heron bit back a gasp. Clear stripes traced down the paintings where he had wiped away the dust. How could he have been so stupid? He wanted to kick himself. He should have planned out the whole thing better. But even if he had, he wouldn't have expected running into his father.

A chair grated on the stone floor. "Thank you for meeting me, Andulza. Go out the south entrance as you came in."

Andulza disappeared down the hall. Father walked toward the paintings. He pulled out Heron's smoldering torch. Heron shuddered. He was trapped. There was no amount of explaining, lying, or making excuses he could do with this one. He glanced toward the door. If he could just find something to distract Father, perhaps he could escape.

His father cast the torch to the ground and waved his lit torch over the room. Heron held his breath. Heavy, confident boot steps neared the table as Father unsheathed his sword. The torchlight glinted off the blade. Flashbacks of Bromlin's tale swirled in his mind. Was this the same sword that slew William Oakheart? If the king killed his own father, would he also kill his only son?

"Show yourself." His voice was low and firm.

Heron looked back toward the door. There was no getting away now. He slowly stood and backed away. Father's surprise melted into a sneer.

"Heron." Donavan stepped closer. "Have you been looking at some pretty paintings?"

"No." Heron took a few steps back toward a bookshelf behind him.

Father placed his blade under Heron's arm.

"Show me your hands."

Heron showed him his dust-covered palms before closing his fingers into a fist.

"I am going to ask you some questions, and you are going to answer me," Father said, lowering his sword. "You have changed. Who have you been talking to? Why are you suddenly so interested in Vickland's past? Who told you about this hall?"

"No one. I found this by myself."

"Don't make me even more ashamed of you than I already am." His brown eyes glinted as he stepped closer toward Heron. Heron took a step back, thankful the overturned table still acted as a shield between them. "You went somewhere when you left on your latest escapade. My soldiers said you went to the Zenia Wood. What's so special in there?"

"Nothing. I just wanted to explore." That was a stupid excuse, but he was running out of options.

Father threw his sword and torch to the floor, leaped over the table, and slammed Heron against the bookshelf. Dusty books rained down on them, and a sheet of dust peppered Heron and fell in his eyes. Father grabbed his collar.

"Do you expect me to believe you?" His voice was filled with a fierce venom Heron had not heard before. He tried in vain to stop trembling. He would rather face that pack of wolves in the Zenia Wood than be in Father's presence right now. At least the wolves would have finished him off quickly.

He blinked away the dust and glanced at the sword on the floor. Father followed his eyes and shoved him harder against the bookshelf. The edge of a shelf cut into his back. The pain dug in deep like a knife. He yelped and tried to push away.

His father dropped his hands and took a step back. "You are no longer any use to me. You are too inquisitive. And curious people are dangerous to me and my reign." His eyes narrowed as he stroked his beard. That look. It was the what-am-I-going-to-do-with-you expression he had seen all too often.

The fallen torch cast a beam of light on the last painting. Heron tore his gaze away from his father's and looked back at the wall. No. The murderer looked like himself. Then, in scribbled black ink were these words: *The king is dead. Whoever sees this wall will not live.*

Bromlin. The peasant's bodies. His grandfather's face painted on shattered pottery. His father's sword. Everything connected. And now his father wanted to end him as well. He stepped forward.

"Haven't I always been a danger to you, like you were a danger to your father's reign?" The accusation and anger felt good coming out.

The king's eyes flashed like stoked embers, and his fist smashed into Heron's jaw before he saw it coming. He fell backward, unsteadying the bookshelf. The heavy, crushing weight of the bookcase fell on him, pinning him to the floor.

The king stormed out of the room and slammed the door. The lock clicked. Heron pushed his back against the bookcase. It wouldn't budge. Something sharp dug into his back and he yelled in pain. He should have never come here. He should have gone with Gressette. No one would find him here. He would just rot. Unless the king came back to finish him off. He would take rotting over death by him any day. But if he had a choice, he'd rather get out of here and escape the castle. He tried rolling over, but the sharp object cut deeper and pinched his skin. After squirming his arms out from under him, he tried to grasp the table leg to pull himself out. But it was just out of his reach.

He groaned. His eyes drifted back to the last painting. Bromlin was telling the truth. The king was a murderer. He couldn't let him get away with this. Were he and

Bromlin the only ones who knew about it? Heron would find a way to ensure everyone in all Vickland, even all of Alastar, knew.

The fallen torch found a dusty book, and it smoldered until it caught fire. That wasn't good. Heron tried again to lift the bookshelf. Something fell from the wall and added to the throbbing pain in his back. The crushing weight knocked out what little breath he had left in him, and searing pain rippled down his back.

He yelled every obscenity he knew. What king would leave his only son to die? What king would kill his own father to gain the throne?

"You're a monster!" Coughing cut off his words.

The fire spread to the bookcase. He tried to wriggle free, but the sharp pain dug deeper with every inch he tried to move. He coughed as his fingers scrabbled uselessly on the cold stone floor. Smothering smoke filled the room. Everything grew hazy. Smoke filled his lungs and fire warmed his face. His eyes darted between the bookcase and fire. He really was going to die here.

No, he couldn't. Someone had to bring his murderous father to justice.

"Help!" His coughs grew deeper, and even when he gasped for air, no relief came to his burning lungs. He frantically shoved against the bookcase again. He tried kicking it.

A voice called to him, but he couldn't see anyone. His lungs were about to explode. He laid his head on the warm stone floor and closed his eyes. The weight lifted off his back and someone pulled on his arms.

CHAPTER 24

THE MEETING

O n the morning of the meeting, thunder rumbled and rain pelted Gwyn as she and River's family traveled in a small wagon. A muscular horse pulled the wagon through the soaked fields.

"River, where's your dagger?" Rose looked at her husband's side.

"I left it at home. Brought a bigger one." He pointed at his feet, where a large dagger rested in his boot. Rose nodded in satisfaction.

The wagon sloshed through a shallow creek and bumped along a dirt path toward a cluster of small buildings made of split logs. A faded wooden sign read "Elgin Village."

The village was not as lively as Nelice, and was smaller and not as dirty as Jalapa. The buildings were not homes; they were merely small wooden structures sheltering booths and tables. Men sat at the booths, smoking long pipes, laughing, and talking, while the women stood in clusters, whispering to each other or chasing after their children. One woman held a distaff and spindle, her fingers moving quickly as she spoke to the other women.

The booths were laden with fresh meats, cages of chickens, jugs of ale, and baskets of herbs, green beans, and peas. One booth contained scythes, axes, hammers, and other tools.

"Where do these people live?" Gwyn asked.

"On farms. We only come here to sell our goods on the third day of the week," River said.

After less than a mile, the path left Elgin and led the travelers to a wood. The cart stopped at a long house nestled in the trees. Once they were inside a room so hot and stuffy that Gwyn could barely breathe, they met a group of about two dozen people forming a circle and sitting on the floor or on rickety benches. Gwyn sat between Rose and Lake.

"That's Crush." Lake pointed to a big, muscular man with salt-and-pepper hair and a full beard. From his authoritative air, he must be the leader of the group. "I don't know what his real name is, but everyone calls him Crush."

Hammer's name must have also been a nickname. He was almost as muscular as Crush and had piercing blue eyes overshadowed by bushy eyebrows. A wispy black-gray mustache underlined his hooked nose. A large war hammer hung across his back.

"Hammer's wife died many years ago, leaving him with two sons to raise," Rose told her. "That's Kegan over there." She pointed to Hammer's oldest son, who sat by the window, staring out with an angry expression.

Gwyn's heart skipped a beat when she noticed the dark eyes and big muscles on his forearms. But he still wasn't nearly as handsome as the rider she had seen in the Zenia Wood.

"Where's his other son?" she asked.

"I just found out his youngest son, Arbor, was kidnapped recently as well," Rose said.

Hammer strode across the floor and faced Crush. "Why wait for Sherard and Anselm? They live farthest away. Let's start the meeting."

"They each have lost a son. It would be insensitive to start without them," Crush said in a calm but decisive voice.

Hammer grunted and sat in a chair near his son. Gwyn could understand his frustration. It didn't seem right for her to be sitting here while Martin was in trouble.

"Wanna know why we have such great names?" Lake asked.

I'm dying to know, she thought. Why hadn't she gone straight to the mountain by herself? Asking River for help was already taking far too long. She looked down at Lake's big, questioning eyes, and for a brief second, she saw Martin. She turned toward him and smiled. "I have wondered about that. Please tell."

Lake grinned. "Only farmers are named after nature. The rich city folk have dull names."

Kegan stirred in his seat. "They're here," he said in a deep voice that sounded surprisingly like his father's.

As Anselm, Sherard, and their wives and children stepped inside and settled their family in the already-cramped room, Lake leaned over and whispered to Gwyn. "They're the best spies in all Vickland. They're woodsmen of the Zenia Wood." Crush stood in the middle of the room. "My fellow Vicklanders, as you know, our children have been kidnapped by the ruthless Black Wizard and sent most likely to the Uziel Mountain. Two of my children were kidnapped, Mica and Anele." Crush's voice wavered for a second, but he cleared his throat and continued. "Hammer's son, Arbor, is gone. Anselm's son, Warrick, and Sherard's son, Riley, were also taken. We can no longer stand idle and watch as the future generation is snatched away before our very eyes."

He pointed to a worn map on the table. "We have no other alternative but to try a rescue attempt. Our biggest concern is the great risk for the women and children left behind."

"What if they were to stay in the tunnels we built last year?" River asked.

Crush nodded. "They aren't the most comfortable living quarters, but they will be the safest."

"The tunnels will be more than adequate for us," Rose said. "We will sacrifice as much as we need to in order to have our children back." The other women nodded in agreement.

"Then the women will stay in the tunnels. I will inspect them and help gather the supplies. Has anyone been in them recently?"

"I 'ave," Sherard said in an accent similar to the woodsman Gwyn had met earlier.

"But you don't have a key," Crush said.

"Do I need one?" Sherard said. Chuckles filled the room. "The tunnel's in the 'zact same state as we left it last spring. 'Tis quite safe."

"Good. What about the armory, Dan?" Crush asked.

"Uncle Dan's name is short for *Dandelion*," Lake whispered with a snicker.

Gwyn frowned at him. "Shh!"

Dan nodded. "Everything is sharpened and ready for action, as usual."

"Your plan's too hasty." Sherard stood. "Ye cain't just go up and storm one of th' most powerful fortresses in all Vickland. Ye need stealth. Skill. Inside sources. Tell 'em our plan, Anselm," he said to his brother.

Anselm stood and walked toward the map. "Sherard and I vis'ted—er, I wouldn't really say we *visited* it."

"Let's jest say we weren't *welcome* vis'tors," Sherard said.

Crush stared at the two brothers impatiently.

"Ahem. Back to the plan. We spied on the castle 'bout eight years ago," Anselm explained. "If things haven't changed, the place is burstin' with maids and cooks and servants to pamper th' Blood Witch. There are also at least a hundred soldiers guarding the castle. We could disguise as servants and soldiers and blend in wit' the rest of them. This way we can get firs' hand information on the location of our chil'ren."

Murmurs of agreement rippled through the crowd.

"Any alternative plans?" Crush asked.

"I have baked several loaves of bread and will bake more for your journey," Rose said. "We also have several cows we can slaughter and beans we can harvest. We will have those ready for provisions for the journey and for our hideout in the tunnels."

"Anything else?" When no one responded, Crush nodded. "Then it is decided. We will leave in four days for the Uziel Mountain."

"Four days?" Hammer leaped to his feet.

Gwyn agreed. This was too much time. By then, Martin might be dead. She bit her lip and looked at Crush.

"That will give us plenty of time to gather supplies for the mission, make plans, and ensure the women and children are safe." Crush frowned at Hammer.

Hammer grumbled under his breath but didn't voice any more disapproval. The group spent the rest of the time discussing other precautions to keep the women and children safe. Gwyn ignored these plans. They should talk more about their attack plan on the Uziel Mountain.

The meeting finally adjourned and the participants dispersed. Gwyn stayed near the group in hopes of speaking to Crush. He finally turned around.

"Ah, Gwyn. River told me about you. I am sorry for your loss and will try my best to find your brother and bring him back to you."

She frowned. "I'm coming too."

"This will be no picnic, my dear."

"I know."

"The climb will be ruthless."

"I've gone mountain climbing many times with my father and brother in Surday."

"The mountains in Surday are hills compared to the Uziel Mountain."

"If I lag behind, you can leave me. I'll catch up eventually." She tried to keep her voice calm and polite, though she spoke through clenched teeth.

"There will be fighting. And blood."

"Blood doesn't scare me. I'm not a little girl." She pulled her shoulders back. "I can handle myself." The roughness in her voice felt satisfying.

Crush shook his head. "I am sure you are a strong young woman, but I think you will be a hindrance more than a help."

"My brother's in danger!" Her voice rose. The room suddenly grew quiet. Everyone turned toward them, but she didn't care. "I have to go. I will not be left behind."

Crush shook his head. "We will try our best to rescue your brother. You will be safer waiting with the rest of the women and children. My decision is final."

River walked to Crush's side. "I agree, Gwyn. You are safest here."

"Unlike everyone here, I am not afraid for my own safety." She turned to River and narrowed her eyes. "You don't really care about your friends' children, do you?"

She hurried out of the house. Her face was warm, and she clenched her jaw. Hot tears traced down her cheeks.

Her mind worked fast. Papa once said, "If you want something done, do it yourself."

She knew what she had to do, but she needed supplies. If she ran to River's house, she would be able to get there before he and his family did.

CHAPTER 25

HERON THE OAKHEARTED

The first thing Heron noticed when he woke was a stabbing pain in his back. He was lying on his stomach, his face buried in the pillow. He had just dreamed he and his mother were having a horseback-riding lesson through the Zenia Wood.

"Heron."

He thought he could hear his mother calling. His heart soared and he jerked up.

"Heron?"

He turned to his side and saw not his mother, but his skinny little servant bending over him.

"Er, excuse me, sire." Dredo seemed to realize he had just called the prince by his first name. "I'm glad you're awake. How are you feeling?"

He leaned on his elbow and looked around the room— some sort of cellar. He was lying on a thin sheet. The hard stones poked through the sheet and into his ribs and elbow. "Where are we?"

Dredo opened his mouth, but closed it. He frowned and was silent a few moments before saying, "We're in some secret tunnels in Lyris. Only the servants know about it."

179

"Why am I here?"

"I thought it was the safest place to hide you."

The incident in the secret room flooded his memory. "What happened?"

"By the way you were talking when I left your quarters, I was afraid you were up to no good—with all due respect, sire. So after I went to the kitchens, I went looking for you to keep an eye on you. I entered the secret tunnel and found you under a bookcase. The whole room was ablaze. I got you out right before guards came in to take care of the fire."

Heron sat up, wincing at the pain in his back. He fingered the cloth bandage encircling his bare chest.

"It's not a deep scratch," Dredo said. "But I fixed it up for you."

"How'd you pick me up?" He coughed several times. It felt like someone had shoved a prickly pine cone down his throat.

"I'm stronger than you think—with all due respect, sire." Dredo added the last part quickly.

Heron took the wooden mug of water Dredo handed him. The water tasted like it had sat too long in an old moldy room.

The king's angry face, the Black Wizard, and the dust-covered paintings swirled in his mind as he fit all the pieces together.

"How did you know about the secret room?"

"All the servants know every crack and crevice of Lyris." Dredo sat cross-legged in front of him.

"Then what do you know about the paintings in the secret room? Who painted them?"

"An artist was hired to paint pictures of King William's life. But as to the last picture depicting King William's and Queen Titania's deaths, no one is certain. The older servants say the king's ghost finished the job. The oldest servant, Birchbark, said he painted the last bit, but no one believes him."

"Is he the forgetful servant who uses a broom as a cane?"

Dredo nodded. "We do not believe the king has even seen the paintings. They have been covered with dust for many years."

"He has seen them now." Heron couldn't get the king's face out of his head.

"One thing all the servants agree on—all the previous king's councillors were murdered along with him."

The slain couple in Jalapa intruded into his thoughts. "My father is a monster."

"Be careful, sire. Your father is a dangerous man."

"I know."

"You don't know the worst of it."

"I know *all* of it."

They locked eyes and were silent a few moments.

"How do you know of my father's ... past?"

Trembling, Dredo looked over his shoulder. "All the servants know. There are still many servants who were here when the ... past ... happened."

All this was still a blur. So much had happened in just a fortnight's time.

"You are not safe here, sire." Dredo's voice lowered. "Not anymore."

Heron nodded as the realization sank in. Lyris was his only home. His safe place. Now it was the most dangerous place for him to be.

"I cannot keep you hidden here forever, sire." Dredo gave him back his shirt and pulled out a faded brown satchel. "I put the pork and bread in here. I wrapped them in cloths to keep everything warm and dry. It's raining outside." He handed Heron his cloak and then fit two canteens of water in the bag. He handed him a horn bearing Vickland's crest.

"If you ever need to play the royal card, then here is something with Vickland's crest. It is an ancient horn, handcrafted by Bromlin and given to King William Oakheart. The servants confiscated it when your grandfather's possessions were burned."

Heron took it and ran his hands over it. It was smooth, and the crest was etched perfectly into the horn. Bromlin made this. Perhaps if he ever came across him again, he could give it back.

Dredo pulled on his own faded cloak and strapped the brown satchel across his chest. "Come, sire, and I will show you the exit into the garden, where you may safely flee Lyris."

Heron slipped on the shirt, fastened his cloak beneath his neck, and followed Dredo down narrow stone passageways smelling of mold and stagnant water. After nearly half an hour of intricate turns, Dredo stopped.

"Here is the door leading out to the garden." His eyes shone in determination. "I am coming with you."

"No. If I am caught, you'll be killed." Heron took the satchel from him and strapped it across his chest. "I'm going by myself."

"Sire." Dredo dropped to one knee. "I swear my fealty to you. You are a kind prince who will be a kind king. *You are my master, not your father.* Please, sire. Let me go with you. You will need someone who is familiar with travel."

A kind king. But would he ever be king? Not after today. Surely the king would find a new heir who was easier to manipulate. Bromlin's words came back to him: *If you were not born into the royal family, what would you do?* Did he want to be king?

"Dredo, I am forever in your debt for saving my life. You have been a faithful servant. However, I must travel alone. I need you to stay here."

From the folds of his cloak, Dredo took out Heron's sword, still in its sheath, and placed it in his hands. He bowed with the respect normally reserved for kings and opened the garden door.

"Then I will wait for your return. The next time I see you, I hope it is with the crown on your head, Heron the Oakhearted."

Chapter 26

A Stormy Heart

G wyn arrived at River's empty house less than an hour after the meeting ended. The door was locked, and she kicked herself for not trying to steal a key. There were a few windows covered by shutters, but they were probably locked. As she walked around the house, she stumbled over a limb long and narrow enough to be a sturdy walking stick. She looked up at the shutters and fingered the stick. All this was Crush's fault. If he had let her go on the mission, she wouldn't have had to steal from River. She didn't need their help anyway. She could rescue her brother herself.

She glanced over her shoulder. She was fast. There was no way anyone at the meeting would be here. Unless they ran. Her stomach churned. How terrible it would be if River or Rose caught her here! What would she say? What would they do to her? Surely they wouldn't kill her, but would they imprison her? Force her to stay behind? Refuse to give her the resources she needed to travel? That would keep her from rescuing Martin. She had to finish quickly.

The stick was sturdy enough to break through the shutters, which were surprisingly fragile. The splintering sound made her wince and check down the path again. After throwing the stick to the ground, she climbed up to the windowsill and dropped inside. The house was eerie without the sounds of pattering feet, Daisy's cooing, and the rumbling boil of pig-foot soup over the fireplace.

She made a list in her head of things she needed: climbing clothes, food, and water.

She came across a chest of clothes in one of the bedrooms and pulled out pants, boots, and a shirt probably belonging to River's oldest son. They were baggy as she slid them on. She stuffed her old clothes in the pack.

The lingering smell of soup made her gag. Did no one have the heart to tell Rose how bad her cooking was? As Rose had mentioned in the meeting, there were several loaves of bread wrapped in towels. She stuffed two in her pack. There were six left. Surely this would be plenty for the mission. "I mean, how much bread can a few men eat?" The sound of her own voice made her jump. She glanced over her shoulder, her heart pounding. *Calm down, Gwyn. There's no one there.* A small canteen rested on the table. She would fill that with creek water on her way out. It fit perfectly between her journal and the bread.

Her hand rested on her journal. Her mother's worn hands had once helped her make it. She looked at the stolen goods in her bag. What was she doing? What would Papa and Mama say?

"I have to find Martin. I won't steal again." Her parents' disappointed faces still frowned in her head. "I promise."

River's baselard sat in its leather sheath on the table, the same dagger she had seen when she first met him in the woods. She picked it up and withdrew the glinting blade. It was definitely sharp. The reflection of her wide eyes stared back at her. She looked different. More serious. Her jaw was tighter. She liked the look. She looked older and tougher. She pushed the knife back into its sheath and ran her hands over the wooden hilt. She had never owned a weapon before. It was scary. And exhilarating. She heard a light step behind her. She jerked around. Leaves filtered in through the broken shutter. The wind must have blown them in. She heaved a sigh of relief.

An overwhelming wave of guilt swamped her. River and Rose had been kind to her. River had been one of her father's dearest friends. The look in his eyes when Gwyn told him of her parents' deaths . . .

She shook her head. If she was able to rescue Martin in the end, then surely it did not matter.

As she climbed out the window again, the wind picked up and blew her hair into her face. She dropped to the ground and took off running through the fields, not sure which way the Uziel Mountain was. But she just wanted to get away. She didn't want to be around when River and Rose returned.

Once in the shelter of a cluster of trees, she pulled out her map to determine which direction the mountains were. Martin should be here to read maps for her. She stuffed it back in her pack and ran through the forest.

An hour or so later, she turned and looked back at the forest from which she had just emerged. The wind tumbled through the trees. It traveled through the forest like an invisible monster, throwing one group of trees into a frenzy, then abandoning those and moving on to the next. They creaked and groaned and swayed with such force she wondered how they still stood. She backed farther away from the forest as limbs broke off and crashed to the ground.

The guilt still clung to her. She looked back in the direction of River and Rose's house. If they truly cared for her and Martin, they would be more willing to help. She shoved away the guilt and turned around.

Just as Gwyn turned toward the mountain, thunder roared like a crashing wave and the cold spray of rain blew in her face. The rain grew heavier as she walked farther from River's house and drew closer to the Uziel Mountain. She trudged many miles up and down slippery hills. Her thighs ached. Would River and the other Vicklanders come after her and punish her or, worse, try to stop her from her mission?

The soggy bag bounced against her side as she plodded up a sloping hill. The bread was probably drenched by now.

When she crested the hill, she gasped at what must be the Uziel Mountain. Outlined by the gray sky, the enormous black mountain loomed a few miles away. Steep paths zig-zagged along its face.

"Crush was right. This is no hill." Her shoulders slumped. Could she do this alone? For Martin. She heaved a sigh and ran down the slippery, grassy slope. Slimy grass wrapped around her shins like the arms of an octopus. As she struggled through it, the medallion bounced against her chest. She broke into a run. Finally, she stopped in a meadow to catch her breath. She collected a few handfuls of berries, until something caught her eye. A ribbon of fire glittered deeper in the woods. It was strange a fire would be able to survive in weather like this.

She would have to travel through part of the woods anyway, so she might as well inspect it. It wouldn't take any time away from her travel, and a warm fire was exactly what she needed. She would just keep a safe distance from it, just in case.

As she edged closer to it, she stopped. There was a man huddled over the fire. His faded red cloak looked more like a limp rag in the rain. He turned around and searched through a damp bag behind him. Gwyn crouched lower to the ground, but he had already seen her movement. Their eyes met.

The Black Wizard leaped to his feet. A sadistic, hungry smile spread over his features. She clenched the medallion and froze.

CHAPTER 27

HERON, GWYN, AND THE BLACK WIZARD

Heron shouldered his pack and shielded his eyes from the pelting rain. He was a day's distance from the castle now. He touched the horn by his side. Besides his sword, this was his only relic from home. But Lyris wasn't his home now.

The sweet tang of honeysuckle in the woods made him smile. He breathed a sigh. He wasn't going back. But where would he go? The king would worry about him, especially now that Heron knew about his dark past.

Bromlin's question gnawed at him: *Do* you *have a purpose for your life?* No, he didn't. He was used to his father carving a path for him. Even when he was being rebellious and stubborn, he at least knew what he was supposed to be doing. Now he had no idea what to do next. He had no idea who he was or who he was becoming. He had never been more alone in his life. Yet he was free. He *should* be feeling free.

He halted his pace. Was he a coward for running away from Lyris? He looked behind him, in the direction of the castle. Thunder rumbled in the distance; the clouds were an angry gray. He clenched his fists. He wanted to bring the king to justice and stop events like the slayings in Jalapa from happening. But he also wanted to put as much distance between him and the king as he could.

Suddenly, an unearthly scream pierced through the rain. He jumped and touched the hilt of his sword. He had never heard anything like that sound before. He squinted through the thick woods. The scream had come from somewhere near. He crouched closer to the ground and crept toward the voices and the light of a dying fire. The pelting rain masked the sound of his footsteps.

"Running is pointless," a deep voice said.

Heron's heart skipped a beat. Running was pointless for him too.

"You have it, I see. My medallion."

"It's my father's." The feminine voice was familiar. "You can't have it."

"Well, your father isn't here to stop me, is he?"

Heron peered around a tree. A man pointed a sword at a girl only a few paces in front of him — the same runner girl he had seen in the Zenia Wood. And there was something strange about the man. As he turned and looked into the woods, Heron could better see his profile.

He clenched his jaw. Coming across Andulza was definitely not something he had planned for. He had never feared the wizard, but after overhearing the meeting with the king, he changed his mind.

"Where's my brother?" The girl backed up to a tree. Her voice quavered.

"Ah, the foolish, trembling boy? I would be more concerned about myself if I were you."

She looked into the woods, her muscles tense. "I know about the medallion. I know you can't touch me," she said.

Andulza lifted an instrument and blew into it, making a horrible, screaming noise. Heron winced. What was that? "No, but my witches can. They will be here soon and can finish the job."

"You are nothing but a coward, hurting children and hiding behind your witches."

Andulza jerked up, clenching his fists.

Without turning around, he slung his knife into the tree Heron hid behind. "I wouldn't be so bold if I were you, you little brat. See, I don't have to be close to reach you, so I wouldn't attempt escape."

Heron stared at the blade, inches away from his face. He swallowed. If only the tree were bigger and he were thinner. Andulza moved to the left and was looking out farther into the woods, cursing and muttering something about witches always being late. The wizard's back was still toward Heron, who could see the girl better. The rain had drenched her hair and clothes, making her appear even smaller than she seemed when he first met her in the Zenia Wood. Even from far away, he could see her trembling.

Her eyes caught his, and her brows rose. She recognized him. Andulza must have seen the change in her expression, because he wheeled around. Heron ducked for cover.

"Who's there? Show yourself!"

Heron's mind raced. The girl. Andulza. The king. Everything he'd overheard in the archive clicked together like a puzzle. He swallowed. It would be a long shot, but he didn't have many options against the Black Wizard.

He stepped out from behind the tree and pulled the dagger out of the trunk.

"Ah, you must be Prince Heron." The Black Wizard gave a mocking bow. "You look just like your father. I see you have escaped the castle walls again. Kindly hand over my dagger."

"What has this girl done?"

"Nothing at all. I just need her."

"*You* need her? I heard my father say he needed her too. You were going to take this girl for yourself and not tell him, weren't you?" He couldn't hide the tremble in his voice. No. He needed to be in charge of the situation. He couldn't appear frightened now.

Andulza smirked. "You think that's my plan, do you?"

Despite his racing heart, he forced himself to step with confidence toward the girl. She shrank back and turned to run, but he caught her by the waist and placed the dagger against her throat. She grasped his arms with her wet hands and tried to pull them away, but he kept a firm hold on her.

"Leave now, without the girl, and I will keep her alive. Come a step closer, and I will slit her throat and call Rinalldo." He motioned to the small horn dangling by his arm. "It won't look good for you if she is killed by your own blade."

The wizard snarled. "Give that back."

Thunder rumbled and the rain made Heron blink. Bromlin had mentioned the Black Wizard's poisoned blade.

"Once the girl is found, your blade's poisonous mark will be quite recognizable on her throat." She sobbed, and he held her tighter. "Be quiet."

Andulza's eyes narrowed. "What are your terms?"

His mind whirled again. He had to get away from Andulza. Runner Girl was a nice distraction. He could use her and the knife as bargaining chips and safely be on his way, if the Black Wizard let him go. He doubted he would stick to any terms Heron put forth. But if he gave the knife and girl back to him, what would the wizard do with her?

Runner Girl trembled against him. Her breaths came in quick, panicked rasps. The Black Wizard would definitely not treat her well. Neither would the king. But he just needed to get out of this situation alive. And if she helped him accomplish this, then he would use her.

"I do not trust you to keep my terms."

"With good reason." The wizard grinned. "You are in a prickly position, young prince."

"I am going to walk away with the girl and knife." The authority in his voice reminded him of his father. He nodded toward his left. "You will go up that hill. I will leave the knife on the ground, but I am taking the girl. I will not tell my father of your whereabouts or treason. Step a pace closer, and the girl will be dead."

"You have too much of your cursed mother in you. She would never be able to kill a helpless girl. How do I know you will?"

Heron firmed his jaw. The Black Wizard laughed.

"Leave now!" Heron's voice was clear and loud without a hint of trembling.

Thunder crashed, and a streak of lightning lit the wizard's sadistic grin.

"You won't kill her." He took a step closer. "You have the flat of the blade against her throat. You don't intend to kill her. You don't have the stomach for killing. You're soft like your mother. Like your cursed grandfather."

The Black Wizard spat on the ground and strode closer. Heron backed away, still holding the girl. His heart pounded, and he clenched his teeth.

"If you get near me, I will touch you," the girl said.

The wizard's grin faded, and he stopped advancing. How could that be considered a threat?

Her eyebrows knitted together. "I get it now," she said. "It's all so clear. You said you couldn't touch me.

It's because of the medallion, isn't it? Martin wore the medallion when he tackled you at Uncle Edwinn's house to save me, and he hurt you. If you touch me, you will get hurt again." Her trembles lessened.

Fear flickered on Andulza's face. Rain continued to pour from the sky. It slicked back his hair and plastered his cape to his clothes, making him look smaller.

"I could have run away at any time, because you can't touch me." Her voice grew stronger. "I could run away now, and there's nothing you can do to stop me." Her confidence made Heron loosen his grip. She squirmed out of his grasp and stood at his side.

"I still have my witches," the Black Wizard said. He searched the woods behind him.

Scurrying sounded behind him.

She looked at him. Her eyes were the most stunning green he had ever seen. "I'm your shield. Run!"

Andulza blew into the horn again. Humpbacked shapes materialized out of the forest.

"Now! We don't want the witches to get us." The girl's voice rose. "Run in front of me."

Heron lowered the knife.

Panic shone in the Black Wizard's eyes. "Stay right there!" he yelled.

The girl elbowed Heron hard. Humpbacked creatures ran toward them.

"Go, go, go!"

Heron grabbed her hand and raced off deeper into the woods. He lost his balance as he leaped over a log and dropped the knife. No time to go back now. He jerked her hand when she also struggled over the log.

"Ow!" She pulled away from him and scowled. "I can run by myself, and twice as fast as you."

He raced through the woods, his heart pounding. She was right. She was fast, but he still easily outran her. Shock and indignation registered in her eyes as he passed her.

"I heard the Black Wizard call you a prince," she called after him as they slid down a leafy ravine. "You're the prince of Vickland, aren't you? How do I know you're not going to turn me in to your father after this?"

"I'm not. I want nothing to do with him."

She stumbled again, and he grasped her arm, keeping her from falling off an edge into a river. He drew his sword and slashed his way through brambles and thorns. Adrenaline rushed through him with each swipe. A thorn sliced into his leg and ripped his pants. Several witches gained on them. There were at least a dozen, and they had their bows drawn.

Fog shrouded the forest and gave them some cover. They leaped over another fallen tree and splashed across a creek. At the crest of the next hill, they found the perfect hiding place—a large rock overhang.

"Follow me!" Heron yelled.

Chapter 28

Witches of the Skull Forest

The rain came down so hard and the fog was so thick that Heron couldn't make out the witches or Andulza. Large thorns snagged his pants. He kicked them away and ran deeper in the woods, Runner Girl close behind. He ducked under a large rocky overhang. She followed him. He drew his sword again and crouched low, searching the fog. His heart sank when the little green lights grew closer. A red cape flashed into view.

"Why, yes! Yes, Master! We smell fear—indeed we do!"

"Shut up and find the girl! We wouldn't be tripping and stumbling through these woods in this pouring rain if you and the rest of your witches had gotten here on time!" Andulza's voice made Heron shrink closer to the ground.

"Yes, yes, Master, but we have excellent smell in the rain. The witches of the Skull Forest are highly trained to smell. We will find the girl."

"Then do so and stop talking to me!"

The green lights halted. "Oh, Master, this way! The trail is fresh! There is blood! Look, look, Master! How tasty it smells."

Runner Girl sucked in a breath. Fear shone in her eyes. Heron touched his stinging leg. Blood dripped into his hands. He ripped off the bloody portion of his pants near his calf and tied it around a rock. Then he flung it as hard as he could. He flattened himself against the ground and kept his eyes on the lights. She did the same. Water droplets traced down his face. The lights began to reveal the humpbacked shapes of the witches.

"The rain has washed away the trail of blood," Andulza said. "Can you smell them?"

"Yes, of course, Master! We have excellent smell in the rain. They are this way!"

The witches hurried closer to the rock but turned sharply right. They passed within a few yards of their hideout. Andulza was close on their heels.

They watched their pursuers as the rain poured down. Heron held his breath until the red splash of Andulza's cape and the glittering green dots of the witches' torches were out of sight.

"That was close." He let out a breath.

They glanced at each other and moved to either side of the rocky overhang. Heron could name many awkward moments. Like the time he accidentally spilled wine down the front of Petunia's dress and tried wiping it off, only to realize everyone at the banquet was watching him as he awkwardly tried to wipe it away. As a prince whose life was always on display, these moments happened quite frequently. However, none of those compared to this one. He had just threatened to kill Runner Girl and had used her as leverage. It had worked out in the end, and they were both alive, but he could definitely see the mistrust in her eyes.

The rain wasn't letting up anytime soon, so he reached in his bag and chewed on some of the meat. The girl also reached into her bag and snacked on a handful of squished berries.

"Why does the Black Wizard want you?" Heron asked.

"If you think I'm going to talk to you right after you threatened to use me as a bargaining chip to get away from the Black Wizard, then you're a fool." She glared at him.

"I don't care if you trust me or not. I'm heading off as soon as this rain ends."

Her expression bounced from suspicion to interest. "What do they call you?"

"My name is Heron."

"Heron, like the bird?" She hid her laughter by coughing on the berries.

He pushed down the anger but couldn't suppress a glare. "It's the ancient Vickland word for 'hero.'"

"Right." She cleared her throat. "I'm Gwyn."

"So where are you going?"

She studied his expression for a few seconds, apparently trying to figure out if she could trust him. "The Black Wizard kidnapped my brother and took him to the Uziel Mountain. I'm on my way to rescue him."

A smile played on his lips. "You're going to storm the Uziel Castle? By yourself?"

"Yes." She raised her chin slightly and squared her shoulders.

"That castle is almost as heavily guarded as Lyris. There's no way you can do that yourself."

"Thanks for the encouragement." Gwyn glared at him.

Heron leaned back and rested his head against the rock. The thunder melted into an ominous rumble, and the rain slackened some. He mulled over all that had happened and tried to form his next step. This girl couldn't survive on her own. And when either the Black Wizard or the king captured her, she might turn him over to his father, especially if they tortured her for information. This meant Heron needed to keep an eye on her to ensure she did not get captured.

There was something about her that scared the Black Wizard. Staying with her would perhaps keep him safe. And protecting her from the king would be a good way to get back at him. That would involve traveling up the Uziel Mountain with her, but he had nowhere else to go besides Bromlin's cabin anyway. Traveling to the Uziel Mountain offered him a purpose. The sense of freedom slowly melted away the weight on his shoulders.

"I'll go with you up the Uziel Mountain," he said.

Chapter 29

The Uziel Mountain

Gwyn was hesitant about the prince coming with her, but he was persistent. She still didn't trust him, but it was nice to have a traveling companion again, even though he always kept his hand on the hilt of his sword. But surely someone who was on the run from Vickland's king must have some good qualities. His face had many good qualities, though she tried not to base her judgment on that.

After traveling for hours through the drenched fields, they came to the foot of the mountain. It wasn't as steep as she thought it would be, but it was a long way to the top. Her legs burned. She had barely made it this far. Would they be able to make it to the top?

"Let's take a break before we start." She sat under a large protruding rock and pulled out the bread. The rags covering the loaves were soaked, but the bread was hard. She took a bite out of it and crunched on it. It tasted like gravel. She'd hate to know what it tasted like when it hadn't been soaked by the rain.

Heron sat beside her and munched on his meat. "Did you bring a disguise?"

Carrie Looper Stephens

"No. I'm still trying to figure things out." Sherard had told her about maids on the mountain. She could steal clothes from a maid.

She studied Heron's face while he looked up at the mountain. Though he had a young face, the muscles in his shoulders and arms and the hint of a beard made him seem old enough to be a soldier. They could find soldier's garb for him.

"I have it figured out. Follow me."

He glowered at her, and she bit back a smile. He obviously wasn't used to being ordered around.

He grasped her arm before she started off on the path up the mountain. "No, you're going to tell me what you have figured out."

Gwyn ripped her arm away from him and glared at him. "Don't touch me again."

Heron put his hands up in mock surrender. "Fine. But I still want to know the plan."

"I'll have a maid's disguise, and you'll get a soldier's disguise. We will get into the castle that way."

"Where will we get those disguises?"

She looked down at her boots and was silent a few moments. They would have to steal them somehow. They'd probably have to infiltrate the castle in their own garb and then find disguises, which would be hard. "When we get to the top, we can better see where a good place would be to steal them." She crossed her arms. "How does that sound?"

He rolled his eyes. "Sure. Great plan." He sauntered in front of her and began the climb.

"I'll come up with a backup plan, just in case we need it. Because I know we will."

She clenched her fists and glared at his back. She was perfectly capable of making her own plans.

204

Slippery rocks littered the narrow path that snaked up the mountain, and the path grew steeper the higher they hiked. Heron stayed several yards in front of her, hiking as easily as if on a flat surface. He kept disappearing around the bends of switchbacks. She forced her legs into a run to keep up, but even then, she couldn't reach him. She was stronger than this! She had traveled weeks on foot. Heron must think she looked weak.

Within a few hours, they were about a quarter of the way up the mountain. The rain slowed to a miserable drizzle, and a thick fog shrouded them. At first she grumbled because she could not see the top of the mountain, but then a dragon roared overhead. Chill bumps trickled up her arms. It sounded like the cry of a linador, only deeper. Maybe the fog wasn't so bad after all.

She strained to see the forms of the dragons, but she could hear only the earsplitting roar and see vague black shadows. All her life she had wanted to see a dragon in person instead of just hearing about them in stories. By the look on Heron's face, he had never seen one this close either. His eyes were wide, and every few moments he threw a glance over his shoulder.

Once they neared the middle of the mountain, the terrain became even steeper. The higher she climbed, the harder it was to breathe. Soon every breath was like a knife stabbing into her chest. She lay down in the path, gasping. Why was she so weak? She punched the ground. She was better than this. Heron also breathed heavily, but he was far ahead of her. He climbed back down to her. She hated the smug look on his face.

"It's the altitude." He shrugged. "You'll get used to it."

"And how would a spoiled prince know about altitude and mountain climbing?" She had to take a breath between each word she said. "You've probably never climbed a mountain in your life!"

"I used to climb in the Oakheart Mountains twice a week for training."

"You made that up!" Gwyn forced herself to her feet and put her hands on her hips. "I bet those mountains don't even exist."

Heron pointed over her head to a range of mountains twice the size of the Uziel.

She clenched her fists. "You think you know how to do everything. You think you're so smart. But you're not the one whose parents were murdered by the Black Wizard. You're not the one who has been on the run for weeks. You wouldn't stand a chance if you had Uncle Edwinn, the witches, the king, and the Black Wizard running after you."

Heron raised an eyebrow and smirked. "About that. Why is the Black Wizard after you? If I'm going to be traveling with you, I at least want to know if I'm traveling with a fugitive or murderer."

"I'm not a fugitive or murderer!" Her yells were muffled by a heavy gust of wind that knifed into her ears. She covered them and winced. "I'm on the run because I have my father's old medallion. No more questions!"

She forced herself forward and brushed past him. But within a few minutes, he had passed her again. By now, her chest hurt so much and her brain was in such a fog that she didn't even care. Her hands were cut and sore from the sharp rocks, but she continued. The rain returned with a vengeance.

One foot in front of the other. Keep going. Don't look down. Don't trip over that rock. Sticky sweat dripped down her sides. Or perhaps it was rain. Or a lot of both. Her breath came in heaving gasps. Nausea swirled in her stomach, and her head felt like it was being squeezed by a giant fist. *One foot in front of the other. Keep going. Don't look down. Look out for that rock. Step over that log. Climb over that boulder.*

206

Heron gasped for breath a few feet in front of her but didn't complain. With every step, her chest tightened. Her breathing turned into gasps. Would this path ever end? Her knees buckled, and she lay down in the middle of the path again. The rain cut into her. Heron sat down ahead of her, his elbows resting on his legs and his head bowed.

She couldn't do this. Why did she think she could climb this mountain? Her chest tightened. She would die here on the mountain. Martin would die too. She had failed.

She pictured Martin's face as he ate his birthday dinner. Was he even alive? Maybe the Blood Witch was beating him to death, and he was lying on a hard, cold stone floor, gasping his last breath. She forced herself to her feet and continued. As he stood, Heron muttered words she had never heard before. Probably some sort of Vickland curse words.

After several hours, the hazy light grew darker.

"Here's a good place to rest for the night," Heron called. There was a small cleft in the rock that would offer a little shelter from the rain.

"We can't stop." She turned toward him and scowled. When she looked how far they had come, a wave of dizziness hit her, and she swayed in the wind.

He held her arm to steady her. "We're stopping."

Gwyn nodded and stumbled into the cleft with him. They ate their food in silence. Heron handed her some of his meat. "You're skinnier than a twig. You need it more than me."

She was too hungry to argue. After she ate the meat and bread, a deeper satisfaction and energy cleared her mind. She offered Heron a handful of her blackberries, which he dismissed with a pompous wave of his hand.

"Who was your father?"

She sighed and stared down at her berry-stained hands. "I honestly don't know anymore. People keep talking about him like he was a magician or something. But that's not the man I knew." Emotion clogged her throat. "No more questions." She scowled and turned away from him.

She searched through her bag and pulled out River's baselard. She slipped it out of the leather sheath and admired the bright silver metal. The blade was double edged and about eighteen inches long. It looked similar to the small dagger her father gave her mother many years ago. She slid the dagger into its sheath and fit the belt around her waist. It fit perfectly by her side—neither too light nor too heavy.

"Where'd you get that puny knife?"

"Someone gave it to me." The lie came off her lips so quickly it surprised her. She used to be such a terrible liar.

"How do I know you're not going to use it against me?"

"How do I know *you're* not going to use your sword on me?" She raised an eyebrow. "And why are you afraid of a girl with a puny knife?"

Heron turned away, but Gwyn caught the small smile on his face.

"Get some sleep," he said.

They curled up in a sitting position as far away from each other and the edge as they could. The pouring rain muffled a dragon's roar. Did Martin hear it too?

She drifted off to sleep, dreaming of Martin riding a fluffy pink dragon.

Chapter 30

The Uziel Castle

Gwyn woke first. Heron still sat against the wall, his head cocked to the right. His brown hair slid into his face, almost covering his eyes. His mouth opened slightly. His snores were louder than Martin's. But he had a nice face. A princely face. A wild face. She had never seen a prince before but had always imagined they would wear rich purple robes and a crown, have perfect posture, and have a sort of noble haughtiness about them. He had the haughtiness all right.

He sat up suddenly and bumped his head. She quickly began to rummage through her bag.

Heron rubbed his head. "I am never sleeping sitting up again."

"Good morning." She handed him a crust of bread. "This is the last of my bread, but I thought maybe you'd like to have it."

"No, thanks." He waved it away and took out his own bread and meat. "Nothing beats the bread from Lyris."

Gwyn stared at her damp bread, and her shoulders slumped. She wanted to feel like she was contributing to this expedition. She didn't like Heron helping her.

Carrie Looper Stephens

Water streamed down the mountain as they climbed. The path grew steeper, forcing her to crawl on her hands and knees. Heron passed her by. She hated the smug look on his face, and she stood and forced her limbs into a faster pace. Her whole body ached, and every step sent shooting pains through her knees.

Her foot slipped in a stream as she reached for a stone. She slid down the rock face, scraping her chin and arms. She grasped for a hold, but her fingers were numb. Heron yelled above her.

She was finally able to grasp a protruding rock before she fell off an enormous drop. She banged her head but managed to cling to the stone and steady herself.

"Gwyn!" Gravel tumbled down as Heron hurried to her. "Here—grab my hand!"

"I can't! I can't let go!" Her hands grew numb, and the hard surface cut into her, but she couldn't bring herself to release her grip. Pebbles slid past her and catapulted off the edge, swallowed by the thick mist obscuring the ground. No telling how far down it was.

"Try!" he yelled. His hand, fingers splayed, was so close—mere inches away—but she didn't dare let go. "Reach for me!"

Sheer terror choked her throat as her fingers cramped and began to lose their grip. "I'm slipping!"

"Hang on!" Heron scrambled closer, sending a spray of sand and pebbles into her hair and eyes. Finally, his strong hands clasped her arms, and he pulled her up to the ledge.

She clung to him for a moment, panting and trembling until her bones rattled. Blood trickled down her forehead, her head throbbed, and her chin and hands stung.

Heron sat beside her. "Are you all right?"

She nodded. "I-I think so."

"You should be more careful."

She was too out of breath and shaky to defend herself.

The lines on his forehead softened. "Can you keep climbing?"

She must. Martin needed her. She forced herself up, and with a final glance over the ledge, she nodded.

Heron stayed closer to her this time as they climbed. He was purposefully climbing slower. Part of her was angry she wasn't strong enough to keep up with him. But another part of her was softening toward him. He did care about her, at least a little.

"If I had fallen and died, would you have gone on to rescue Martin? Or would you have given up and gone back home?"

He frowned. "I don't have a home anymore."

They hiked in silence. Night fell, but they continued their ascent. She counted the days and realized she was behind schedule. Two days had passed, but she was still not at the top.

After climbing a few more hours, they neared a ledge. By now, her lungs had gotten used to the elevation. The climb was still hard and Heron was still a better hiker, but at least she wasn't as miserable as she was before. They took sips of water from their canteens and refilled them with the water streaming down cracks in the mountain. They settled back on the ledge and ate the last bit of their food.

"Uh, you have blood on your head."

"Oh, sorry." She wiped her sleeve on her forehead.

His eyebrows knitted together as he stared at her. He searched his bag and brought out the cloth that had been keeping his bread dry. "Here."

"Thank you." She took it and dabbed at her brow. "Is it gone now?"

He nodded.

Voices sounded above. She and Heron scooted closer to the side of the mountain so its shadow could hide them.

They must be near the top. She caught his eye. He reached for his sword.

"We need another shipment of tobacco," a man said. Gwyn could smell the sickening scent of tobacco smoke.

"Low again? It seems like just a fortnight since we left to get the stuff from Jalapa," his companion said.

"That's the good thing about being stationed up here. There are so many soldiers, you can go missing for a while and no one notices."

"And if they do notice, no one cares."

"No one's stupid enough to attack anyway."

"I don't know. With the new additions to our prison, I've been on edge."

"Do you honestly believe those puny villagers are going to try to rescue their kids?"

"I've heard they've proved a strong group of people so far. I've heard their leaders are mighty warriors."

"True. I'm starved, and our watch is almost up. Want to hit the kitchens?"

"Sure." The light clinking of their armor faded into the distance.

Heron released the breath he'd been holding. "We have to have a more definite plan."

"Let's see what's at the top, and then we can make a plan."

His whisper tickled her ear. "Let me go first."

"Fine."

They scrambled upward. She tried not to think about what would happen if she fell again.

They finally reached a small cleft. Just above, lights flickered in a small tower. She strained her sore muscles and climbed up the last ledge.

As she came nearer the top, she stood in awe of the huge towers. Candlelight, like the blinking eyes of a dark monster, brightened hundreds of windows.

Fear twisted in her again, but she whispered, "You can do this, Gwyn. For Martin."

"Be quiet," Heron snapped.

She scrambled higher and rested on a ledge three feet from the top. A thin, dirty girl her own age walked across the lawn in front of the castle, carrying a basket of kindling. An idea leaped into Gwyn's mind.

"Hey, you!" she whispered.

The girl jumped and looked like she was about to scream. Gwyn climbed onto the ledge. She motioned for Heron to stay.

"It's okay." She hid behind another bush. "I'm not going to hurt you."

"What do you want?" Red scars traced down the girl's face and arms, and fear shone in her eyes.

"You hate it here?" she asked.

The girl nodded. "It's impossible to escape, though. The soldiers keep a close eye on everyone."

"Listen, I need a job. You want to trade places?"

"You're mad!"

"I know. But I have to get in there."

A soldier's voice made Gwyn duck deeper into the bushes. "Hey, you! Hurry up, you filthy rat! The kitchens need that wood."

The girl shuddered and turned back to her. "Fine. What's the plan?"

"We can trade clothes. Be careful climbing down the mountain."

The girl slid behind the bush, and they swapped clothes. The maid's dress came to Gwyn's knees. The sandals were worn and pinched her feet. She tied her baselard's belt around her leg and strapped her satchel across her chest.

She looked at the girl's pale complexion and curly, red hair. "We look nothing alike." She picked up the basket of kindling.

"It doesn't matter," the girl said. "No one will realize I'm missing. There are so many of us, you'll blend in perfectly. Tell Madam Crocker you are new. She won't think twice about it. We're due to have a new maid soon anyway. One died recently."

Gwyn dropped the basket of kindling. "Died? How?" Being a maid wasn't supposed to be dangerous work, was it? What was she signing up for?

"Never mind." She put the basket back in Gwyn's arms and took a step back. "Thank you. I've been waiting for this day. My family is from Jalapa, and I haven't seen them in three years."

The girl scooted down the ledge and disappeared, half-sliding down the mountain. Gwyn had freed a slave. But her words were not comforting.

Heron scrambled up the ledge and joined her behind the bushes. "So you have a disguise. What about me?"

"Who goes there?" The voice came from the tower.

Gwyn jumped, then whispered to Heron. "Stay here. I'll bring a disguise out to you."

He looked at the flickering lights of the castle, then back at her, his brow creased. "Be careful."

"I will."

She stepped out from the cover of the bushes and shielded her eyes against the bright lights of the castle. Her heart pounded as she watched the soldier lean out the battlements. No turning back now. She held up the basket of kindling in her trembling hand. "I was just collecting wood."

"Open the gate!" the soldier yelled below.

Gwyn heaved a deep breath and stepped up toward the gate.

"For Martin."

Chapter 31

Inside the Castle

Protruding metal spikes lined the doors, and carvings of skulls and swords were etched into the gateposts.

Gwyn hesitated in front of the open gate. The inside did not look like the castles she had read about in books. Torches cast ominous, bouncing shadows across the hallway behind the guards. Someone screamed, and then several loud voices erupted, and then an explosion shook the walls.

The screaming stopped.

Every bone in her body and what little shred of sense she had left told her to turn around and climb back down the mountain. Her whole body switched into escape mode. She had to flee. With each beat of her heart, a voice in her head screamed *Run. Run. Run!*

Who did she think she was? She had never read any stories about a fifteen-year-old girl who stormed a castle. Only knights did that. She was nowhere near being as brave or strong or clever as a knight. The guards frowned at her and reached up to close the door. She imagined Martin cowering in a dungeon and slipped into the gate, keeping her face down as she passed the dozens of guards inside.

She ducked under the arms of several guards and sidestepped two men wrestling in the hallway. Several men marched past her, carrying spears twice her size.

"Lavida? Is that you? Are you dawdling again?" A hoarse, older woman's voice. A rotund woman appeared down the hall, pushing a cart laden with linens. A younger maid carried some linens behind her.

"I'm new," she squeaked.

"I think that's Lavida's replacement, Madam Crocker," the young maid said.

"Ah yes. I keep forgetting Lavida is dead. I knew we'd be getting a replacement maid soon. Well, don't just stand there, girl! Get to work!"

"Yes, ma'am." Gwyn dipped a curtsy. Was that how she was supposed to behave in a castle? She had no idea. And why did Lavida die?

"Two doors down and turn to the left. You can smell the rest of the way there. I'm cooking collard green stew." She threw her hand in the direction of the kitchen. "I've been waiting a full ten minutes for that blasted kindling. The fire is about to die."

Her heart pounded fast as she dashed toward the reeking smell of collard greens. Inside the kitchen was a huge fireplace where a bubbling cauldron hung over the flames. Clean dishes, fresh herbs, and lumps of dough filled a long table in the middle of the room.

Gwyn built up the fire as best as she could. She had never been good at this. Her brother and father could start up a roaring fire even with wet wood.

The younger maid scurried around, mopping. Several other maids scattered to and fro—sweeping, putting away cooking utensils, hanging fresh herbs up to dry, and chopping dried herbs and putting them away in a spice cabinet.

"Stir the pot. Stoke the fire. Knead the bread. Wash that pan." Madam Crocker's loud voice made Gwyn's already-aching head pound even more. She was so exhausted she could barely walk. Her legs wobbled like jelly.

She glanced out the window. It must be near midnight. She had to find a way to get a disguise for Heron.

"All right, bedtime! Everyone out!"

Gwyn walked down the hallway, following Madam Crocker and the rest of the maids to a small room near the kitchen. A lone candle illuminated a dozen narrow beds lining the walls . There were no windows.

Madam Crocker closed the door and the lock clicked. Gwyn's heart sank. No chance of meeting Heron tonight.

After an uneasy night's sleep, she woke to the sound of Madam Crocker's hoarse voice and the crash of pots and pans. She could barely lift her head. She had never been sorer in her whole life. Her neck, arms, back, legs, and feet hurt with a dull ache. She dragged herself out of bed and stepped into the kitchen.

"Drelina, I told you to sift the flour!" Madam Crocker yelled to an older girl with black hair. The fat cook slapped the youngest maid, who looked only a little older than Martin. "Nadine, a boil! It must come to a rumbling boil before you pour it over the salted pork. Saskia, run down to the wine cellar and get the queen's best wine. And be careful you get the right kind this time or she might have your head too." She placed a chubby hand on her hip and glared at Gwyn. "Well, well. Good morning, beautiful."

She rubbed the sleep away from her eyes and tied on an apron.

"When you work in the kitchen, you wake before dawn." Madam Crocker pointed a dripping wooden spoon at a pile of dirty cauldrons and bowls. "Dishes."

Gwyn hurried to the pile of dishes. She brushed her hair away from her face and threw it up in a quick, sloppy bun.

"What's your name?" Madam Crocker asked.

She jumped. She hadn't realized the woman was still standing behind her. "Gw-uh, Sara."

"Well, Gwasara, finish the dishes and sweep the kitchen, and then Saskia will show you the garderobe. It needs to be cleaned out once a day. Since our last maid died, things have started piling up."

"Garderobe?"

"The sewer," Madam Crocker said. "Haven't you any experience in castles?"

The sewer. Great.

As Gwyn washed the dishes, she wondered about Martin. What part of the castle was he imprisoned in? How would she get there? Was he still alive? Because of her distracting thoughts, the excess of soap, and trembling hands, she accidentally let a plate slip. It crashed on the ground and sent shards clattering over the kitchen floor.

Madam Crocker swung around, her eyes bulging and bloodshot. She turned a bright red, stormed over to her, and slapped her hard. Gwyn touched her stinging face and stared at her in shock. She had never been slapped before.

"You drop one more plate, and I'll have you hanging from the ceiling with that ham over there!" she yelled, pointing to a dripping ham dangling near the fire.

Gwyn muttered her apologies and swept up the shards. She normally would have wanted to fight back, but she had never met a woman like Madam Crocker, and she terrified her.

As she washed the three-foot-high pile of dishes, she noticed Nadine glancing at her. The younger maid, about Martin's age, blushed and turned back to the soup she was stirring. "Sorry to stare."

"That's fine." She touched the scar on her face and winced. She had forgotten about the wound she received while climbing down the tree at Uncle Edwinn's house.

"What happened?"

"Lightning bolt."

Nadine's eyes widened. Gwyn enjoyed lying to kids. She used to tell lies to Martin all the time. He was usually gullible enough to believe just about anything.

Nadine's cheeks grew redder and she stirred the pot faster.

"What?"

"What happened to your arms?"

Her dress's sleeves had been rolled up to just below her shoulder. "What do you mean?"

"Why are they so big and so, uh … dark?"

Everyone in Surday had the same light-brown skin tone, but the Vickland people were much paler. "My mother was from Surday. Also, I've been in the sun many times because I lived near the coast. My arms …" Her biceps had definitely become more defined the past couple of days, especially since her mountain-climbing adventure. "I suppose my arms are big from fishing at the coast. The fishnets are heavy."

"Tell me more about the coast."

"No talking! We have deadlines, girls," Madam Crocker said as she swatted the table with her big wooden spoon. She pronounced each word slowly as she hit the table with the splintering spoon. "And the queen will not have her dinner late."

After finishing her kitchen duties, Gwyn followed Saskia down the hall. Saskia led her through the intricate and confusing passageways of the castle. Several dozen soldiers marched past them. How was she going to get past all this to find Martin?

"The sewer." Saskia gave a pompous bow as she opened the door. A horrid stench filtered out behind the door. "We are all *so* very glad you are here."

Gwyn pinched her nose.

"The sewer is a state-of-the-art amenity. The queen hired the best engineers to create a system of pipes that drain down to the sewer. Someone on the tippy top of this castle can take a bath, and then it drains down the pipes to this place right here. The only downside? Someone has to clean it out." Saskia gave a smug smile and handed her a shovel. "And today, that someone is *you*."

"The queen's smart engineers could have extended the pipes farther and drained the sewage out of the castle and down the mountain," Gwyn said as she picked up the shovel.

Saskia frowned. "I didn't think of that. I suppose they could have. There's a small door where you shovel the stuff out. The guards come in here when they need to." She pointed to a wooden seat over a wide bowl. "Don't let the Ghost of Uziel get you when you open the door."

"Ghost?"

Saskia's smugness made her want to push her into the sludge of the sewer. "Uziel was a witch who was killed here. Several soldiers have seen her wandering near the edge of the mountain. They have seen her snatch soldiers near the edge of the cliff. They were never seen again."

"Thanks," she grumbled as Saskia slammed the sewer door.

She marched through the gloopy, stinking mess, opened the window-sized sewer door, and began shoveling the stuff out. She gagged at the putrid smell and brushed away wisps of her hair that kept escaping her bun.

She was supposed to be finding a disguise for Heron, spying out the castle, and trying to find the prison and Martin. First her parents died. Then her brother got kidnapped. Now she was in enemy territory and shoveling gross sludge. Things couldn't get any worse.

Finally she shoveled the last pile out the door. She threw the shovel at the wall, watching with satisfaction as it crashed and fell to the ground with a loud clatter. She stomped over to the small sewage door and slammed it shut. But then she reopened it. It could be opened only from the inside, but it led outside to a garden. The door was about two feet by two feet. Too small for a grown man, but a child could easily crawl through.

She had an escape route. And a way to give Heron his disguise. Now all she had to do was find a disguise and then find the prison.

Chapter 32

Kitchen Duties

After Gwyn washed off, Madam Crocker told her she was to help take dinner to the queen. "Put on your best apron and look nice and tidy. The queen is not to be trifled with. She likes everyone to look and smell nice and clean."

"Gwasara doesn't smell nice, even after a bath." Saskia snickered.

"This is true." Madam Crocker tapped her chin with her wooden spoon. "Saskia, you will come with me tonight. Gwasara can meet the queen another time."

Saskia sneered. "Oh, I'm *so* very sorry, Gwasara. You'll have to meet the glorious queen another time."

Gwyn narrowed her eyes but bit back a retort. Madam Crocker was standing near, and she didn't want to risk getting slapped again.

That was fine with her anyway. She imagined the queen, who was probably the Blood Witch, as some spoiled, fat woman with expensive clothes. And by the way Madam Crocker talked about her, she probably had a temper.

Madam Crocker and Saskia left with a cart of food, and Gwyn helped the other two girls with the dishes.

"Nadine, make sure you don't forget the laundry," Drelina, the oldest of the maids, said. She was probably second in command. "We'll also need to take the food to the prisoners in a few hours."

Gwyn almost dropped another plate. She tried to think of a discreet way to ask about the prisoners.

"You can come along if you want." Drelina's black hair swished down the middle of her back as she scrubbed a pot.

"I will." She said it too fast. Drelina and Nadine turned toward her. She bit her lip and shrugged. "This castle is so large, I would think it is easy to get lost here. I need to know my way around."

"You'll get used to it," Drelina said. "Nadine, the water is coming to a boil. Gwasara, hand me that towel."

Nadine scurried over to the bubbling pot over the fire. Gwyn tossed a towel to Drelina. She had never seen a girl wash dishes so fast. Drelina was even faster than her mother used to be. An image flashed in her mind. Her mother's dark brown hair fell below her waist and was tied halfway back with a blue ribbon. A faded brown apron was tied around her tiny waist, and she swayed back and forth as she hummed a tune.

Gwyn pushed away the memory and bit her lip.

"The upper stories are the most confusing. There are so many twists and turns." Nadine said. "I got lost for a whole day one time. It was scary."

"Here, take this to the cellar." Drelina handed Gwyn a jug of wine.

She carried it down the hall and placed it on a shelf in the cool cellar. As she returned to the hall, a soldier marched toward her. As he passed, a strong hand grabbed her arm and yanked her into a room. Before she could let out a scream, the hand covered her mouth. The door closed. A grungy window allowed the only light in the room.

A whisper tickled her ear. "Thanks for coming for me."

The hand left her mouth, and she swung around, breathing a sigh of relief. But Heron's scowl was deeper than she had ever seen it.

"I couldn't get away! Everyone always watches you here."

"I could've told you that. Castle life is not private."

Gwyn wrenched away from him. "I really was going to find a disguise and bring it to you. I found an escape route. The sewers."

His scowl faded. "The sewers? Not bad. We'll have to make a more definite plan, but it's a good start."

He wore an oversize tunic, brown pants, and knee-high boots. His sword sat in the sheath along his waist.

"Where'd you get the disguise?"

"There were a group of soldiers bathing in a lake on the north side of the mountain. They left their clothes in the bushes."

She touched the hilt of his sword. "Why are you using your own sword? Won't people notice?"

He pulled his tunic over the hilt. "It is a little fancier than the soldiers', but I'm not going anywhere without it."

She shrugged. They were silent a few seconds.

"Have you seen Marvin?"

"Martin," she snapped. "And no. But I'm going with the other maids to feed the prisoners soon."

Heron nodded. He glanced at the closed door, fear shining in his eyes. He was just as alone as she was.

"We can meet up here again." Her statement sounded more like a question. The space was a storage closet, holding mops, rags, and a few buckets.

"Yes. Meet me after you've gotten back from the prison."

"I will. You be careful."

He opened the door for her. His expression softened, and the flicker of a smile lit his face. "You too." His stern expression returned almost as quickly as it left. "Hurry up. I want to leave here as soon as possible."

She stepped out of the room and hurried back down the hall, dodging the swarm of soldiers. Heron melted into the crowd. Despite his roughness, she liked having at least one familiar face. But could she trust him?

He hadn't abandoned her thus far.

CHAPTER 33

DAY-OLD BREAD

When Gwyn returned, the kitchen sounded like a battleground. Drelina and Nadine were sobbing as Madam Crocker yelled at them. An overflowing pot dripped broth into the hissing fire below, and something burned in the oven.

"What's wrong?" she asked.

"Where've you been?" Madam Crocker put her hands on her hips.

"Saskia is dead!" Nadine's face was red and splotchy with tears.

She gasped. "How?"

"The queen was in one of her moods. Saskia spilled a drop of wine on the tablecloth, and that was it." Madam Crocker drew a finger across her chubby neck. "It's the second time this week we've lost a maid."

Gwyn took a step back and held on to the doorway. That was almost her.

"Well, don't just stand there! Snap out of it. Next one who cries will have to do Gwasara's sewer duties."

Madam Crocker's bloodshot eyes and angry scowl were enough to keep Gwyn motivated in her duties. She helped dispose of the burning food and rolled out some dough. The crashes and yells in the kitchen faded into a blur.

So many times, she had dodged death. Rylith had warned Martin and her of their parents' deaths. A tree near the roofline and a cart that happened to be passing by had helped them escape Uncle Edwinn and Andulza. The mysterious man had saved her again and brought her to the Zenia Wood. The Woodsmen of Vickland had saved her from the border guards. She almost didn't make it in Jalapa, but she did. Fog had protected her and Heron from being spotted by dragons and soldiers as they climbed the Uziel Mountain. Perhaps Martin had the same luck she was having. But the fact that the queen often killed her servants at random did not give her much hope.

After the chaos in the kitchen settled down, Gwyn and the other maids stacked loaves of bread in baskets.

"Those aren't fresh, are they?" Madam Crocker snapped. She clenched Gwyn's arm with a greasy hand.

Gwyn shook her head.

"Good. Day-old or older for the prisoners. Queen's orders."

Gwyn, Nadine, and Drelina walked down the stone halls and came to a winding staircase. The steps were made of a smooth, light-gray stone, and the railings were made of stone with a few sparkling jewels embedded in the stonework. A strange metal track lay along the bottom of the railing.

"This staircase goes up twenty-three floors. Are you prepared for the climb?" Drelina asked.

"Yes, I'm used to it," Gwyn said.

As they climbed, she realized the reason for the tracks along the stairwell. Some of the queen's personal maids escorted large carts with sheets covering them. Each cart's wheels ran down metal tracks along the railing. Inside the carts were laundry, dishes, and bottles of ointments and flowery oils.

At the top, she looked down the staircase. Soldiers marched around like little ants. A loud bell rang. She winced. It sounded like the bell from the Aberdeen Temple in Surday.

"What was that?"

"The bell tower. One ring means supper is ready. Two rings mean armor check for the soldiers. Three rings mean the castle is under attack, and four means the prisoners have escaped," Drelina explained.

They continued up the stairs for nearly an hour. A left turn, up two flights of stairs, then turn to the right. Then turn to the fourth door on the right. Once down this hall, take the first door to the left. Then climb one flight of stairs. Drelina opened a door and led the way. The stairs were in a sort of tunnel and became dirtier, less maintained, lit by only one torch. A stale smell wafted through the stairway. Goosebumps rose on her arms and her heart pounded faster. This was it. She could finally see Martin.

At least a dozen soldiers guarded the prison. Drelina and Nadine handed their baskets to the guards, who gave empty ones back. Gwyn reluctantly handed hers to the soldiers. She had hoped for just a peek at the prisoners, perhaps a glimpse of her brother's brown hair or the sound of his hoarse, high-pitched voice. But there was nothing but eerie silence.

The guards pocketed some of the freshest bread and opened the prison's gate. She stared at the keys jingling in one guard's hand. The girls turned and trudged back down the hall. Her heart sank.

"So have you ever seen the prisoners?" She tried to maintain her nonchalance, but her voice sounded panicky. It took all her strength not to rush back into the prison. But she had to be calm. Have a plan.

"No. None of us have," Drelina answered. "We've been told they are cruel murderers and thieves who have threatened the queen."

"I'd be scared to meet them. Wouldn't you?" Nadine asked.

"Maybe." She turned her face away and pretended to study the grungy stains on the walls as they walked. Her hands shook, and she tried to control her breathing. She was so close. Yet so far away.

That night, by the dim candlelight of the kitchen, Gwyn mapped out parts of the castle in her journal. Unfortunately, this was only according to what she had seen and not the whole castle. She stuffed her journal under the table and went back to the small pile of unfinished dishes. Madam Crocker would be back any minute, and she definitely wanted to be finished before then. This was just her first full day here. She had accomplished a lot in one day. Now she had to figure out how to let Martin know she was here. That would be dangerous.

After the dishes were finished, she ripped a sheet of parchment from her journal. With her charcoal pencil, she drew a little imaginary creature she and Martin had made up when they were younger. It was furry, had a long neck, short body, small head, and long legs. Its tongue was sticking out, and it had wild eyes. She laughed at the familiar memories and wrote "grocledeboo" underneath her masterpiece. Only Martin would understand this drawing.

After hiding the map and her drawing in her pocket, she slipped down the narrow hall. She found the room Heron had been in before and peeked in. He stood and picked up a stubby candle sitting in a bowl. The lines on his forehead smoothed.

"Well?"

"I know exactly where the prison is but didn't see Martin." She closed the door behind her, pulled out the map, and handed it to him.

He took it and brought the candle closer. He frowned. "It doesn't make sense. What are these zigzags?"

"Stairs. What? You think you could draw a better one?"

"Definitely. But this is a start."

She yanked the map out of his hand and pocketed it. Why did he always make her feel incompetent? "It is a long way to the top, and the prison is guarded by tons of soldiers."

"What is *tons* supposed to mean?"

"A lot. Maybe two dozen?"

He sighed. "Two people can't take on two dozen." His tone grew serious and businesslike. "If there were four of me, we might be able to break in, but then we would need to escape the hundreds of other soldiers in the castle, get through the sewer, and then climb back down the mountain."

"So maybe if I were a Heron, we would have half a chance." She glared at him.

"Why are you mad at me?"

"You are just so full of yourself. *It could take four Herons.*" She mocked him in a deep voice.

"Well, it's true!" His voice rose.

"Be quiet. You think you can just barge in and fight your way out."

"I never said that! When did I say that?"

"We need to have stealth. Spy out the land. That's what Sherard and Anselm said."

"Who are they? Never mind. I don't care." Heron threw his hands up in the air. "Listen, I don't care what you do. As long as I get out of here alive, I am happy."

"You're nothing but a spoiled prince. You're not doing anything to help! You just complain about everything

231

I do. You don't care about Martin. All you care about is yourself."

"Don't call me that again." He shot back with a venom she had not heard him use before. "I'm not a prince anymore. Princes are weak, and I am not weak. Besides — you're the selfish one. You were too busy to bring me a disguise. Why? Because you had yours, and you were happy and thought you didn't need me."

"Well, I don't! And I don't trust you anyway." Gwyn stormed out of the room, slamming the door hard. Everything was hopeless. Heron might be a complete jerk, but she didn't want to be alone, especially not in a foreign castle inhabited by hundreds of soldiers and ruled by an evil witch.

CHAPTER 34

THE BODY

The next morning, Gwyn helped prepare the prisoners' loaves. She picked the moldiest piece of bread so the guards wouldn't snitch it, then cut a small portion out. Then she pushed her small folded grocledeboo drawing deep inside it, along with a piece of charcoal for Martin to write a response with. She placed it at the bottom of her basket and hoped he would find it. If he didn't get the bread, perhaps one of the other prisoners would find it and give it to him. As usual, the maids and the guards exchanged baskets—their full ones for the guards' empties. Gwyn watched hers as it was being taken away. If she were caught, that would be the end of it. She dared a peek into the prison. A body lay against the wall, covered by a dingy white sheet.

Her heart slipped down to her toes. It took every ounce of strength for her to not run into the prison and rip off the face cloth. Surely it wasn't Martin. It wasn't. It couldn't be.

"Please no," she whispered.

"Gwasara?" Nadine asked.

She shook herself. "Glad I'm not in there."

"Me too," Drelina said as they turned back toward the stairs.

"Me three." Nadine shuddered. "I hear screams all the time."

Gwyn bit her lip.

"They must've done really bad stuff to be in there," Nadine said.

"What do the voices sound like? The screams, I mean," Gwyn asked.

"I've never thought about it." Drelina frowned. "Recently the voices have sounded young."

Gwyn continued walking along with the other two, but every step took her farther away from Martin. She couldn't get the image of the body out of her head. She had to break into the prison—tonight.

She slid into the room where she and Heron met earlier. He wasn't there. He probably escaped and was on his way down the mountain. And she didn't blame him.

She groaned and stepped back into the hallway. Three soldiers marched single file down the hall, going the opposite direction as her. The third caught her attention. Heron's brown eyes shone with fear. He reached out and pushed something metallic into her hand. Once the soldiers had passed, she dared a look—a black key. Sharp black spikes decorated the top, and swirls that looked like bones wrapped around the body. She shoved it in her pocket and turned around. Heron threw a glance over his shoulder before turning the corner and disappearing.

That night, Gwyn made corrections and additions to her map in bed. Drelina mumbled in her sleep and Nadine whimpered. The candle in her left hand dripped hot wax on the map. She slid her map in her pocket and sneaked toward the door. Madam Crocker hadn't locked it yet. Now was her chance. But as she reached the door, Madam Crocker shoved another maid into the room.

"No wandering at night, you foolish little imp!" And then the door slammed and locked.

Her heart sank as she climbed back into bed. She had been stupid to think she could do this by herself. She needed help.

When cleaning out the sewer the next morning, she slipped out the small door, taking the shovel with her. She left a rock on the threshold so she wouldn't be locked out. As she stepped into the foggy morning, a few raindrops splashed on her arm. When she passed the main gate, a soldier called out, "What are you doing?"

She jumped. "I, uh, I'm checking on a place to put the sewage."

"We have a room for that," one of the soldiers said with a suspicious glare.

"I know. But you see, my job is to shovel out the sewer. When I shovel it out, it lands in one big mound. Eventually, the mound will turn to a huge hill, and it will be too hard for me to shovel it out. So I was trying to find a good place to shovel it over the mountain."

The guards looked at each other. The main one shrugged. "Go ahead."

She walked near the edge, pretending to study the decision. Several carts rested in the garden and near the gate. Some carried vegetables and herbs, while others carried wood and kindling. A very dirty plan formed in her head.

As she walked back, the cool air brushed against her hot skin. She had forgotten how clean and clear the fresh air smelled. She wanted to stay here longer and allow her brain to clear, but she walked back to the sewer. She took the carts to the garden and settled them by the small door, then slipped back in.

"You look pale." Heron's voice made her drop the shovel.

"Don't scare me like that!"

He closed the garderobe door after him and crinkled his nose at the smell. "We need to talk, but let's do it in the broom closet."

"Heron, there was a body in the prison. I couldn't see it well at all. Do you think it's Martin?"

He averted his gaze. "Actually—"

"Gwasara!" Madam Crocker's voice filtered through the door. "Time to help with food for the prisoners!" She didn't even look in the garderobe as she clomped by. "I shouldn't have to remind you. Goodness, maids these days. They don't make them like they used to."

Her footsteps retreated back toward the kitchen.

"I've got to go. I have to go to the prison to see if Martin wrote me a note."

"Gwyn, wait." Heron took hold of her arm but much more gently than normal. She pushed him away and hurried to the kitchens. There was no time to wait.

Chapter 35

The Uziel Prison

While climbing the stairs to take the prisoners their bread late that afternoon, Gwyn's legs ached. Each step sent sharp pains from her calves to her back. All the adrenaline of mountain climbing, spying, and walking up what seemed like thousands of stairs every day was taking its toll on her body. She lagged behind the other girls.

"Tired?" Drelina said with her nose in the air. "Maybe you're not cut out for maid work."

"No, I'm not," she muttered under her breath.

After the many twists and turns Gwyn had memorized, they arrived at the prison gate. The guards took the breadbaskets and returned the empty ones. As the three girls walked back down the stairs, she searched through the baskets to see if Martin left anything inside. She spotted a loose piece of paper stuck in the intertwining branches of the basket Nadine carried.

When they arrived at the kitchen, she pulled out the paper and unfolded it in the hallway. Her drawing was on one side, and a message was scrawled in Martin's sloppy handwriting on the other. Her heart leaped at the sight of the familiar writing.

"You're alive," she whispered. She hadn't come for nothing. He was alive.

The wetch is gong to kil us tonit. Hury.

Her chest tightened. He was alive, but who knew for how long? She reread the note several times, then folded it and slipped it into her pocket. This changed everything.

Heron approached her. She started toward him, but someone grabbed her hair.

"And what do you think you're doing out here?" Madam Crocker yelled.

Gwyn jumped and stifled a scream.

The cook brandished her dripping wooden spoon. Her jowls trembled. "Are the dishes out here in the hall, missy?"

"No, ma'am." Gwyn backed into the opposite wall.

"Then get in the kitchen," she ordered, drawing her fat face close to Gwyn's. She let go of her hair and clenched her arm with her greasy hand. "I'm watching you, little missy." She shook her hard. "One more mistake, and I'll send you to the queen. She is good at dealing with unruly servants."

Heron's hand was on his hilt. Thankfully, Madam Crocker hadn't seen him. Gwyn hurried into the kitchen, trying to keep her hands from shaking as she washed the stack of dishes. Madam Crocker stomped out of the kitchen with a tray on her arm and her spoon clenched in her hand. Something had to be done fast. Gwyn watched through the small window in the kitchen as the light faded. It would take her almost half an hour to climb the steps and get to the prison.

She turned to Nadine, the only other person in the room. "How would you like to escape this dreadful place?"

Nadine searched the kitchen to see if anyone was near. "Of course. But where would I go?"

"Home. Do you have any parents?"

"Yes. I was kidnapped several years ago."

Gwyn looked over her shoulder again. "You can escape with me."

"Really?"

"If you help me."

"Help with what?"

She eyed the dishes. "Wash my dishes for me. I'll be back by nightfall. If Madam Crocker questions you, tell her we switched chores. I'm going to take the fresh linens upstairs."

"All right," Nadine said. "Be careful."

Gwyn hurried into the maids' sleeping quarters and pulled out her bag. She slipped the belt and dagger under her skirt and fastened the belt around her waist. She strapped her bag across her chest and dashed out into the hallway. Heron stood near the stairs.

"Slow down. Act natural." His voice was calm.

"Act natural?" Her voice cracked as she handed him Martin's note. "Martin wrote this."

He stared at the wrinkled paper. "How do you know it's not a trap?"

"That's Martin's handwriting!"

"Someone could've forced him to write it. We need to slow down and come up with a plan."

She scowled at him. "We can't slow down!"

They were silent as two soldiers passed them.

"Gwyn, we need to work together on this. You can't do this alone, and neither can I."

She only half listened to what he was saying. She remembered Martin's hand slipping out of hers as she fell into the hole, and she pounded up the stairs.

"Please be safe, Martin," she whispered.

Heron jogged beside her and took her wrist, pulling her to a stop.

"Slow down. You're going to get us caught."

She tried to wrench out of his grasp, but he held her tight. "Stop making a scene."

"I need you to listen to me." His voice was stern, but not angry. She turned toward him. He swallowed and took a deep breath. "I've been trying to tell you this, but you won't stand still long enough to listen. I was sent to the prison yesterday. That's how I got the key."

She checked her pocket to make sure it was still there. The metal spike poked into her leg. "What did you see?"

His face softened, and something akin to sympathy shone in his eyes. "I also saw the body. It was wrapped in shrouds. We took it and burned it outside the castle."

"Who was it? What did he look like?" The words tumbled out in a panicked flurry. A lump formed in her throat. She pictured the body. It was an image she would never be able to get out of her mind.

"We did not see his face. He felt heavy, about your age or older."

She breathed a sigh of relief. "It's not Martin. He's only ten and really short. Plus, he returned my message to me, remember?" Heron breathed out heavily, and she embraced him. "He's all right. My brother's all right."

"Next step, we need a plan." His voice took on that businesslike tone again.

She slowed down her pace, though every nerve in her body told her to run as fast as she could into the prison and rescue Martin. Heron let go of her hand and stayed a few steps behind her. He described some complicated-sounding plan he had concocted.

How on earth were they going to get the guards away from the prison door? As they meandered through the passageway, she brought the map to the forefront of her mind. Then it hit her. Of course!

"Heron, where's the bell?"

He halted. "That will work. Follow me."

Finally they came to the top, and Gwyn leaned over the railing, gasping for breath. She brushed her hair out of her eyes and retied it into a loose bun as she tried to catch her breath. Several soldiers passed by, casting curious glances at her. She must look more frazzled than she thought.

Heron pointed at a door. "That one."

She dashed down the hall to the door and threw it open, screaming as two bats fluttered out.

Heron came behind her and put his hand over her mouth. "Shut up! You want to get caught?"

She pulled away from his grip, and he closed the door behind them. More stairs. The air was cool and damp, and the steps were slick. Thankfully the bell tower contained only a few flights.

The bell was bigger than her father's old fishing boat. A thick rope dangled from its center. *One ring means supper is ready. Two rings mean armor check for the soldiers. Three rings mean the castle is under attack. Four mean prisoners have escaped.*

She looked up at the bell. "Two rings mean armor check. Where is the armory?"

"Near the entrance."

"Far enough away from the sewers?"

He shrugged. "Too close for comfort. But we don't have much of a choice. Once we infiltrate the prison, I know how to get everyone down the stairs without being noticed."

"Do even the prison guards get checked during an armory check?"

"I don't know. I've never seen an armory check before."

"But you lived in a castle!"

"This is a different type of castle than Lyris." His tone turned defensive again. "This is more like a fortress."

She took hold of the thick rope and yanked. But the bell moved only a few inches.

Heron pushed her out of the way and pulled hard on the rope.

Dong ... Dong. They dashed down the stairs and peeked out the door. The soldiers had gathered their weapons and were rushing to answer the call for an armory check. When the hallway was clear, she slipped out and darted ahead of Heron through the maze, sliding to a stop at the prison door.

The soldiers were gone. She stood on her toes and peeked through the bars. "Martin!" she whispered.

"Who goes there?" a gruff voice from inside said.

Heron snatched her bag and strapped it across his chest. He roughly forced her hands behind her.

The guard opened the door. She was too confused to fight against Heron's tight hold.

"Another prisoner? I wasn't notified."

"This is one of the maids. Madam Crocker said she wasn't doing her job."

Gwyn caught on quickly and stared at the floor.

The guard opened the door wider. "Cell thirty-two is open."

Heron nodded and shoved her through the door, which clanged shut behind them. Keeping her hand locked behind her back, he marshaled her toward the cell the guard had indicated. As soon as they were out of the guard's sight, he released her, and they hurried down the hall.

Around the corner stood long lines of prison cells. She drew a deep breath. Dirty hay littered the cold stone floor, and a horrid stench made her gag. Heron coughed behind her and held his hand up to his nose. Each cell was empty. Several voices sounded outside the door.

"We are posting twenty soldiers by the prison door. Do not remove yourselves from this position until further notice." An authoritative female voice said behind her. "I will go in alone." Gwyn's heart skipped a beat, and she picked up her pace. She had to see Martin before the extra guards came.

She came to a locked door at the end of the room and yanked on it, wincing when it made a jerking noise. Locked. She stared through the rusty keyhole to see several more rows of bars.

"Try the key," Heron said. She slipped it out of her pocket and inserted it. The door unlocked with a quiet click.

Inside was another locked, barred room. She peered inside the cells.

There he was. His blond-brown hair was covered in hay and dirt as he sat among a group of dirty children.

She ran to the cell. "Martin!"

"Gwyn!"

They clasped hands through the bars. She touched his bruised, thin face and ran her hands through his dirty hair. It was him. He was alive. It didn't seem real.

"Are you all right?"

He nodded. "I knew you'd find me. I just knew it!" He was thin and his hands were so cold. But he was alive. "The Blood Witch is scary, Gwyn."

"That's why I'm here. We're going to escape together and everything will be fine."

"These are my friends Stream, Clover, Falcon, Will, Anele, Riley, Warrick, and Arbor ... Wait—how'd you get here?" He frowned at Heron. "Who is he?"

"Long story." There was quite an assortment of dirty children and young people. A few looked younger than Martin.

Arbor stood from the corner and smiled at her. He looked like a miniature Hammer, minus the mustache and much friendlier. Not to mention ten times better looking.

"I never thought I would be rescued by a girl. And a pretty girl at that," he said with a wink. Gwyn's cheeks grew warm.

Before she could place the key in the lock, the main door creaked open. She released Martin and hid with Heron behind a bale of hay.

Dressed in purple robes, a lithe woman with long, flowing black hair and bright red lips unlatched the prison door and stepped inside. If it weren't for her cold gray eyes, Gwyn wouldn't have recognized her. Cyrilla Coastworthy?

CHAPTER 36

THE BLOOD WITCH

The Blood Witch circled the small group, clenching a black dagger. She left the door slightly ajar and faced the prisoners.

Gwyn slipped closer and hid behind another clump of hay. Heron followed her and quietly drew his sword. He held her arm. By now she could read his expressions well. His look said not to try anything stupid.

"When and if your parents come up to this tower, they will realize they are too late." The Blood Witch's voice dropped like smooth stones on a cold lake.

She took Martin's collar and raised her dagger. "You, young one, are the lucky one my father said to keep alive." She tapped the flat of her blade against his cheek. "But all your weak little friends here have to die. Which one should I kill first? You pick."

Martin's teeth started chattering, and his eyes grew wide.

Gwyn clenched her jaw. The strength of adrenaline flowed through her veins. Regardless of whether the witch intended to kill her brother or not, no one was going to treat him like that. She stood from behind the hay. Heron stood beside her and let go of her arm. He touched the hilt of his sword.

"Choose now, little weakling," she said with a smirk.

Without any forethought, Gwyn slipped the dagger out from under her skirt and ran into the cell. "Drop the knife!"

The witch spun around, her gray eyes wide in shock. She dropped Martin and turned toward Gwyn.

"What tyranny and betrayal in the Uziel Castle! My own maid about to—" She narrowed her eyes and studied Gwyn's face. "No, you are not my maid. You are the daughter of the cursed Dylan."

Her wicked smile made Gwyn shudder. Heron stood beside her. His presence reminded her that he was here with her and wasn't going to abandon her. She wasn't alone. But would a sword and dagger be enough against a witch?

"Come to rescue dear little brother, have you?" The Blood Witch strode closer. "Step near him and you both will die." She dragged Martin to his feet and held him around the chest with her dagger to his throat. Her eyes darted toward Heron. "You too, you traitorous little prince. Your father will hear of your antics, and my father will ensure there is a grave punishment."

She looked around the room and laughed. Her red lips were as bright as fresh blood. "All of you are weak little mongrels. Look at you, cowering in the corners. Dirty and disgusting. Your families will not rescue you. You will all die by my hand. And it will be a painful, slow death. Your screams will fill the castle."

She eyed Gwyn's medallion and drew in a breath. What fear was left melted from Gwyn when the Blood Witch started trembling. Perhaps the medallion held power against her as well. Gwyn dared to move closer.

"Do not get near me, filthy little peasant!" she hissed like a cornered snake. Her eyes turned wild like a hunted animal.

Gwyn looked at the terror on Martin's terrified and bruised face.

"Your threats are empty. You don't scare me." She took another step closer. "You think I am just a weak little girl like I was at Uncle Edwinn's house. But now I understand the medallion. I know of the power I can wield against you."

"Stay back!" The witch backed up but still held Martin tightly. Her eyes darted to the door. Her once smooth and well-groomed hair fell into her face. "Don't touch me."

"Release my brother *now*."

The Blood Witch's back hit the wall. She sucked in a breath and her eyes darted toward the door. Heron stood in front of her only chance of escape. She squeezed Martin closer. His face crinkled in pain. Something snapped deep within Gwyn. She had given her enough time. She lunged toward the woman. The witch recoiled from Gwyn, dropping Martin, who scurried toward a corner. Her dagger fell into clumps of dirty hay. As soon as Gwyn gripped her arm, the medallion grew warm against her chest, and a flash of blue light filled the cell. The Blood Witch's eyes fluttered, and she fell to the ground, still. Gwyn backed away and stared at her, a crumpled heap on a pile of dirty hay. Had she killed her? She had never killed anyone before. She clenched her unused dagger.

Everything inside her warned her to take Martin and escape, but she forced herself to check the witch's pulse. Her skin was cold as ice, but her pulse was still healthy. Why did she feel relieved?

"She's still alive."

Heron drew his sword. "She will not be for long. She has tortured Vickland and her people for far too long." He held his sword above the witch's pale face, but paused.

He wore a look Gwyn had seen only glimpses of. Pity.

She couldn't understand it. This witch had tortured her brother and kept him away from her. She deserved to die. Yet her own dagger hung limply in her hand. She couldn't do it either. She was too weak.

Heron lowered his sword and stared at the ground. No one spoke. Suddenly someone ripped Gwyn's dagger from her hand. She stepped back in surprise as Will rushed toward the limp form of the witch and stabbed her in the chest.

"Who is the weak one now?" Will roared as he stabbed her again and again. His eyes flamed like freshly lit torches.

Blood mixed with dirty hay. The prison cell was silent, besides a few whimpers from the younger children. Everyone stared at Will's bloody hands and the dagger protruding from the witch's chest. Will looked at the horror-stricken faces in the room. He stared at his hands with a look of disbelief and turned as white as the witch. He knelt by the hay and desperately tried to clean the blood off.

Gwyn looked at her own hands, dirty but blood free. Her anger matched Will's, yet she did not act on it. Why? How was she different? She had more reason to kill the witch than anyone else.

Heron shook himself and turned toward the group. "Follow me. We have to move fast." He opened the prison door wider and stepped out.

"Quickly," Falcon said. He knelt down to let a younger boy crawl onto his back.

"There are still soldiers. We should be careful," Stream said.

"We'll cross that bridge when we come to it." Gwyn reached down and pulled Martin to his feet. He was so light.

"Are you hurt?" He shook his head and rubbed his chest. "Just sore."

Heron led the procession toward the door. Gwyn took her bag from him and strung the strap across her chest.

She searched for the guards. They were lying dead on the floor, arrows protruding out of their backs.

"This is too easy," Will said. "It's a trap."

"You want to go back?" Clover snapped. Will shuddered and glared at her.

"Shh," Stream whispered. She hiccupped every few seconds.

A soldier stepped out of the shadows and grabbed Gwyn around the waist. She gasped and tried to push away, but he was strong. Where had he come from? He placed a dagger to her neck and called out for reinforcements. Heron clenched his sword.

"You touch my sister and you'll be sorry!" Martin yelled.

The soldier backed away, pulling Gwyn with him. "You think you can get away with rescuing your friends, don't you? Well, the guards around here are not like your little toy soldiers back home." Several other guards encircled them.

"Just wait, and —" The guard suddenly shrieked and the dagger clattered to the floor. Gwyn swung around and watched him crumple to the ground, an arrow protruding out of his neck. The other guards tried to flee, yelling in confusion as they fell to the ground, hit by even more arrows.

She looked around the corner. A man wearing a hooded black cloak and clenching a bow disappeared around the corner. His presence filled her with a conflicting sense of relief and dread. Martin grabbed her hand.

"Hey, that's the same guy who—"

"Yes, I know." She tightened her grip on her brother's hand. She wasn't about to let him out of her sight.

"Follow me," Heron said. "I have a plan."

The small group ran through the twists and turns of the passageway. They came out at the main hall and stopped, scanning the area for soldiers. Heron led them to the stairwell and opened a closet, motioning everyone to hide in there. Once everyone was in, Gwyn closed the door. It was a sort of linen closet, with towels, maids' uniforms, and tablecloths piled on shelves that reached the ceiling. Several carts covered with sheets rested by the back wall. Her father's fishing boat would have fit in the closet, but it seemed smaller with all the extra people.

"Do you still have the medallion?" Martin whispered.

"Yes," she said.

The sudden reality sank into her. She and Heron had about ten prisoners to smuggle out of the castle and down the mountain.

Heron pulled some maids' clothes off a shelf and threw them to Clover and Stream. "Put these on."

Stream blushed deeply, and Clover gave Heron an incredulous look.

"Excuse me?" Clover said. "And who are you? Why are we supposed to listen to you?"

"He's the prince of Vickland. Obey him," Gwyn said. Heron shot her a look of anger and hurt. She winced. She shouldn't have called him prince again knowing how much he hated it.

"Prince of Vickland?" Will scowled at Heron. "Why are we trusting him?"

"Listen here, we don't have a choice," Falcon said. "Let's go with the man. He's helped us so far."

"He did just rescue us," Stream said in a quiet voice between hiccups.

Dong ... Dong ... Dong ... Dong.

Gwyn closed her eyes and groaned. It would be impossible to get past all the soldiers now.

Heron muttered a curse under his breath. "Put the clothes on," he ordered the two girls again. "The rest of you, besides Gwyn, get in the carts and don't make a sound."

The ex-prisoners crammed into three different carts, trying and failing at being quiet. The two youngest boys, Warrick and Riley, whined and fought over which side of the cart to sit in.

Gwyn watched as everyone entered the carts. "Why didn't I think about that?"

"I'm no help, eh?" Heron said, a faint smile on his face.

She couldn't help but smile in return.

"Can you please not look?" Stream said in a voice barely above a whisper.

Heron rolled his eyes and turned around to face the boys in the carts. "Anyone want to die?"

The two boys fell silent.

"Then keep quiet."

Gwyn also turned her back toward Clover and Stream as they put on their clothes and instead watched Martin situating himself in a cart. Falcon pulled the sheet over his cart. Now everyone was hidden but Gwyn, Heron, Stream, and Clover. All the carts looked normal with sheets over them. No one would know that escapees hid underneath. The door groaned on its hinges. "And what, pray tell, are you doing in the linen closet?"

She swung around and faced Madam Crocker. She held a pile of laundry and glared at Gwyn. She swallowed and forced herself to take a breath.

"I—Drelina told me to get a new dishtowel."

She narrowed her eyes. "Oh, she did, did she?"

Gwyn eyed the carts. "A lot of dishtowels. I'll need three carts to carry them all."

"Drelina is not supposed to touch the linens. I put her on a strict cleaning duty. She's supposed to be in the queen's chambers, polishing the floor. I'd better put that girl back in her place."

She stopped at the door and turned toward Heron, who stood with a calm look on his face. Her eyes narrowed in suspicion. "What are you doing up here?"

"I needed to clean a mess in the dining hall before you got there," he lied. "I didn't want to make you angry."

Madam Crocker's face softened. "Well, well, well! I've never heard of a soldier cleaning up after himself. Come to the kitchens after supper, and you will get a chocolate pastry and a pound of cheese."

"I will."

"And what about you two?" Madam Crocker eyed Clover and Stream, who had just tied on their aprons.

Stream seemed about to faint. Clover looked down at her feet.

"New recruits, ma'am," Gwyn said. "I've been training them for you."

Madam Crocker scowled at her. "You're the last person I want training my maids. Send them down to the kitchens. Drelina will work with them once she's finished cleaning."

Madam Crocker left the room in a huff.

"You three push the carts to the stairway." Heron maneuvered one cart toward Gwyn. She tried to push it, but it wouldn't budge.

"It's too heavy."

He groaned and instructed some of the older prisoners to come out. Falcon, Will, and Arbor climbed out.

Riley, Warrick, Anele, and Martin were chosen for the first ride. Heron placed his hand on the door.

"I will walk down behind each of you and cover for you should any trouble happen. Everyone ready?"

The girls nodded.

He opened the door, and the procession headed down the hallway.

Heron helped fit each cart on the track, then followed silently behind. Gwyn led the way, pushing the cart carrying Martin. It took all her strength to hold the cart without it speeding down the steps.

"Gwyn, don't let go," Martin whispered from underneath the cart.

"I won't."

He had said something similar when they were in the woods running away from the witches. She wasn't letting go. Not this time. Not ever.

Stream yelled, "Oh, look out!" Her hands had slipped and she had fallen backward. Her cart rolled down and crashed into Clover's cart. Clover tripped and fell to the steps. Both carts barreled toward Gwyn, the wheels screeching on the tracks.

Gwyn stepped out of the way so she wouldn't get smashed but tried to keep a hold on the cart. But the impact of the carts colliding with hers was too much and she was forced to let go.

"Hold on!" she yelled.

The three girls dashed down the steps, Heron close behind. The pile of terrified children tumbled out of the cart and landed at the bottom of the steps. When the guards marched down a nearby hallway, Gwyn yelled, "Back in the carts!"

They hurried back into the carts just in time as the soldiers passed by. After the soldiers were gone, she led them into the garderobe room.

"This stinks!" Warrick wrinkled his nose.

"This is the only safe place," she said. "At least I cleaned it out today."

Heron peeked in. "Hurry."

After settling the children in, Heron closed the door.

The girls pushed the carts back up the stairs to get the others. Heron stayed posted at the sewer door, attempting to act nonchalant as he leaned against the wall, but his eyes darted to and fro, and he clenched the hilt of his sword with white knuckles. She noticed he had acquired a bow and quiver.

Even without passengers, pushing the cart up the stairs was much more difficult than pushing it down.

"All that's left is Will, Falcon, and Arbor," Stream said, gasping for breath.

"They're not heavy, are they?" Sweat dripped down Gwyn's face, neck, and sides.

"Will is," Clover said. "I think we should let them slide down next time."

Several soldiers raced up the stairs, passing the maids.

One of them stopped Gwyn. "All maids were ordered to stay in the kitchen. There's been a prison break."

She swallowed. "Yes, sir, we're on our way to the kitchen after we make this delivery. The queen said it was important."

The soldier nodded to her and followed the rest of the soldiers up the stairs.

Upstairs, a soldier issued orders in a commanding voice. "I want every closet searched. Look under every bed. Every room. They can't have gone far."

"We need to do this quickly," Gwyn said once they had passed. She had a sudden urge to run back down the stairs, take Marlin, and escape by themselves. That was what she had come to do. But what about Stream? She had a brother waiting for her upstairs. Gwyn couldn't abandon them. She threw her strength into pushing the cart up the stairs. Sweat dripped down her back and made her hands slippery.

After Will, Falcon, and Arbor were loaded on the carts and the carts were hooked to the rails on the stairs, Gwyn leaped on the front cart and held on to the sides, motioning for the other girls to do the same. The carts whizzed down the stairs along the track much faster than they had before.

"Whoa, this is going way too fast," Arbor's voice came from inside Gwyn's cart.

"Shh," she said. More soldiers marched up. She checked to make sure the girls were following. They were behind her, but one of the boys was slipping off the cart. Falcon, the tallest, placed his feet on the cart in front of him to keep from falling off. Soldiers climbed the stairs, passing the maids riding the carts as if they did not even exist.

She looked over her shoulder again in time to see the sheet slip off the cart, exposing Falcon. The soldiers yelled and began chasing the carts.

Her heart pounded as she tried to keep from falling. Her feet were slipping off the front, but she held on to the back. She turned over and lay on her stomach, facing forward. The steps flew under her, and her head spun. Her arms tensed and ached from her viselike grip. She couldn't hold on much longer.

Farther ahead, a soldier held his sword in the track. Great. Her eyes darted around her. If she could throw something at the soldier, he would move. An arrow whizzed from below and struck the man's arm, causing him to fall backward down the stairs. Gwyn looked over the railing to see Heron's bow in his hands. She blew a sigh of relief. He was a good shot. She and the others slid past the fallen soldier and barreled down toward the bottom. Near the bottom, she sat up and got ready to tumble off the cart.

"Be prepared for a sudden stop," she shouted to Arbor.

Right before the end of the track, she leaped off. The three carts slammed to a stop, tossing the passengers out onto the floor.

She led them to the sewer, where Heron stood with the door open.

After everyone got in, Martin sighed in relief and hugged her. She ruffled his hair and kissed his forehead. Her shoulders relaxed. So far, so good.

"Now what?" Falcon asked.

"They're going to find out sooner or later that the queen's dead," Gwyn said.

"The queen? You mean the Blood Witch." Will scowled.

"Yes, the witch. Is this all of you?" She lifted her apron and rubbed the sweat out of her eyes.

"Except Mica," little Anele said. Tears shone in her eyes. "My brother was killed by the witch."

"I'm so sorry."

"We need a plan," Martin said. He was pale, but something had changed since the last time she had seen him several weeks ago. His bright green eyes sparkled with a bravery and resilience that reminded her of their father. She smiled at him.

"We have a plan." She slid the latch and opened the door. "It's still nightfall, but your fathers probably won't be here until tomorrow morning. I doubt we'll be able to stay hidden that long."

The door opened. Heron drew his sword. Gwyn was relieved to see it was Nadine. Drelina stood behind her.

"It's all right, Heron. They're going to escape with us."

"You almost forgot me. Can Drelina escape too?"

"Sorry, Nadine. I was about to come get you. And yes, Drelina can come."

CHAPTER 37

DRAGON ATTACK

Gwyn ran through the plan in her mind. Would this work? She had had this planned out for a while, but now with all the faces looking expectantly at her, she wasn't so sure. There were more prisoners than she thought.

"We'll use whistles to communicate with each other on the mountain," Heron said.

She nodded. "Good idea."

"But I can't whistle!" one of the younger children whined.

"I'll whistle for you," Stream said.

Gwyn opened the sewer door and peeked outside. The wheelbarrows were still there.

"Everyone except us maids get in the carts."

"I'll keep guard." Heron squeezed out the hole. Martin squirmed through next, then one by one each person climbed through the door and clambered into a cart.

"I don't see how this is going to work," Will said from his cart. "The guards are going to see us as soon as we're out in the open."

Gwyn picked up the shovel.

Stream gasped. "You are not about to—"

Gwyn shoveled the sludge on top of Will's cart first.

"Are you serious?" His gagging voice was muffled.

Clover smiled and muttered, "That was the most satisfying thing ever."

After each cart was piled high, Heron helped her and the other girls through the door. Muffled whimpers came out of one of the carts.

"Follow me," Gwyn said as she and the older girls each took a load of manure toward the edge of the mountain. A dull, burning ache settled in her shoulders. Her grip on the wheelbarrow's handle slid and she stumbled. No. She had to keep going. They just had to get down the mountain and they would all be safe. She firmed her jaw and kept advancing toward the edge of the mountain.

Heron stood in the shadows of the castle, keeping an eye on the guards above. He held a bow nocked with an arrow. Torchlight flickered above.

"Who goes there?"

Gwyn blinked in the light. "I'm dumping the sewage over the side of the mountain."

"At this time of night?"

"Well, yes. Because …" She clenched the wheelbarrow. "It's not raining. The rain has put me behind in my duties."

"No one's allowed out of the castle at night. How'd you get out?" another guard asked.

"Madam Crocker told me to." Her voice grew shrill. *Please believe me.*

"Get back inside!" one of the soldiers called. "I don't like this. Graden, bring those maids back!"

"Come on, faster!" She yelled to the girls and put all her weight into pushing the wheelbarrow. At the edge, she dumped sewage, Martin, and Anele off the side of the mountain. They fell a few feet to a small landing and whistled that they were fine. She helped the others with their wheelbarrows and stowaways.

An arrow pierced the ground near her foot. Another thudded into her wheelbarrow.

"Jump!" Heron ran up and gripped Gwyn's and Stream's arms, and they all leaped off the ledge.

She scrambled down the mountain beside Heron and the others. Farther down, Falcon helped two of the younger boys, Warrick and Riley. Martin held Anele's hand and helped her down to the next ledge.

"This is insane." Drelina glared at Gwyn as she stumbled. "You do know none of us are going to make it down alive. If we don't get shot first, the dragons will bring us right back to the castle."

"Thanks for your optimism." Clover returned the glare.

"It's worth a shot," Gwyn said. She noticed one of the younger children trying to wipe manure off. "The soldiers will be down any second. We need to hurry."

"They won't be coming anytime soon." Heron's voice held a smile.

"What did you do?"

"Jammed the front gate."

She smiled. Had he thought of everything?

Dozens of arrows and spears spun toward the escapees.

"Look out!" Heron pulled Gwyn and Stream under him to shield them from the volley.

A spear bounced off a rock near her head. Arrows peppered the rocks like metallic raindrops. At least they still had darkness as cover.

"Keep climbing down! We'll be out of range soon," Heron ordered.

Falcon yelled. Warrick and Riley screamed.

Gwyn swung around. In the dim moonlight, Falcon yanked an arrow out of his arm while shielding the two youngest underneath him. Will was still hightailing it down the mountain without even a look back.

"Falcon!" Stream yelled and rocks scattered as she rushed toward him. Gwyn and the rest of the girls scaled down after her. Heron stood on a ledge and fired several arrows up. He was a good shot. Though the fact that the soldiers were lit up in the moonlight and torchlight did make them an easier target than the escapees.

Gwyn slid down and hurried to Warrick and Riley, who were still screaming.

"Shhh. It's okay. Keep climbing." This was chaos. Where were Anele and Drelina? She had lost track of Heron too. She supported Warrick as he stumbled down toward Falcon. At least, she thought she was getting closer to Falcon. Everyone was quiet so the arrows wouldn't find them out.

Arrows fell like hail around her. One sliced into her skirt and nicked her skin. She bit her lip and shuddered. Just an inch more and she would have had an arrow sticking out of her leg. How on earth were they going to make it? It was up to her and Heron to get all these kids to safety. Their families were counting on her. Rose. River. She wouldn't let them down. Not this time.

For at least half an hour, the group half slid, half climbed down the mountain. The blinking eyes of the castle grew smaller, and the arrows and spears grew sparser. The sky turned gray, and morning mist rinsed off the remaining manure from the ex-prisoners.

"There's a cleft we can rest under." Arbor's voice sounded below. He and Stream must be helping Falcon.

Whispers sounded near her and she directed Warrick and Riley toward the rock overhang. The other girls climbed down beside her, and everyone crowded underneath the rock.

Heron stood guard at the entrance of the cave. A dragon's roar pierced the night, followed by a bright flame.

"Coward!" Clover yelled down to Will. He hid behind a rock about a hundred feet below them. "Don't you care your cousin's been shot?"

Will peeked out from behind the rock but ducked back.

"Falcon, oh, Falcon!" Stream put an arm around him and pulled him close. Blood gushed out of his wound.

Gwyn pushed away images of Mama and Papa and crawled over to them. Papa had tended to wounds like this after an invasion in Sunday. She had to stop the blood flow, or Falcon would bleed to death.

She snapped her fingers. "Fire."

Martin pulled his piece of flint out of his pocket and struck it against some rocks. He caught some dried leaves and twigs on fire and warm orange light brightened Falcon's pale face and red wound.

She pressed hard on the wound and ripped her apron off.

"Arbor, double this until it's thick," she ordered as she tightened her grip on the wound.

Arbor did so and handed it back to her. She wrapped the wound tightly.

"Please don't die. Please, Falcon," Stream whispered as she stroked her brother's hair.

Gwyn's vision blurred. She wiped her eyes, but the blood on her hands made things worse. This could have been Martin. She couldn't tell if the blood was stopping. Her heart raced. Come on—work!

Falcon closed his eyes.

"Falcon, stay with me." Stream's tears dripped on her brother's face.

Above them, dragons roared and the guards yelled.

"I'll watch your backs." Arbor stood in the entrance of the overhang. Will pushed past Arbor and rushed to Falcon's side.

"Look who finally showed up," Clover scolded. "Just in time to say goodbye."

Will shoved Gwyn out of the way. "Falcon, don't you dare die on me!" He gripped Falcon's shoulders and shook him.

Clover grabbed his arm. "Stop!"

A shadow passed over the overhang. Heron ducked. Gwyn caught a glimpse of a black, clawed foot. An earsplitting roar made her ears ring. Great. Falcon groaned again. He sat up and ripped the bandage off.

"No, don't do that!" Stream said.

"It stopped bleeding." Clover gasped. "Gwyn, how'd you do that?"

Gwyn peered over Will's shoulder. Falcon's wound had already formed into a small red scar.

"I—I just did what Papa taught me." She looked down at her bloody hands. Clover handed her her apron, and Gwyn wiped the blood away. This was weird. But at the same time, it was normal. She had seen Papa do this many times. Perhaps Martin was right. She was like Papa.

Stream hugged her brother. Will looked pale.

"I'm not about to abandon you, Will," Falcon said with a weak smile.

Will stared at the ground.

Heron studied Gwyn's hands, then his eyes rested on the medallion. "How?"

Gwyn fingered the medallion's cool metal. Papa's smiling green eyes drifted into her memory.

A dragon roared above them. The rock shuddered.

"We've got to get out of here," Drelina said.

Nadine nodded in agreement. Martin stamped out the fire.

Arbor dared a look down the mountain. "Ho!" His face creased into a grin. "Look who's here!"

Will and Gwyn crawled toward Arbor and stood on either side. Several men clambered up the mountain, illuminated by the awakening morning light. She squinted at the men. She still couldn't make them out, but by Arbor's excitement, he must have recognized them.

A volley of arrows whizzed past, though only a few reached the advancing men. Will frowned. "Why'd they come? They're gonna get killed."

As the morning light filtered through the darkness, Gwyn searched the mountain. The fog was gone. Not good. The bell tolled. That wasn't good either, though it was too far to hear the number of times it rang. At least the rain had halted again.

As the men advanced and the sun grew brighter, Gwyn recognized River, Dan, Crush, and all the men who were in the meeting in Vickland several days ago. They zigzagged between boulders, and a man with an eye patch covered them with his longbow. Hammer and his oldest son, Kegan, climbed side by side up to a cleft. Hammer helped Kegan when he slipped, and he held his father's hammer when Hammer leaped to the next ledge. They took turns holding a shield to protect each other from the arrows.

Kegan yelled as a black dragon swooped down and carried him off. Hammer took his war hammer out of his belt, but the sun was now too bright, and she was sure he was afraid of hitting his son.

Gwyn watched in horror as the dragon dropped Kegan off the mountainside. His father gave a fierce yell and threw his hammer into the chest of the dragon. The dragon roared and spiraled to the ground. It crashed into the mountainside and limped away.

"No, you don't!" Hammer yelled as he ran toward it.

The rock cracked and shifted.

"There's a dragon on the ledge," Falcon said.

"It's a trap," Heron said. "It just wants us to get out."

"If we don't leave, we'll be smashed as flat as Mama's bread," Falcon said. "We've got to go."

The escapees poured out of the cleft and slid down the mountain. The fathers were only a few yards below them.

"Papi!" Anele squealed.

Clover put a hand over her mouth. "Hush."

Several black dragons attacked the travelers. Fathers sheltered their children with their bodies, while the one-eyed archer and Heron shot several arrows toward the dragons. Gwyn pulled Martin to her side and placed an arm over his back. Both ducked to avoid the claws of the swooping dragons. One dragon's black scales reflected the sun like tiny mirrors, blinding her. The beasts were bigger than the Aberdeen Temple back in Surday, their claws as long as swords.

Gwyn ducked as one dragon dove toward her. Heron stood in front of her and raised his sword. The dragon banked to the left and retreated back to the skies. In the brief instant before she hurried back down the path, she noticed Heron standing there, sword raised high, his biceps bulging and a fierce look on his face. He did not look like a prince anymore. He looked like a king.

Chapter 38

Escaping Down the Mountain

"Gwyn!" Martin's squeaky voice was never sweeter.

She looked down to her right and watched him climbing down next to River. The Vicklanders' arrows had caused the dragons to back off, though they still swarmed the mountainside.

"Come, dear Stream," River said in a tender voice in front of her. "Keep climbing. We need to get off the mountain. Your mother will cook up a fine dinner when we get home."

In River's kindness she saw her own father's kindness. She longed for her father's strong arms to wrap around her. She longed for him to wipe away her tears and tell her she was safe now and a warm supper would be waiting at home. She suddenly felt small and out of place. All these people were part of families. They had a home to go to after this. She climbed down and jumped to Martin's side. River nodded in greeting, but a frown passed over his features.

A jolt of guilt burned in her chest. "I'm sorry I stole from you."

Carrie Looper Stephens

Martin swung around and frowned at her. "What?"

"I know you were desperate." The normally polite, kind River spoke in a stern tone. "But the missing food made us a day late to leave. The food was made specifically for the trip."

The scowl on his face made her take a step back. The guilt turned into a stinging, gnawing feeling that made her feel sick.

"I'm really sorry. It did work out, though. Everyone's safe."

"Except Kegan and One Eye's son, Brant." River clenched his jaw and motioned to a ledge a little below them.

The two young men were bloody and pale, and their fathers and siblings knelt over their bodies. Hammer, who looked tough enough to beat up a dozen dragons, wept.

The sudden realization hit her like a lead weight. If she had not stolen the food, the rescue group would have left on time, and perhaps these young men would still be alive.

"Keep climbing! Save your grieving for a safer time," Crush yelled. Arrows held off the dragons in the sky, but that didn't stop them from attempting to dive at the escapees. "Carry the bodies!"

Watching the heartbreaking scene of grieving fathers and dead sons, Gwyn felt like a heavy stone was strapped to her shoulders. "Is there anything I can do?"

"Not unless you can bring the boys back to life." River's tone was sharp.

She followed him down the slope and spoke to his back. "I-I didn't know this would happen."

River turned around. His eyes softened, though his jaw was still clenched. "I know you didn't plan for this to happen. I know you love your brother and wanted him safe at all costs. However, your actions, no matter how

266

well intended, always have consequences, not only for you, but also those around you."

"I'm so, *so* sorry." Her voice trembled. He reached up and helped her and Martin down to the next ledge.

"Rose and I still want you and Martin to live with us," he said.

"Really?" She had never thought to enter the Glendower house again. She could never pay back the food or clothes or River's baselard, which was still embedded in the Blood Witch's heart on top of the Uziel Castle. How could she accept his generosity now, after all she'd done? "No, I don't deserve it."

"No, you don't. But you wouldn't expect me to abandon the children of my best friend, would you?" River said.

"Thank you. We are very grateful."

She turned toward Martin. He smiled, and the two descended side by side. There wasn't a dragon in sight. The arrows must have injured enough of them to cause them to pull back.

Heron stood behind her. Dirt and sand from the descent made his brown hair look gray.

"Martin's safe," she murmured. "We did it."

Heron turned toward her and, for the first time, gave her a real smile. Her stomach flipped and the words caught in her throat.

"Thank you."

He gave her a regal nod, then shook Martin's hand. "Nice to meet you."

Martin's eyes were wide. "I've never talked to a prince before."

Heron glanced at Gwyn with a sparkle in his eye. "Well, I won't force you to bow to me now, but next time will be different."

"Stop holding up the line!" Will shouted. He and Arbor stood near the rear of the line.

Gwyn, Martin, and Heron continued traveling down the mountain. She needed to introduce Heron to the rest of the group. Everyone besides the rescued children probably thought he was another prisoner. Introducing him could potentially be awkward. What would she say? *Hello, this is the son of the king. Yes, his father is evil, but he is on our side.* Would they accept him? Would they kill him? Would they imprison him? She watched him staring at Stream, and a squirmy, angry feeling writhed in her chest. She hadn't looked closely at Stream until now. Even though mud and grime covered her dress, hair, and face, her eyes shone like bright blue gems. Her demeanor only added to her beauty. She held the younger children's hands and talked softly to them.

"It won't be much longer," she said when one of the children had fallen and sprained an ankle. "Then we can all go home to our mothers and have delicious meals and warm baths and nice soft beds."

Heron walked beside Gwyn, clenching his sword and throwing furtive looks over his shoulder.

"Crush," Gwyn said.

Crush looked up at her and frowned. Her last conversation with him pricked her conscience.

She nodded toward Heron. "This is Heron."

Crush's nostrils flared and he touched his sword. "What's an Oakheart doing here?"

Several of the men who had overheard stopped in their tracks.

"He is the one who rescued us, Father," Stream said to River. "Don't hurt him."

River's eyes softened, but the rest of the fathers looked like they were about to slaughter Heron then and there.

"He's not bad. He's good." Gwyn's face grew hot as she tried to think of some better defense for him. This was just like being back at home, trying to fit in with the girls in Nelice. These Vicklanders would be her new family. "He really is."

Heron raised an eyebrow at her and turned toward the angry fathers. "I'm not going to hurt you. I have seen what my father does. I am not like him."

He could have made a much better speech in his defense, but she couldn't think of anything else to say either. Fortunately, Hammer was farther down the mountain. Heron would not have lived this long if Hammer had known who he was.

"Let him come down with us, Crush," River said. "He has a bow and has been no trouble so far. Once at the bottom of the mountain, we can decide what to do with him. We need to focus on our retreat."

Crush glared at Heron but nodded. "Very well. But one false move, and your royal head will be lifted off your shoulders and roll down this mountain."

CHAPTER 39

THE ABANDONED PRINCE

Heron hated how Gwyn was completely ignoring him. If Stream hadn't told her father that he had rescued them, then he would have probably been left on the path, filled with the arrows of protective fathers. When Gwyn decided to rescue all the prisoners, not just Martin, she started changing. He'd seen glimpses of her kind heart. But that kindness seemed to fade once she was in relative safety with her new friends.

He couldn't blame her. She had her brother, was accepted into the Vicklanders' group, and had no need of an outcast like him. He stayed toward the back of the group, his bow in hand to help defend against the dragons.

All he got were looks of mistrust from the fathers. He wanted to yell, "Next time, *you* risk your lives and rescue your own kids." It didn't matter what they thought anyway. His strength and cunning had saved the lives of about a dozen children. Gwyn had helped, but without his strength or superior plan, none of this would have come to fruition.

The Vicklanders and their children scurried down the mountain as quickly as they could. Gwyn looked back at him, a look of guilt on her face. He looked away to hide his hurt pride. He didn't belong here. But he didn't belong with the king either. The only place he truly belonged was at Bromlin's house. If the villagers didn't kill him first, perhaps he could go there. The thought of warm mushroom stew made his shoulders relax.

An earsplitting roar made him jump. Air rushed over him, and he ducked. But the claws found his shoulders and jerked him upward. He gasped as the claws knifed into him and ripped at his skin. The pain took his breath away.

He clutched his sword's handle and swiped at the dragon's legs. The dragon roared and flew faster toward a sharp ledge. The beast intended to drop him off the side of the mountain.

The villagers scurried down the mountain, hurrying away from another dragon pursuing them. The dragon holding Heron swerved around the mountain, and the group vanished from sight.

He swiped again at the leg, this time cutting a chunk into the scales. The dragon roared and the pressure of the claws lessened. Heron slipped, but the dragon grasped his leg, hanging him upside down. Pain seared through his leg and he yelled. Black spots blurred his vision.

He swiped one more time at the dragon's leg. The claws released and he fell headfirst down to the mountain. A small, knobby tree softened his fall but earned him several scratches and cuts. He dropped to the ground and lay by the tree's trunk, clutching his leg as the pain ripped through. Blood pooled in his hands and spilled on the rocks. The dragon roared above him. The tree was in a rocky valley too small for the dragon to enter. Heron was safe, if he didn't bleed to death. He had never seen so much blood in his life.

He rolled over to his side and tried to stand, but his leg kept giving way. He clenched handfuls of rocks and tried to crawl, but his leg scraped against the gravel. He lay still, shivering in pain. He wasn't supposed to be weak. When Gwyn needed him, he had been strong—and clever enough to outrun the Black Wizard. He should be able to get himself out of this. But he grew weaker and weaker.

Was this it? Was he dying? He wasn't ready to die, especially not here, bloody and exposed on an evil mountain, alone and abandoned by those he had saved.

Everything around him was slippery with blood. A tremor of pain sliced into his leg again, and he yelled louder than he ever had in his life. The tree above him started spinning.

CHAPTER 40

GWYN'S DECISION

Gwyn climbed down with the others but kept looking behind her.

"He's a goner."

"He would have betrayed us all anyway."

"Your life and safety, and your brother's, are more important," River told her.

She couldn't push away the guilt gnawing at her and making her chest hurt. She couldn't just abandon him. But the other villagers mistrusted him. This would be her future family, and she wanted them to think well of her.

She roved the mountainside in search of the last place she saw the dragon. Heron's eyes had been so sympathetic when he told her about the body. He might have irritated her at first, but she couldn't have rescued Martin without him. Once in the castle, something had changed in him. He didn't seem as concerned about just finishing the job. He seemed more invested in her and her mission.

He was so different from her friends in Nelice. They wanted to be her friend only if they could gain something from her. Now that she thought about it, this was why she had never had many friends. She had nothing to offer. She had nothing to offer Heron, yet when she needed help, he helped her. Maybe that's what it meant to be a friend. It was not about what she could get out of them, but what she could give. She turned to Arbor, who was walking down the path behind her. "Protect Martin."

Arbor raised an eyebrow. "Sure."

She hugged Martin tight. "I have to save Heron."

"But you said you weren't going to leave me again!" Panic laced Martin's voice.

"I'll be back. You have to trust me." She leaped up to a cliff and dashed up the path. The dragons had carried Kegan and Brant away and dropped them off the side of the mountain. Surely Heron hadn't endured the same fate. Her muscles ached, but she pushed herself into a faster run.

"Wait, Gwyn!" Martin called after her. "Don't leave me!" An image of a terrified Martin by the White River flitted through her head. No. He would be safe with River and the others. Heron needed her more right now.

"Gwyn!" River's voice echoed over the mountain.

"Stupid girl," Will shouted. "You're going to die!"

She looked back. She couldn't even see the other villagers now. She climbed along the path and tried to guess where Heron was. A strong whoosh of air almost knocked her down. She swung around. The ground trembled as a dragon landed in front of her, its tail lashing and red eyes gleaming. She reached for her dagger, but the sheath was empty; the dagger was still in the Blood Witch's chest.

The dragon spit a ball of fire, and she dodged its flame. She tripped over a rock and tumbled down to the next ledge. The dragon circled above, preparing for its next attack. Gwyn jumped to the next ledge and continued running as it circled above her, like a buzzard circling a carcass. But as it drew nearer, it didn't seem as terrifying. She expected a dragon to be smoother and lither like a linador, yet this one was big and clumsy. She'd take a dragon over a linador any day. Dragons were easy to see and predict.

She stopped as the circles grew smaller and closer. The dragon dove toward her, its teeth grinding and snapping and its razor claws extended to snatch her. She pressed against the side of the mountain. Her heart somersaulted as it continued diving toward her, its red eyes glinting. She threw her hands over her head.

Footsteps sounded behind her—a man in black clothing jumped in front of her and brandished a black-bladed sword that gleamed and changed to a bright, blinding green. At the sight of it, the dragon frantically pumped its wings backward in an attempt to undo its dive. It roared in anger, banked left, and retreated back toward the castle.

The sword sent a stream of green light into the sky. Six more dragons attacking below also fled to the refuge of the castle, as if they knew the light meant trouble.

Rylith's hood fell off and his dark eyes shone. "Why do you keep saving Martin and me?"

"My motives are my own."

"But you tried to kill me in Jalapa." She hadn't forgotten the evil look on his face while he chased her.

"Sorry about that." He averted his eyes. "I was possessed by my father, the Black Wizard."

"Oh." There was a few seconds silence. "So mind reading is a real thing."

"Basically. They're different concepts but accomplished the same way. I learned something about the medallion that day. While the Black Wizard was controlling me, I couldn't touch it. It threw me to the ground. I'm not sure what happened. I suppose I passed out. It protects against dark magic being used against the person wearing it."

"You were using dark magic?"

"No, but my father was."

"And he was in your mind, using dark magic."

Rylith nodded. "I am trying my best to watch over you and Martin. But there is only so much I can do without my father catching me."

Gwyn frowned at him. "Rylith means *son of darkness*, right? Can I call you something else?"

He shrugged and looked above for any sign of the dragons.

"I'll call you Jason," she said. "My mother always liked that name."

He stared at her and seemed lost for words. "Your mother liked that name?"

"She did. I don't know why. I've always liked it as well. It sounds brave and mysterious. Can I call you Jason?"

"Call me what you like."

She shook herself. "I've got to find Heron."

"But first, listen," he said. "The medallion is more important than you realize. Be warned. The Black Wizard wants you and your brother, as does the king of Vickland."

"I already figured that out, but why?"

"You will soon find out. This medallion is not just any medallion. It is a shade stone. The last one left. It is the only thing that can kill a witch or wizard who has the Dark Shadow. But only people of great gifts can wield the shade stone effectively."

"I injured the Blood Witch. Does that mean I have great gifts?"

"I believe you can answer that question."

She raised an eyebrow.

"You went after him—the prince." Jason's eyes were kind.

She nodded.

"You have your father's heart. Do not let the pain in your life change that." He turned and disappeared down the path.

She continued running in the direction she thought Heron would be. She tried to fit the pieces together. Her identity was wrapped up tightly with the medallion. If she did have great gifts, what were they?

She pushed away the thoughts and tried to focus on where Heron might have landed. Would she be able to find him? Would he still be alive? She walked along a steeper portion of a path and came across a small valley with a tree. A gasp mingled with a sob caught in her throat. There was Heron, sprawled in a pool of blood.

Chapter 41

The Test of True Friendship

Heron vaguely noticed someone rush into the valley. He closed his eyes. Someone slapped his face.

"Heron, stay with me!"

His eyes flicked open. Gwyn pressed her hands against his leg, sending a shooting pain through him. He cried out.

"What are you doing?"

"Shut up and be still! Do you want to die?"

Pain jolted through him again and blackness swirled his vision.

His eyes fluttered open what seemed like seconds later. He moaned.

"The bleeding has stopped, but it's going to be hard to walk. You lost a lot of your skin and some muscle." Her voice sounded miles away. She shook his shoulder. "Heron!"

His eyes opened. Gwyn sat by his side. Her concerned expression softened when their eyes met.

"You lost a lot of blood. You're going to be weak for a while."

He sat up with his back against the tree. There was no skin on his leg, only old red blood. It looked like someone had dipped his leg in strawberry jelly. But at least it had stopped bleeding. The rough bark pinched his back. His shirt was off. Gwyn wrapped it tightly around the wound.

The pain exploded through his body. He groaned.

"I'll find some herbs when we get home, but this will have to do for now."

"Home?" His voice sounded faint.

Gwyn tied the knot and looked up at him. "Wherever that is."

She looked down at his bandaged leg. Wisps of brown hair swept across her tanned complexion. Blood smudged her cheek. Probably his blood. She looked back at him, studying his eyes as if trying to figure out what he was thinking. He tried to form his gratitude and relief into words, but talking took too much energy.

Her concerned expression deepened. "I can try to help you walk, but I can't carry you."

"I don't need to be carried." His tone sharpened. He used the tree to stand. But as soon as he put weight on his leg, pain shot through him. He closed his eyes and sucked in a breath. She clenched his arm, steadying him. She was stronger than she looked.

"You helped me up this mountain. Now I'm going to help you down."

He tried to keep his tough expression as they slowly made their way to the path. They had barely walked half an hour before the pain grew too great. Trembling from the agony, he sat down and gritted his teeth.

"You shouldn't have come back for me. Now we're both going to die. You have your brother. Just leave me here." He put his head in his hands.

She gripped his shoulder. "We have to keep going."

"Go!" He pushed her away.

The pain was the most intense he had ever experienced. He hated Gwyn being there, watching his weakness.

Several seconds passed as he breathed heavily yet she remained beside him.

"I'm not leaving without you."

"You should."

"Your stubbornness can't beat mine. I'm not leaving you."

He grabbed a fistful of gravel and threw it down the mountain. "Then help me up."

She put her hands under his arm and helped him to his feet. Her forearm muscles bulged. He didn't like to admit it, but she was strong. Definitely stronger than he was right now. He was supposed to be the strong one. Weakness was something he thought he had left behind when he escaped Lyris. But it had followed him here.

Hours of slow, painful traveling passed. Darkness came back over the mountain. Gwyn's breathing grew heavier, and she stumbled almost as much as he did. They had to stop for a break every half hour or so.

The path eventually grew less steep, and by dawn they had come to the foot of the mountain. Her grip lessened, and she collapsed. Heron fell face first beside her.

"We made it." Her voice came in rasped breaths.

"We're near Lyris." He wasn't sure why that was the first thing that came to his mind. It was strange being an outcast. He didn't even feel like a prince anymore. Any dignity he had was gone. His father would be disgusted with him if he could see him now, lying dirty, bloody, shirtless, and lame on the ground.

Hoofbeats sounded. Heron rolled to his side, and Gwyn stood and drew his sword. He hadn't realized she had taken his belt and sword and carried them for him. She wore a brave, confident expression. She wasn't the same scared little girl he had met in the Zenia Wood. He lifted his head. A horse and two riders emerged over a hill.

"Who's there?" Gwyn's voice wavered, but she kept the sword drawn and pointed at the riders.

"Gwyn!"

Heron recognized Martin's squeaky voice. Gwyn sheathed his sword and ran toward them.

Martin clumsily dismounted and hugged her.

Arbor dismounted and held the reins. "You said to protect him, and that I did. No one wanted to come after you. I took ... my brother's horse"—his voice faltered—"and the rest went on toward home."

"Thank you," she said.

"I don't want to go home anyway." His voice was barely above a whisper.

Heron thought it strange, considering Arbor had just been imprisoned for who knew how long. But then he felt the same about his own home.

"What happened to Drelina and Nadine?" Gwyn asked. "Did they make it safely down?"

"Who?"

"You mean the maid girls?" Martin asked. "They went home to their families in Jalapa."

"Good."

There was the kind smile on her face again. Despite his pain, he gave a small smile too.

Arbor and Gwyn helped him mount, and the four traveled slowly all day toward River's house. Arbor knew some back roads that would keep their traveling secret, but the roads were rocky and filled with roots and overgrown shrubs. Every step the horse took sent rippling pain through his leg. He clenched the reins and bit back the groans as best he could. As the sun began to set, a small cottage came into view. He vaguely heard Gwyn speaking to him.

"This is our new home. I know River will let you stay, but I should check first."

Chapter 42

Runaway Prince

rbor held the horse for Heron as Gwyn and Martin walked into River's house.

"I don't need you to hold the reins. I can do it myself," Heron said.

Arbor shrugged and dropped them. "River is a kind man, but don't be surprised if they don't let you in. I know my father wouldn't. Your father is not too popular around here, no offense."

Heron heaved a sigh. He was too tired to tell Arbor that he didn't even know the worst of it. Several silent moments passed. More than anything, he just wanted a bed and water.

Eyes narrowed and jaw clenched, Gwyn stormed out of the cottage with Martin close on her heels.

"At least they say *we* can stay," Martin said. "Even after you stole from them."

Gwyn marched up to the horse and led it by the reins to River's barn.

"I'm taking it they said Heron couldn't stay?" Arbor asked.

Martin shook his head. "River said he could come in. Rose said he couldn't take a step inside but could stay in the barn."

"You need a safe place to stay, and your wounds need tending. You would think they would let an injured man stay one night in a bed." She opened the barn door, and she and Arbor helped Heron into the barn.

They helped him lie on some bales of hay. Gwyn laid his sword by his side. "I'll be back with some food."

As they walked toward the barn door, Martin's squeaky voice asked, "You're not going to steal again?"

"No, Martin. My stealing days are over."

...

Heron lay in the barn for nearly half an hour. Here he was, the prince of Vickland, lying shirtless and cold on dirty hay. He laughed bitterly. At home he had a plush bed and an infinite supply of quilts and blankets. But Lyris was not home anymore. He was no longer safe or wanted there.

The pain zipped through his leg again. He gasped and clenched his fists. He was a powerless, helpless cripple, lying here in a rickety barn in a remote village in his father's kingdom. What if he were never able to walk again?

Angry energy swirled in his chest. He wanted to throw something. Break something.

He had been foolish to leave the castle, foolish to go with Gwyn to the Uziel Mountain to rescue the children. He punched the ground with his clenched fist and kicked a column with his good leg. A few disgruntled chickens voiced their disapproval with whining clucks.

He wanted to pull this barn down on top of him. He wanted to catch the whole kingdom on fire, including Lyris. He wanted to torture every dragon in Alastar. He wanted everyone to pay.

The barn door creaked on his hinges. He clenched his sword's hilt and tried to calm his heavy breathing.

Light, bare feet trod on the floor, and his grip loosened on the hilt. Gwyn peered behind the bales of hay. A small candle illuminated her. He hated her look of concern. He was not supposed to be taken care of. He was supposed to be strong. Resilient. Independent. He was supposed to be protecting her.

When she was trembling and wet, cowering underneath the rocky overhang, he had wanted to protect her for his own selfish reasons, but now his protective desire was different. He had never felt it before.

She looked at his hand on the hilt. He drew his hand away and slid it under the back of his head. She climbed over the bales and sat on her knees beside him, then unwrapped a roll and a hunk of cheese.

"Stream is the only person besides Martin and me who trusts you. She gave me this and some cloths for bandages from her mother's kitchen."

"She is a kind girl."

Gwyn frowned. "Yes, I suppose she is."

"Have you eaten?" he asked.

"Yes, don't you worry about me. Eat."

He tried to eat slowly, but in less than a minute, the food was gone. She handed him a small clay cup filled with water. He drank it and then lay back down. She unwrapped his bandages, wiped his leg with a wet cloth, and put some herbs on it.

"The blood stopped fast. I'm not sure what I did." She rewrapped it with a clean cloth.

"Oh. Thanks for that," he said between gritted teeth. The herbs stung.

She gave him a side glance. She held the candle in her lap and stared at the flames. Maybe it was the strength from the food or the warmth from the candle or the presence of a familiar person, but his heart rate calmed, and with it, his heavy breathing. Yes, he was weak. He couldn't take care of himself, and it made him furious. But Gwyn had endangered her relationship with her new family by helping him. She had sacrificed the home she wanted to save him. Despite this, she wore a calmer, kinder look. The muscles in her face were not tight anymore.

"I know no one else is going to thank you, but I ..." She paused and looked down at the flickering flame. The light bouncing off her face gave him glimpses of the tears. And something else he had never seen in her eyes. He wasn't sure what it was. She still had blood on her face.

"Thank you for helping me rescue Martin." Her eyes met his. "I am sorry I—well, I don't know what to say." She looked down again and her cheeks turned red. "I am sorry I kind of abandoned you when we met up with the Vicklanders."

"Kind of?" But he regretted his tone when the hurt shone in her eyes. "It's fine. Don't worry about it. You kind of saved me, so I guess you made up for it."

"Kind of?" She raised an eyebrow.

He couldn't resist a smile. He put both hands behind his head and stared up at the ceiling.

"Does the medallion have healing powers?" he asked. "Is that why you could heal Falcon and me so quickly?"

Gwyn touched it and frowned. "I was told it is a shade stone."

He shook his head. "I've never heard of that."

"Me neither. It's the only thing that can kill a Dark Shadow witch or wizard, whatever that means. But I was told only people with great gifts can use the shade stone. And I hurt the Blood Witch. Just a mere touch, and she went unconscious."

"But that didn't kill her. Will did."

Gwyn nodded. "Then maybe I don't have any gifts." She looked at Heron's bandaged leg. "There's nothing special about me. I must just have a talent for healing like Papa."

"What you did is more than a talent. And even if you can't kill witches and wizards, you have a knack for escaping them."

Gwyn smiled. "True." They were silent a few minutes.

Heron stared at the ceiling. Now to come up with a plan. Where would he go? There was no way he could travel alone. He winced as he tried to move his leg.

"I don't know why you decided to save me. I can't help you anymore. I can't walk. I'm not strong. I'm a runaway prince. A nobody." The dark despair came back to him. It was true. He had nowhere to go.

"I am a nobody as well." She breathed a long sigh. The flickering flame cast trembling shadows over her face. The hurt in her eyes made him forget about his pain, at least for a few moments.

"Where will you and Martin go?"

"The Vicklanders are moving to the Zenia Wood for safety. It is too dangerous for them to stay here. Martin wants to go with them. I don't know where else we would go. The Zenia Wood is safe. It is quite beautiful there." Their eyes caught again, but both quickly looked away. "I promise I'm not a fairy." Her eyes shone with a playfulness he had not noticed before.

He hid his smile, but a small laugh escaped him.

"I don't know where I would go. Your Vicklanders don't want me. My father doesn't want me." But he didn't care anymore about what the king thought about him. Here he was, the very picture of weakness, yet he was free.

"Is there anyone? Anyone who can hide you and keep you safe?"

"Any place but Lyris." He thought about the booming laugh and mushroom stew. He had been at Bromlin's cabin for just a few days, but it was the only place he had ever felt safe. Safe from his father. Safe to ponder his own path, not the path the king wanted for him.

But the image of the lifeless couple in Jalapa came back to his mind. The king had to be stopped. He was hurting his people. Heron's people. A shooting pain ripped through his leg and he winced. Someone had to stop the king, but he was not that person. At least not now. He was in no condition to challenge the king of Vickland and his mighty army. He needed a place to rest. A place to figure things out.

"You have to promise not to tell anyone, but there is a man who lives in the Zenia Wood. I will be safe there."

"How will you get there?"

"That's what I've been trying to figure out."

Gwyn stood and stepped outside the barn. She returned with a long stick. "I found a cane for you. I can take you there."

Heron took it and fingered the knobby branch. It would make a sturdy walking stick.

She checked under his bandages again and felt his forehead. Their eyes met.

"I'm going to take care of you." Her voice grew quiet. She kept her hand against his forehead. Her touch was cool, soothing. "Everything is going to be fine."

The look shone in her eyes again. Fondness. Compassion. Concern.

The fact that she was here, when no one else wanted to help him, calmed his heart. No matter what happened, she would do whatever she could to take care of him.

"Get some rest and be ready at dawn. We will walk with you to the Zenia Wood and take you to your friend's house." She left the candle by his side and stepped outside the barn.

CHAPTER 43

TRAVELING HOME

River and most of the rest of the people Gwyn had met at the meeting left that night to go to the Zenia Wood. They didn't want to risk staying in Vickland any longer for fear of retaliation from the king and the Black Wizard.

Arbor had returned with his brother's horse in the morning. He offered the steed to Heron, and this made traveling much faster. But because they avoided the roads, it still took almost a week of exhausting travel. His leg hurt with every step the horse took. Gwyn, Martin, and Arbor walked beside him and took turns keeping watch at night.

Arbor brought a bow and caught rabbits and squirrels that Gwyn cooked in the evenings. Martin was in charge of collecting wood and building a fire each night. Gwyn tended to his wounds, collected wild berries, and made sure everyone had a blanket in the evenings. Besides excruciating pain, the journey wasn't too bad.

When they finally arrived in the Zenia Wood, Heron kept imagining he could smell the mushroom stew and hear the jovial, booming laugh.

"So who is Bromlin?" Martin asked.

"A wise old man who lives alone deep in the woods."

Martin didn't look impressed. "Oh. I thought he'd be some mighty warrior who could protect us."

Heron chuckled. "He is not that. But he is the kindest man I have ever met."

The deeper they walked into the wood, Heron noticed new, half-finished wooden structures wrapped around the ancient trees. Each tree house was about a quarter of a mile apart. Temporary tents and lean-tos were set up on the ground, and livestock was tied to trees or put in makeshift fences. River and Falcon hammered boards down on the roof of a tree house. Falcon looked down and waved.

"Hullo, Martin! Welcome home!" Falcon yelled. He would have fallen off the roof if River hadn't grabbed his arm.

Martin laughed and waved back. "That's Falcon," he told Gwyn. "He's my friend."

Gwyn studied the tree houses. "This *is* our home." Her voice was barely above a whisper. "*Our* home."

As midmorning approached, the old cabin came into view. Heron smiled, and the despair evaporated. He was home. The old, dark wood of the cabin contrasted with the bright green of trees and a vegetable patch near the porch.

And there was Bromlin, sitting on the porch, snapping beans. A steamy cup of black brew sat by his side. Marrok sat alert and looked straight at Heron. At the sight of the wolf, the others stopped.

But Marrok's tail started wagging, hitting the porch with a *thump thump thump*.

Bromlin peered at the wolf. "What is it, my boy?" He looked out into the woods and dropped his basket as he stood and shaded his eyes from the sun. "Well, bless my soul. What have we here?" He chuckled. "Well, I'll be. It's good to see you again, young sir!"

"Bromlin." Heron had a foolish grin on his face, but he didn't care.

"I feared I'd never see you again, Heron." His deep brown eyes shone as he shuffled toward them. "And these are your friends?"

"Gwyn, Martin, and Arbor." Heron pointed to each.

Bromlin and Marrok stopped a few feet in front of Heron and his friends. Marrok's tail wagged harder, and he barked at Heron. Heron had never seen Bromlin smile so much.

"It is so good to see you all. Well, then, come in, come in. I have a cauldron of mushroom stew cooking, and I'll put on another pot of brew for us all in just a moment. I'm sure there are plenty of stories to go around the table."

As they neared the cottage, Bromlin eyed Heron's bandaged leg. The wrinkles in his brow furrowed. He looked back up at Heron, and a twinkle sparkled in his eyes.

"You know, Heron. You don't have to get hurt to have an excuse to visit me." A playful smile twitched beneath Bromlin's shaggy beard.

Chapter 44

Time Will Tell

The tree houses are interesting, but Martin and me felt more at home in Bromlin's cabin. He insisted he had plenty of room for Heron, Martin, and me. We are all settled in and are starting our first day as citizens of the Zenia Wood. I actually have my own room! Poor Heron has to share a room with Martin. He is being nice, but I think Martin gets on his nerves quite often. I can tell by the way he clenches his jaw. Heron has changed, though. His leg heals slowly, and he still limps. He is quieter, and his haughtiness has diminished, though I still see traces of it. He smiles more. His smile makes me smile. It makes me feel calm yet excited on the inside. I just realized that he is my first real friend. I don't know if he feels the same way.

I can't believe we actually have a roof over our heads. And not only a roof, but a home. A real home. Bromlin is kind and wise like Papa. He smiles so often. I think he likes having a full house.

So many questions still swirl in my head. Will I see Jason again? What is the history behind the medallion, and how will we keep it away from the Black Wizard? Do I have the gifts I need to defeat the Black Wizard? And if I do, do I have the courage *to do so? How long will we be safe here before the Black Wizard and Heron's father find us? I hate unanswered questions and uncertainty. The world is not as simple as I thought.*

Despite all these questions, I think I'm beginning to understand who I am now. I'm strong. I'm brave. I am good at thinking fast. But I am not independent. I need friends. I can't go through life on my own without them. And my friends need me too. It's really hard for me to admit that I need other people. But it's freeing in a way. I don't have to go through life alone.

Gwyn closed her pencil inside her journal. She looked at the early-morning fog outside the open window. Bromlin came to the kitchen table and placed four mugs of black coffee down. Then he brought a platter of eggs and spooned them onto four plates and passed them around the table.

"Eat up!" He sat down and took a long draft of coffee.

Martin poked at the eggs with his spoon.

"Those are mushrooms," Heron whispered.

Martin crinkled his nose.

"I'm sure it's better than pine needles," Gwyn said.

Martin nodded. "Anything's better than pine needles."

The eggs were gone in a moment, and Bromlin couldn't look happier that so many people were enjoying his cooking.

"Now then, dear girl. You wanted to ask me about a medallion?"

Gwyn slipped the necklace over her head and handed it to him. His eyebrows furrowed as he took it.

"You said this was your father's?"

"Yes, sir," she said.

He quickly handed it back to her as if he were afraid to keep it in his hands too long. "I wonder how Dylan came across it."

"What is it?" Martin asked. "What's so special about it?"

He frowned and glanced out the window like he expected the Black Wizard to be eavesdropping. "There is much about this medallion we don't know. I have heard the rock has some strange qualities that could make it appear magical. In Alastar, there are certain things black magic cannot touch. These things are not necessarily magical, but they appear this way since they are immune to the deepest, darkest magic."

"Why does the Black Wizard want it?" Gwyn asked.

Bromlin frowned. "That is the part that confuses me. I have my theories, but nothing solid. Time will tell." He looked at them with warm brown eyes. "Did you know your father was a gifted healer?"

A lump grew in her throat. "He never told me. But I watched him heal lots of people."

"Ah, I suppose he wouldn't," Bromlin said.

Heron looked at Gwyn. She touched the medallion. Just the feel of the cool metal made her feel closer to Papa.

"How did you know him?"

"I raised him when he was just a wee lad. My wife and I started a sort of orphanage back in the day." He stared outside and smiled. "A talented young man. Such a shame. But as long as you two are alive, he lives through you. You both have his eyes. You both are brave and kind like he was."

Everyone was quiet again. She blinked several times and was glad Heron was looking away.

...

Later that evening, Gwyn and Martin stood on the porch of Bromlin's cabin and watched the sunset.

Martin turned to her. "Where's the medallion?"

She took it off and slipped it over his head. "I know Father would want you to wear it."

Tears shone in his eyes. All the pent-up emotion rushed through her like a hundred-foot wave. She pulled Martin into a tight hug and let her tears fall.

"You could've died," she whispered.

"I knew you'd find me." His voice trembled.

She held him tighter. What if she had been killed by the border patrols or the Black Wizard or fallen off the mountain or not gotten to him in time? She shuddered.

"I learned what it means to be brave." Martin pulled away.

Gwyn stared at her little brother's tear-stained face. Her throat tightened. He looked so much like Papa.

"Watching Heron made me want to be brave like him someday."

"You already are."

He gave a small smile. "I guess I am."

They were quiet a few minutes. She wasn't sure what to say. But they were together. Martin was alive. And that was all that mattered. He fingered the medallion. "Why does the Black Wizard want it?"

She tried to push away the uneasiness that often intruded into the daydream of the Zenia Wood. She decided not to tell him what Jason had told her about the Black Wizard wanting them.

Gwyn stared out at the purple stain of the sunset. "Time will tell."